THE G
DICTIC
OF
THEATRICAL
QUOTATIONS

THE GUINNESS
DICTIONARY
OF
THEATRICAL
QUOTATIONS

COMPILED BY
MICHÈLE BROWN

GUINNESS PUBLISHING

DEDICATION

For Noel Davis, who for nearly twenty years has kept me
laughing with an inexhaustible repertoire of theatrical
stories.

Editor: Beatrice Frei
Design: Mandy Sedge

Typeset in Monotype Bembo by
Ace Filmsetting Ltd, Frome, Somerset
Printed and bound in Great Britain by
Cox & Wyman Ltd

A catalogue record for this book is available from the British Library

ISBN 0–85112–596–4

CONTENTS

FOREWORD

To paraphrase Shakespeare, if I may be so bold, 'If it be true that a good wine needs no bush, 'tis true that a good compilation needs no introduction.'

So let me be brief. The authors of the quotations gathered here are past masters of the art of saying a great deal with wit and admirable brevity; the credit is all theirs. As compiler I take responsibility for any errors and omissions. I have added a biographical index of authors and subjects which I hope will shed additional light on the quotations by putting them in context. It will also help those readers who wish to pursue particular subjects or authors through the book.

As with everything to do with the theatre, compiling this dictionary of quotations has been a great pleasure. I hope it will also give pleasure, both as a volume to dip into and as a source of reference. My aim has been to produce a light-hearted book which rings true with the received wit and wisdom of the theatre. And for those who choose not to agree with my selection let me finish as I began, by paraphrasing another writer featured in the pages which follow. 'Asking an author what she feels about critics is like asking a lamp-post how it feels about dogs.'

HOW TO USE
THIS BOOK

The primary aim of this book is to reflect the wit and wisdom of the theatre in a wide-ranging selection of quotations which can be dipped into at random or read section by section. The titles of the sections are found in the contents list at the front of the book.

There are two indexes. One is biographical, giving the dates where known, and a brief description of the person concerned, then listing all references to them in the book. This index includes details of people written about (e.g. Mary Betterton) and of people quoted (e.g. George Jean Nathan). Obviously there are many people who come into both categories (e.g. Olivier). Including biographical information in the text would mean cumbersome repetition. However, understanding the wider context of the quotations enhances their value and I recommend using this index extensively.

The index of plays is for those interested in tracking down references to particular works. Both biographical and play indexes refer to the sections in which quotations can be found rather than to specific page references. In these sections quotations are listed alphabetically by author unless indicated otherwise.

A few conventions have been used which might possibly be unfamiliar to some readers. *Ibid* means that a quotation comes from the same author and source as the quotation immediately preceding it; *fl.* in the biographical index means that I do not have exact dates of birth and death of the person named but that he or she flourished around the date indicated.

ACTING

In London acting is not a capricious, freakish, or Bohemian way of life. It is an ancient and honourable profession that is accepted by the public as a normal part of the life of London.

Brooks Atkinson *Broadway* 1970

Acting is a bum's life. Quitting acting – *that* is a sign of maturity.

Marlon Brando

When you act in the West End you pick up your coffee cup in exactly the same way for nine months.

Richard Briers *The Times* 6 May 1992

I am acquainted with no *im*material sensuality so delightful as good acting.

Lord Byron letter to Thomas Moore 1814

All acting is a question of control, the control of the actor of himself, and through himself of the audience.

Noël Coward quoted in *Great Acting* (ed. H. Burton) 1967

Acting is the shy person's revenge on the world.

Sinead Cusack *Daily Mail* 16 February 1991

I think I love and reverence all arts equally, only putting my own just above the others. . . . To me it seems as if when God conceived the world, that was Poetry; He formed it and that was Sculpture; He coloured it, and that was Painting; He peopled it with living beings, and that was the grand, divine, eternal Drama.

Charlotte Cushman

An actor with no insecurities would be lost.

Judi Dench *Daily Mail* 21 January 1992

It is easier to get an actor to be a cowboy than to get a cowboy to be an actor.

John Ford attrib.

Of all the arts I think acting must be the least concrete, the most solitary.

John Gielgud *Early Stages* 1938

When you finally learn how to do it you're too old for the good parts.

Ruth Gordon quoted in Leonard Lyons' column, 21 June 1972, when she was 76

The terrible thing about acting in the theatre is that you have to do it at night.

Katherine Hepburn *New York Times* 16 January 1976

Acting isn't really a very high class way to make a living, is it?

Katherine Hepburn

Life's what's important. Walking, houses, family, birth and pain and joy. Acting's just waiting for the custard pie. That's all.

Katherine Hepburn

Acting is painting, not photography.

Derek Jacobi *Sunday Times* 24 May 1992

It is a most unholy trade.

Henry James

Acting more than any other art is a demonstration of rebellion against the mundanity of everyday existence.

Michèal MacLiammoir

I think the whole business of being an actor and being part of entertainment, whether it be TV shows or stage shows or movies, is noble. You learn about everything, and you're involved in something. You know what it is – it's acting. Look at the doctors and the lawyers. *They* think they're real people.

Walter Matthau 1979; quoted in J. Green, *A Dictionary of Contemporary Quotations* 1982

Acting is therefore the lowest of all the arts, if it is an art at all.

George Moore *Mummer Worship*

The whole matter of acting is enveloped with written and oral bosh.

George Jean Nathan *Encyclopaedia of the Theatre* 1940

Acting should be seen and not written about.

Ibid.

If somebody asked me to put in a sentence what acting was, I should say that acting was the art of persuasion.

Laurence Olivier quoted in K. Tynan, *Curtains* 1961

It does seem sometimes that acting is hardly the occupation of an adult.

Laurence Olivier 1970

Acting – the ability to keep an audience from coughing.

Ralph Richardson *Observer* 1947

Acting is like roller skating – once you know how to do it, it is neither stimulating nor exciting.

George Sanders quoted in J. Green, *A Dictionary of Contemporary Quotations* 1982

Highly paid casual labour of the most casual sort.

George Bernard Shaw

Shouting in the evening.

Patrick Troughton (definition of acting)

I love acting. It is so much more real than life.

Oscar Wilde *The Picture of Dorian Gray* 1891

Acting is like painting pictures on bathroom tissues. Ten minutes

later you throw them away and they are gone.

Shelley Winters *The Saturday Evening Post* 1962

ACTORS

The aim of an actor should not be the part, but the whole.

Peggy Ashcroft 1961

A good French actor is merely a French barrister who has missed his vocation.

Arnold Bennett *Journals* 1896–1928

An actor is a sculptor who carves in snow.

Edwin Booth

An actor is a guy who, if you ain't talking about him, ain't listening.

Marlon Brando *Observer* 1956

An actor is something less than a man, while an actress is something more than a woman.

Richard Burton

The better the actor the more stupid he is.

Truman Capote

They are a race apart, doomed to go through life pretending to be someone else.

R.F. Delderfield

He speaks all his words distinctly, half as loud again as the other. Anybody may see he is an actor.

Henry Fielding *Tom Jones* 1749

Show me a great actor and I'll show you a lousy husband.

W.C. Fields

The more you do for an actor the worse it hates you.

Percy Hammond quoted in *Selected Letters of James Thurber* 1981

Anyone who has been an actor any length of time does not know whether he has any true emotions or not.

Cedric Hardwicke

Only a true actor with a deep-seated compulsion is going to stick out the struggle that goes with being in the theatre. It's brutal, it's worse than a Marine boot-camp.

Helen Hayes

An actor-manager is one to whom the part is greater than the whole.

Ronald Jeans

Players, Sir! I look on them as no better than creatures set upon tables and joint stools to make faces and produce laughter, like dancing dogs.

Samuel Johnson quoted in James Boswell, *The Life of Samuel Johnson* 1791

If there is anything I think I'd hate as a son-in-law, it's an actor, and if there's anything I think I'd hate worse than an actor as a son-in-law, it's an English actor.

Joseph P. Kennedy whose daughter Patricia married English actor Peter Lawford

An actor can remember his briefest notice well into

senescence and long after he has forgotten his phone number and where he lives.

Jean Kerr

Although his traffic in entertainment can lead one to forget it, the great actor is one of nature's miracles. He brings aspects of music, poetry, literature and sculpture within the capacity of a human being and transmits them to the crowd. . . .

Laurence Kitchin *Mid-Century Drama* 1960

Actors should still be called comedians – wit and inventiveness are the attributes they most need.

Joan Littlewood *Esquire* 1964; quoted in J. Green, *A Dictionary of Contemporary Quotations* 1982

Actresses will happen in the best regulated families.

Addison Mizner and **Oliver Herford** *The Entirely New Cynic's Calendar* 1905

Some of the greatest love affairs I've known have involved one actor, unassisted.

Wilson Mizner quoted in A. Johnson, *The Incredible Mizners* 1953

It is a great help for a man to be in love with himself. For an actor it is absolutely essential.

Robert Morley quoted in his obituary, *The Times* 4 June 1992

Actors and boarding school misses keep scrapbooks.

George Jean Nathan

The autobiographies of English and American actresses appear to differ chiefly in one important detail. Whereas English actresses all seem to have had fathers, American actresses seem for the most part to have had only mothers.

George Jean Nathan
Encyclopaedia of the Theatre 1940

[English actors'] clipped speech, over-precision of diction and congenital and apparently unconquerable chill of comportment combine in American eyes and ears to make their dramatic protestations of heat and passion often indistinguishable from so many cucumbers.

Ibid.

Like most actors she (Mary Ure) was hysterical when unemployed and resentful when appearing every night to full houses.

John Osborne *Almost a Gentleman* 1991

Actors like Shakespeare because they can gum on a lot of crepe hair, bellow almost anything that comes into their heads, and then have their Lear taken seriously by the critics.

J.B. Priestley

An actor is not quite a human being – but then, who is?

George Sanders quoted in J. Green, *A Dictionary of Contemporary Quotations* 1982

A man is an actor as he is a prince: by birth.

Jean Paul Sartre *Kean* 1954

A woman cannot be an actress and a respectable woman at the same time

Clement Scott

There are thousands of respectable women on the stage and only about six actresses.

Robert Buchanan response to the above

The stock actor is a stage calamity.

George Bernard Shaw

You will never be an actor until you have learnt to get through your part though the snow comes through the roof; with an audience consisting of only two or three drunks, who are not listening; while the sparrows twitter and flutter round the auditorium before settling to roost in the flies; while rats trot across the footlights carrying your pet powder-puff in their mouths. You have got to learn to act though none of the company except yourself are sober; when no one gives you your proper cue; when you have not had a square meal for a month and will probably get no salary on Saturday; when you are sent on to play a part of two or three hundred lines with one night's study and no proper rehearsal. When you can do this, and not dry up, but hold an audience, great or small, drunk or sober, stalls or gallery, or Royal Box, whether the play is good or bad, and your part actor-proof or impossible, then, and not till then, may you call yourself an actor.

Mrs (Fanny) Stirling quoted in Sir Frank Benson, *My Memoirs*

When you're an actor you cease to be male or female . . .

Sybil Thorndike quoted in R. Findlater, *The Player Queens* 1976

Give an actress a round, resonant voice and a long Shakespearean part, and she will have to enter smoking a pipe to avoid being acclaimed.

Kenneth Tynan *Curtains* 1961

An actor is a man who can walk to the side of the stage, peer into the wings filled with dust, other actors, stagehands, old clothes and other claptrap and say, 'What a lovely view there is from this window.'

Variety

Very good actors never seem to talk about their art. Very bad ones never stop.

John Whiting *John Whiting on Theatre* 1966

English actors act quite well but they act between the lines.

Oscar Wilde

You can pick out actors by the glazed look that comes into their eyes when the conversation wanders away from themselves.

Michael Wilding

Actors act too much.

Nicol Williamson *Now* 1981

ACTORS – *Individuals*

EDWARD ALLEYN
And present worth in all dost so
*   contract*
As others speak, but only thou dost
*   act.*
Weare this renowne. 'Tis just, that
*   who did give*
So many Poets life, by one should
*   live.*

Ben Jonson *To Edward Alleyn, Epigrammes* 1616

JULIE ANDREWS
Working with Julie Andrews is like being hit over the head with a Valentine's card.

Christopher Plummer quoted in *Celebrity Gossip* 1984

FRANK BENSON
When he dies, five thousand creditors will follow him to the grave. And all will shed a tear because they can't lend him a bit more.

Harold Neilson quoted in R. May, *The Wit of the Theatre* 1969

MARY BETTERTON

Having, by nature, all the accomplishments required to make a perfect actress, she added to them the distinguishing characteristic of a virtuous life.

Charles Gildon *The Life of Mr Thomas Betterton* 1710

MASTER BETTY

The popularity of that baby-faced boy, who possessed not even the elements of a good actor, was a hallucination in the public mind, and a disgrace to our theatre history.

Thomas Campbell

I am disposed to think his talents were not fairly appreciated. It seemed as if the public resented on the grown man the extravagance of the idolatry they had lavished on the boy.

William Charles Macready

EDWIN BOOTH

But as for all the rest,
There's hardly one (I may say none)
*   who stands the Artist's test.*
The Artist is a rare, rare breed. There
*   were but two forsooth,*
In all me time (the stage's prime!) and
*   The Other One was Booth.*

Edmund Vance Cooke *The Other One was Booth*

ANNE BRACEGIRDLE

She seems to have been a cold, vain and interested coquette, who perfectly understood how much the influence of her charms was increased by the severity which cost her nothing, and who could venture to flirt with a succession of admirers in the just confidence that no flame which she might kindle in them would thaw her own ice.

Thomas Macaulay *History of England* 1852

RICHARD BURBAGE

Which is your Burbage now? Your best actor?

Ben Jonson *Bartholomew Fair* 1614

RICHARD BURTON

Richard Burton is so discriminating that he won't go to see a play with anybody in it but himself.

Elizabeth Taylor on her then husband

CAROL CHANNING

Carol never just enters a room. Even when she comes out of the bathroom her husband applauds.

George Burns

COLLEY CIBBER

Colley Cibber, they say, was

extremely haughty as a theatrical manager, and very insolent to dramatists. When he had rejected a play, if the author desired him to point out the particular parts that displeased him, he took a pinch of snuff and answered in general terms, 'Sir, there is nothing in it to coerce my passions.'

George Coleman *Random Records of My Life* 1830

Cibber had the misfortune to have Fielding as a persistent enemy. Fielding was severe on him for his alterations to Shakespeare's plays, of one of which Cibber self-complacently said 'I have endeavoured to make it more like a play than I found in Shakespeare.'

David Patrick *Chambers Encyclopaedia of English Literature* 1903

Less human genius than God gives an ape.

Alexander Pope *Dunciad* 1743

KATHERINE CORNELL

The first lady of the American theatre (as I sometimes think of her). . . .

Kenneth Tynan *Show* November 1961

GÉRARD DEPARDIEU

The excitement in every Depardieu performance is somehow rooted in this contradiction between the powerful physique and the sensitivity of the spirit within.

David Robinson *Daily Mail* 5 January 1991

More than any other actor since Jean Gabin, Depardieu is a national institution.

Ibid.

CHARLES DICKENS

Ah, Mr Dickens, if it hadn't been for them books what an actor you would have made!

Anonymous admirer quoted in J.B. Van Ameronger, *The Actor in Dickens* 1926

PHYLLIS DILLER

Like an old Chevrolet starting up on a below-freezing morning.

Anonymous description of Phyllis Diller's laugh

I treasure every moment that I do not see her.

Oscar Levant

JOHN DREW

The Beau Brummel of the American Stage.

Margaret Case Harriman

GERALD DU MAURIER

When one knew him, one knew that the stage meant nothing to him but a means of getting money; he never pretended otherwise.

A.A. Milne *It's Too Late Now* (autobiography) 1939

ROBERT ELLISTON

His feelings follow each other like the buckets on a water-wheel, full one instant and empty the next.

Leigh Hunt

EDITH EVANS

As earthy as a potato, as slow as a cart-horse, and as cunning as a badger.

W.A. Darlington reviewing her Nurse in *Romeo and Juliet* 1935

To me, Edith looks like something that would eat its young.

Dorothy Parker

BARRY FITZGERALD

He could steal a scene from a dog.

John Ford attrib.

MINNIE MADDERN FISKE

Somewords she runstogether,
Some others are distinctly stated.
Somecometoofast a n d
S o m e   t o o   s l o w

And some are sy$^{n\ o\ a}_{c\ p\ t}$ed

And yet no voice – I am sincere –
Exists that I prefer to hear.

Franklin P. Adams *c.* 1918; quoted in Brooks Atkinson, *Broadway* 1970

FRÉDÉRICK

There was always something offensive to good taste in Frédérick's acting – a note of vulgarity, partly owing to his daring animal spirits but mainly owing, I suspect, to an innate vulgarity of nature.

G.H. Lewes *On Actors and the Art of Acting* 1875

ALEC GUINNESS

The number of arrests following the circulation of his description would break all records.

Kenneth Tynan

NELL GWYNNE

. . . so great performance of a

comical part was never, I believe, in the world before as Nell hath done this, both as mad girle, and then, most and best of all, when she comes in like a young gallant; and hath the motions and carriage of a spark, the most that ever I saw any man have. It makes me, I confess, admire her.

Samuel Pepys on Nell Gwynne's performance as Florimel in Dryden's *Mayden Queene* in *Diary* 2 March 1667

CEDRIC HARDWICKE
You are my fifth favourite actor, the first four being the Marx Brothers.

George Bernard Shaw

RICHARD HARRIS
He's something of a f...-up, no question.

Charlton Heston quoted in *Celebrity Gossip* 1984

KATHERINE HEPBURN
Katherine of Arrogance.

Anon.

She has a cheekbone like a death's head allied to a manner as sinister and aggressive as crossbones.

James Agate

She has a face that belongs to the sea and the wind, with large

rocking-horse nostrils and teeth that you just know bite an apple a day.

Cecil Beaton

HEDDA HOPPER
Hedda Hopper was a dud actress who swapped the stage for journalism.

Simone Signoret

CELIA JOHNSON
She was the middle-class doctor's daughter who became an actress because she thought it would be 'rather wicked'.

Kate Fleming (daughter) *The Mail on Sunday* 13 October 1991

JOHN KEMBLE
Frogs in a marsh, flies in a bottle, wind in a crevice, a preacher in a field, the drone of the bagpipe, all yielded to the inimitable soporific monotony of Mr Kemble.

George Coleman *Random Records of My Life* 1830

Kemble turned his head so slowly that people might have imagined he had a stiff neck, while his words followed so slowly that he might have been reckoning how many words he had got by heart.

Leigh Hunt *Critical Essays on Performers in the London Theatre* 1807

He never pulls out his handkerchief without a design upon the audience.

Ibid.

DEBORAH KERR

Miss Kerr is a good actress. She is also unreasonably chaste.

Laurence Olivier

LILLIE LANGTRY

I would rather have discovered Mrs Langtry than have discovered America.

Oscar Wilde October 1882

GERTRUDE LAWRENCE

Most actresses when they write a book about their youth recall the crunch of carriage wheels in the drive. Gertie recalled eating kippers in the gutter, which, of course, was completely untrue.

Noël Coward *Present Indicative* 1937

She had this shimmering kind of sexual, sensuous elegance, like a perfume wafting over you.

Daniel Massey BBC Television, 1 March 1992

BEA LILLIE

She could make me laugh reading from the telephone book.

Ashton Stevens review 1926; quoted in Bea Lillie, *Every Other Inch a Lady* 1972

WALTER MATTHAU

He could play anything from Rhett Butler to Scarlett O'Hara.

Billy Wilder *Time* 24 May 1971

DAVID NIVEN

I always knew that if all else failed I could be an actor – and all else failed.

David Niven

IVOR NOVELLO

The two most beautiful things in the world are Ivor's profile and my mind.

Noël Coward

PETER O'TOOLE

The very stereotype of the ham.

Omar Sharif quoted in *Celebrity Gossip* 1984

ANTHONY QUAYLE

You'll never be out of work for long, and I'll tell you why. Because you are a bloody good actor: – and you haven't enough personality to worry a leading man.

Laurence Olivier quoted in A. Quayle, *A Time to Speak* 1990

RACHEL
The strife, the mixture in her soul, are ours; Her genius and her glory are her own.

Matthew Arnold quoted in M. Billington, *The Guinness Book of Theatre Facts and Feats* 1982

Her range, like Kean's, was very limited, but her expression was perfect within that range.

G.H. Lewes *On Actors and the Art of Acting* 1875

BASIL RATHBONE
I don't know what his name is but he has a face like two profiles stuck together.

Mrs Patrick Campbell

VANESSA REDGRAVE
She's a marvellous actress and she never stops coming out with new plays, and she manages to find time for all that political rubbish as well.

John Gielgud *Daily Mail* 16 August 1991

MARGARET RUTHERFORD
A British comedienne whose appearance suggests an overstuffed electric chair.

Time 1962; review of *Murder She Says*

ATHENE SEYLER
An irritable hippopotamus.

Anonymous critic quoted in her obituary, *The Times* 13 September 1990

THOMAS SHERIDAN
Sherry is dull, naturally dull; but it must have taken him a great deal of pains to become what we now see him. Such an excess of stupidity, sir, is not nature.

Samuel Johnson 28 July 1763; quoted in J. Boswell, *Life of Samuel Johnson* 1791

ELIZABETH TAYLOR
She has an incipient double chin, her legs are too short and she has a slight pot belly.

Richard Burton Miss Taylor's husband at the time, 1967

She's not acting at all. She doesn't know how.

Walter Kerr

MARIE TEMPEST
Every new appearance of Miss Marie Tempest is a fresh delight. True, she is always presenting the

same thing – herself. But hers is a very various self, and she can always find you some unanticipated *nuance*, some very latest fashion of herself, like the very latest fashion of her gowns.

The Times 6 September 1891

SYBIL THORNDIKE
She could act with a tailor's dummy and bring it to life.

Ralph Richardson

PETER USTINOV
I was irrevocably betrothed to laughter, the sound of which has always seemed to me the most civilized music in the universe.

On himself *Dear Me* 1977

ORSON WELLES
He is too big for the boots of any part.

Kenneth Tynan reviewing Welles as Captain Ahab in the 1955 London production of *Moby Dick*

I started at the top and worked down.

Orson Welles

MAE WEST
A plumber's idea of Cleopatra.

W.C. Fields

Because my plays have dealt with sex and the dregs of humanity, some persons see fit to assume that I write vividly about such subjects because I know them by experience. . . . People who know me will bear me out that there is no star who is less of an exhibitionist, or who shows herself less in public places than myself. I am, in fact, retiring by nature in my private life to the point of shyness. . . . I do not drink. I do not smoke. I have my books, my writings, my friends – that is my private life.

On herself

I'm just a campfire girl.

On herself attrib.

DONALD WOLFIT
At the end of every barnstorming performance Wolfit would stagger back on stage clinging to the curtains as though drained to the dregs and on his knees.
The audience would clap in tumultuous applause as he gazed down at them with tears in his eyes. When the final curtain went down Wolfit would say: 'Coughing bastards', and leg it at full speed to his dressing room and a drink.

Alan Ayckbourn *Daily Mail* 7 October 1991

Olivier is a *tour de force* and Wolfit is forced to tour.

Hermione Gingold after Olivier's amazing success as Richard III 1944; quoted in R. Harwood, *Donald Wolfit* 1971

MONTY WOOLLEY

Mr Woolley reduced the nurse in *The Man Who Came to Dinner* to the potency of a pound of wet Kleenex. It was probably the best thing that happened to the art of the insult since the Medicis stopped talking in the 16th century.

Richard Severo recollection of Monty Woolley in the role based on writer Alexander Woollcott, obituary *New York Herald-Tribune* 7 May 1963

See also: Peggy Ashcroft, Tallulah Bankhead, The Barrymores, Sarah Bernhardt, Mrs Patrick Campbell, Critical Abuse – Actors; Garrick, John Gielgud, Irving, Kean, Vivien Leigh, Oscar Levant, The Lunts, Laurence Olivier, Ralph Richardson, Shakespeare's Plays, Sarah Siddons, Ellen Terry, H.B. Tree.

ADAPTATIONS

Dramatisations as a rule prove more like sieves than containers for the virtues of a book.

John Mason Brown

I don't want to see the uncut version of ANYTHING.

Jean Kerr

ADVICE

Remember, Ernest my boy, steak and stout for tragedy.

Henry Ainley to **Ernest Milton**; quoted in D. Blakelock, *Acting My Way*

Get on, say the wordies loud and clear, and get off.

Pamela Brown

Forget about the motivation. Speak the lines clearly and don't trip over the furniture.

Noël Coward attrib.

You've got to keep surprising them. Always come out of another hole.

Noël Coward to **David Lean**; recounted by David Lean at the 1989 Academy Awards Dinner

Don't put your daughter on the stage
Mrs Worthington,
Don't put your daughter on the stage,
The profession is overcrowded
And the struggle's pretty tough
And admitting the fact
She's burning to act,
That isn't quite enough.

Noël Coward *Mrs Worthington*
(song) *The Lyrics of Noël Coward*
1965

My entire success is based on one
rule: never take advice from
anybody.

W.C. Fields to **Paul Muni**
quoted in Jerome Lawrence, *Actor:*
The Life and Times of Paul Muni
1974

Well, of course, if you can't love
him you'll never be any good in
him, will you?

Tyrone Guthrie to **Laurence**
Olivier on his Sergius Saranoff in
Arms and the Man 1944. Olivier
later called this 'the richest pearl of
advice in my life'. Quoted in A.
Holden, *Olivier* 1988.

My boy listen to me. In the next
twenty or thirty years you may be
called upon to perform some eight
thousand times, and as you may
possibly not feel inspired each
time you perform you may,
during the course of a very stren-
u-ous role, not feel inspired more
than – er – let us say – um – ten
minutes per act. I think therefore,
you will do well to remember that
by taking great pains you can, shall
we say – um – design a part, a
role, so carefully that, inspired or
not, you'll be demmed interesting.
The less 'feeling' the better. See
what I mean, my boy.

Henry Irving quoted in Edward
Gordon Craig, *Henry Irving* 1930

Watch, watch always, and if you
see nothing worth copying, you
will see something to avoid.

Henry Irving to **Constance**
Benson quoted in Constance
Benson, *Mainly Players* 1926

I once got a letter from Richard
Burton. . . . He had seen me in a
student *Hamlet*, and he wrote that
I suffered from the same thing he
did: a voice too melodious, easy
to listen to and liable to send
people to sleep. He advised me to
roughen it up a bit.

Derek Jacobi *Sunday Times* 24
May 1992

Anyone who works is a fool. I
don't work – I merely inflict
myself on the public.

Robert Morley

My dear boy, why don't you try acting – it's so much easier.

Laurence Olivier to **Dustin Hoffman**. (For the film *Marathon Man* Dustin Hoffman had stayed awake for several nights in order to be convincing as a man who had had no sleep.)

If you're going on the stage, read Dickens, and you'll never lack for a characterisation.

Laurence Olivier quoted in *Great Acting* (ed. H. Burton) 1967

Just remember there's many an actor sleeping on the embankment tonight, with no soles to his shoes, for lack of an upward inflection.

Douglas Quayle to his son **John Quayle** when he decided on an acting career; recalled by **Donald Sinden**

The most important advice I ever had came from a Hungarian teacher who told me every actress has to be aware of outside influences, or poodles. If you are to be a good actress you must let your poodles off the leash and stop thinking about them.

Vanessa Redgrave *Evening Standard* 13 November 1991

. . . the greatest difficulty is to keep sober enough in the one hour twenty five minutes wait you have before the end to take your curtain call without falling into an orchestra pit. This takes years of skill and cannot be over-estimated, as much of the effect of the poetic 'Mab' speech may be lost by such an incident. . . .

Ralph Richardson to **Laurence Olivier**; letter on his experience playing Mercutio in *Romeo and Juliet*; quoted in F. Barker, *Laurence Olivier* 1984

Speak the speech, I pray you, as I pronounced it to you, trippingly on the tongue; but if you mouth it, as many of your players do, I had as lief the town-crier spoke my lines. Nor do not saw the air too much with your hand, but use all gently; for in the very torrent, tempest, and as I may say, the whirlwind of your passion, you must acquire and beget a temperance that may give it smoothness.

William Shakespeare *Hamlet* Act III, Scene 2

Suit the action to the word, the word to the action, with this special observance, that you o'erstep not the modesty of nature.

Ibid.

There are no small parts, only small actors.

Constantin Stanislavski; often attributed to other actors e.g. **Ginger Rogers**

The three great I's are Industry, Intelligence and Imagination: and the greatest of these is Imagination.

Ellen Terry 1907; advice to **Gwen Ffrangcon-Davies**; recalled by her in *The Times* 26 January 1991

Keep your bowels and your vowels open.

Herbert Beerbohm Tree

I always pass on good advice. It is the only thing to do with it.

Oscar Wilde *An Ideal Husband* 1899

AMATEURS

A professional is a man who can do his job when he doesn't feel like it; an amateur is one who can't do it when he does feel like it.

James Agate (the difference between professional and amateur actors)

The artistic temperament is a disease that attracts amateurs.

G.K. Chesterton *Heretics*

Those brave individuals who always step in where audiences fear to tread.

Seymour Hicks *Chestnuts Reroasted*

AMBITION

I am only interested in two kinds of people; those who can entertain me and those who can advance my career.

Ingrid Bergman

I think I've left it a bit late. I might play the nurse in *Romeo and Juliet*.

Noël Coward when asked if he still had any ambition to play a Shakespearean role

To be Bernard Shaw is honour enough.

George Bernard Shaw when offered a knighthood

I've been offered titles, but I think they get one into disreputable company.

George Bernard Shaw on his 90th birthday, 1946

You know, you get frightfully cocky, but if you haven't got that in the theatre, if you don't feel, 'I've got something to say that nobody else on this earth knows how to say,' I don't think you're any good.

Sybil Thorndike quoted in R. Findlater, *The Player Queens* 1976

ARTISTIC INTEGRITY

My memory is full of beauty – Hamlet's soliloquies, the Queen Mab speech, King Magnus's monologue from *The Apple Cart*. Do you expect me to clutter up all that with this horse-shit?

John Barrymore when refusing to learn the lines for his movie roles

PEGGY ASHCROFT

She was a great actress because she was a great woman; so when we are responding to Ashcroft the actress we are also responding to a unique woman.

Michael Billington television obituary 17 June 1991

What a huge hole she's left. She was more than an actress. She rallied the troops.

Judi Dench *Sunday Times* 15 December 1991

In her steady progress towards the heights of her art Peggy Ashcroft learned to subsume her youthfulness, charm, delicacy and Englishness in the truths of the characters that she not only played but lived.

Richard Findlater *The Player Queens* 1976

When Peggy came on in the Senate scene it was as if all the lights in the theatre had suddenly gone up.

John Gielgud on her Desdemona in *Othello* 1930

It was like being butted in the stomach by a young calf.

John Gielgud on acting with Peggy Ashcroft in *Romeo and Juliet* 1932. Television obituary 17 June 1991

More than any other actress on the stage she has the moral alertness which separates the tragic from the merely melodramatic or pathetic.

Penelope Gilliatt review of *The Duchess of Malfi* 1960

When I told her that she was a potato in Leicester – that the theatre bar there had a 'Spud Ashcroft' stuffed with prawns, she took both hands off the wheel and waved them about with pleasure and amazement. We nearly hit a lorry.

Peter Hall *Diaries* 21 April 1974

She cared more about the play than the part, and more about the company than being a star. She fought tirelessly for serious theatre, and was always there when a new start was made.

Peter Hall *Sunday Times* 16 June 1991

AUDIENCES

Long experience has taught me that in England nobody goes to the theatre unless he or she has bronchitis.

James Agate *Ego 8* 1947

The best audience is intelligent, well-educated and a little drunk.

Alben W. Barkley

Audiences, no, the plural is impossible. Whether it is in Butte, Montana or Broadway it's an audience. The same great hulking monster with four thousand eyes and forty thousand teeth.

John Barrymore quoted in R. May, *The Wit of the Theatre* 1969

How many idiots go to make up a public?

Pierre Beaumarchais quoted in A. Houssaye, *Behind the Scenes of the Comédie Française* 1889

In the theatre the audience wants to be surprised – but by things they expect.

Tristan Bernard *Contes, Répliques et Bons Mots*

The Marquess and Marchioness of Empty are in front again.

Mrs Patrick Campbell usual remark when faced with a thin house

Those who have free seats for the play hiss first.

Chinese Proverb

Just say the lines as written. There will be some in the audience who won't understand yet will deeply admire them.

Corneille, admitting to an actor that he did not always know the meaning of what he had written; T. Revesz, *Bolcsek Mosolya* 1960, quoted in P. Hay *Theatrical Anecdotes* 1987

The great public refuse to be impressed by the Brechts and the Anouilhs and all the rest of the defeatists, and continue unregenerately to enjoy being amused in the theatre. I expect that the public will win in the long run; it usually does.

Noël Coward *The Noël Coward Diaries* February 1957 (pub. 1982)

The audience was tremendously fashionable, and for the first part of the play (*Bitter Sweet*), almost as responsive as so many cornflour blancmanges.

Noël Coward

Now the common haunters [of the theatre] are for the most part, the lewdest persons in the land, apt for pilfery, perjury, forgery, or any rogueries; the very scum, rascality, and baggage of the people, thieves, cut-purses, shifters – briefly an unclean generation, and spawn of vipers. . . . For a play is like a sincke in a Towne, whereunto all the filth doth runne: or a boyle in the body, that draweth all the ill humours to it.

Henry Crosse 1603

By sitting on the stage, if you be a Knight, you may happily get yourself a Mistresse: if a mere Fleet Street Gentleman, a wife.

Thomas Dekker *The Gull's Handbook* 1609

No one can fully appreciate the fatuity of human nature until he has spent some time in a box office.

St. John Ervine

It is extraordinary how an audience as a whole is sharper than any single member of it.

Peter Hall *Diaries* 19 October 1977

The author seeks to keep from me
The murderer's identity
And you are not a friend of his
If you keep shouting who it is. . . .

A.P. Herbert poem *To the Lady
Behind Me at the Theatre*

I always enjoy appearing before a
British audience. Even if they
don't feel like laughing they nod
their heads to show they've
understood.

Bob Hope

I would produce *Noah's Ark* in
modern dress. The curtain will
not rise until the last straggler is in
his seat. Then Noah will appear
and announce, 'Now it's going to
rain for forty days.' At this point
the ceiling in the theatre will open
and drench the entire audience. If
they try to escape I will be
standing by the exit with a hose to
catch them.

George S. Kaufman planning
his revenge on habitual latecomers

The critic says: this is an
extremely bad play – why is that?
The audience says: this is an
extremely bad play – why was I
born?

Jean Kerr

It is well understood by every
dramatist that a late-dining

audience needs several minutes of
dialogue before it recovers from
its bewilderment at finding itself
in a theatre.

A.A. Milne

Besides this perpetual pelting
(with rotten oranges) from the
gallery, which renders an English
playhouse so uncomfortable, there
is no end to their calling out and
knocking with their sticks 'til the
curtain is drawn up.

Dr Moritz on 18th-century
English audiences *The Era
Almanack* 1872

Adulterers, Whore-masters,
Panders, Whores and such like
effeminate, idle, unchaste,
lascivious, graceless persons were
the most assiduous Play-hunters in
their time.

Ovid *Ars Amatoria* 1 BC

*There still remains to mortify a wit,
The many-headed monster of the pit.*

Alexander Pope *Horace* Epistle I,
Book II

Aunt Edna – a nice, respectable,
middle-class, middle-aged maiden
lady with time on her hands and
money to help her pass it.

Terence Rattigan on a typical
member of the London audience

I don't think actors really love their audience; they are more in the nature of a lion-tamer.

Ralph Richardson quoted in *Great Acting* (ed. H. Burton) 1967

It is clear to me that we shall not become a play-going people until we discard our fixed idea that it is the business of the people to come to the theatre and substitute for it the idea that it is the business of the theatre to come to the people.

George Bernard Shaw

I regret to say that the patrons of the gallery at the Princess's, being admitted at half the usual West End price, devote the saving to the purchase of sausages to throw at the critics. I appeal to the gentleman or lady who successfully aimed one at me to throw a cabbage next time, as I am a vegetarian, and sausages are wasted on me.

George Bernard Shaw

*In other things the knowing artist may
Judge better than the people; but a
    play,
(Made for delight, and for no other
    use)
If you approve it not, has no excuse.*

Edmund Waller prologue to *The Maid's Tragedy*

I want to thank you for your very generous applause – and your very heavy breathing.

Mae West

The play was a great success, but the audience was a total failure.

Oscar Wilde after the unsuccessful first night of *Lady Windermere's Fan* 1892

The audience strummed their catarrhs.

Alexander Woollcott

AUDIENCE ASIDES

Thank goodness I have at last found a place where I can see and hear comfortably.

Anonymous woman who had just fallen from the overcrowded gallery into the pit. *The Era Almanack*, 1872; quoted in G. Snell, *The Book of Theatre Quotes* 1982

How different, how very different, from the home-life of our own dear Queen!

Victorian theatre-goer after watching Sarah Bernhardt's frenzied performance as the

Queen of Egypt in Shakespeare's *Antony and Cleopatra*

How different, how very different, from the home life of our own dear queens.

Member of the audience at Wyndham's Theatre after a performance of the American homosexual comedy *The Boys in the Band*

Rather an unpleasant family those Lears.

Comment during a performance of *King Lear*; quoted in W. Pett Ridge, *A Story Teller*

And the funny thing is (pause) — exactly the same thing happened to Dorothy.

Comment after a performance of *Vivat Vivat Regina* 1970 (in which Mary Queen of Scots is beheaded); recalled by **Eileen Atkins**

Well Mildred, that was the worst play I've seen since *King Lear*.

Overheard by director **John Fernald** after a Saturday matinée of his production of *The Cherry Orchard*, Liverpool Playhouse, 1948; recalled by Noel Davis

Look, here comes old Ginger again!

Reaction to the carrot-red wig sported by Olivier for Hotspur in *Henry IV* Part I 1945. Overheard by **John Mills** and quoted in A. Holden *Olivier* 1988

AUDITIONS

The nicest words I know in the theatre are 'That's all, sir, which signify the end of a mass audition. It means we shan't hear *Phil The Fluter's Ball* again that morning.

Noël Coward

Don't worry my dear, I know how frightening this is: I had to audition for Ellen Terry.

Gwen Ffrangcon-Davies while conducting a master class on *Romeo and Juliet* in 1988 at the age of 97; quoted in her obituary in *The Times* 28 January 1992

Aspiring player auditioning for James Quin at Drury Lane: To be or not to be, that is the question. **James Quin:** No question, sir, 'pon my honour — not to be, most certainly.

Callow young director to veteran actress Athene Seyler: And what

have you done Miss Seyler?
Athene Seyler: Do you mean
this morning?

AVANT-GARDE

Avant-garde is French for off-
Broadway garbage.

Line from the Dick Van Dyke
television show; quoted in D.
Richards, *The Curtain Rises* 1966

The dead theatre is always with
us, and what blazes from the stage
today becomes an orthodoxy
tomorrow.

Peter Brook quoted by **Howard
Brenton** in *The Times* 13 April
1992

I have never written for the
intelligentsia. Sixteen curtain-calls
and close on Saturday.

Noël Coward

The Theatre of the Absurd strives
to express its sense of the
senselessness of the human
condition and the inadequacy of
the rational approach by the open
abandonment of rational devices
and discursive thought.

Martin Esslin *The Theatre of the
Absurd* 1962

The one thing constant in a
changing world is the avant-garde.

Louis Jouvet

BAD HABITS

Cocaine isn't habit forming. I
should know – I've been using it
for years.

Tallulah Bankhead

He was suffering from the effects
of nervousness and its antidotes.

Constance Benson about
George Weir after he had
forgotten all his lines

Ladies and gentlemen, you see
that I am not in good condition to
play tonight. But if you will only
wait five minutes, while I go
behind the scenes to cool my head
in a pail of water, I'll come out
and show you the damnedest King
Henry you ever saw in your life.

Junius Brutus Booth after being
hissed for his inebriated
performance in *Henry IV* at the
Old Bowery Theatre, New York

Where's the stage – and what's the
play?

Junius Brutus Booth arriving at
the theatre to play in *King Lear*

When I played drunks I had to remain sober because I didn't know how to play them when I was drunk.

Richard Burton

My idea of a good afternoon's exercise is 50 Turkish cigarettes and a box of marrons glacés.

Noël Coward quoted by Daniel Massey, television interview, March 1992

Sobriety's a real turn-on for me. You can see what you're doing.

Peter O'Toole

It is better to drink a little too much than much too little.

Herbert Beerbohm Tree attrib.

Cocaine is God's way of saying you're making too much money.

Robin Williams

TALLULAH BANKHEAD

More of an act than an actress.

Anon.

A parrot around Tallulah must feel as frustrated as a kleptomaniac in a piano store.

Fred Allen attrib.

I'm as pure as driven slush.

Tallulah Bankhead *Observer* 24 February 1957

Don't look now, Tallulah, but your show's slipping.

Heywood Broun review of *The Exciters*

Watching Tallulah on stage is like watching someone skating on thin ice – everyone wants to be there when it breaks.

Mrs Patrick Campbell quoted in Bankhead's obituary, *The Times* 13 December 1968

My messages to Congress
Are a lot of boola-boola.
I'm not so fond of Bankhead,
But I'd love to meet Tallulah.

George M. Cohen (Tallulah's father was Speaker of the House of Representatives.)

With Tallulah a leading man has an exhausting time off-stage.

Donald Cook attrib. *c.* 1950

A day away from Tallulah is like a month in the country.

Howard Dietz attrib. *Show Business Illlustrated* 17 October 1961

She learned how little it takes to make people bleed, and sometimes she could not resist demonstrating her skill at this unpleasing game.

Brendan Gill *New Yorker* 17 October 1972

Tallulah was crowding seventeen when she arrived from Alabama, stage-struck, sultry-voiced, and brimming with a rose-leaf beauty which she determinedly hid under the then fashionable mask of white powder, blue eye-shadow and beef-coloured lipstick. She fondly believed that this made her look more like Ethel Barrymore, who was her idol.

Margaret Case Harriman *The Vicious Circle* 1951

Tallulah was sitting in a group of people giving the monologue she always thought was conversation.

Lillian Hellman

I've just spent an hour talking to Tallulah Bankhead for a few minutes.

Fred Keating

I've staged shows that called for the management of a herd of buffalo, and I've shot actors out of cannons for fifty feet into the arms of an adagio dancer, but both of them were easier than saying 'Good morning' to Miss Bankhead.

Billy Rose

I suppose you could say Tallulah was a tramp, in the elegant sense.

Tennessee Williams

[She was] talking so ceaselessly that you had to make a reservation five minutes ahead to get a word in.

Earl Wilson

J.M. BARRIE

What I think I liked best was tearing up the programme and dropping the bits on people's heads.

Anonymous child who had been taken to see *Peter Pan* by J.M. Barrie

The ideal audience for this would be a house composed entirely of married couples who had never had any children, or parents who had lost them all.

James Agate on *Peter Pan* in *Ego 3* 1937

In the days when Bernard Shaw was a critic he began an article on a play of mine with the words: 'This is worse than Shakespeare.' I admit that this rankled.

J.M. Barrie quoted in R. May, *The Wit of the Theatre* 1969

Dinner guest: Not all your plays are successes I suppose, Sir James?
J.M. Barrie: No, some Peter out and some Pan out.

Attrib.

A little child whom the Gods have whispered to.

Mrs Patrick Campbell letter to George Bernard Shaw, January 1913

The cheerful clatter of Sir James Barrie's cans as he went round with the milk of human kindness.

Philip Guedalla 'Some Critics', *Supers and Supermen* 1920

Oh, for an hour of Herod.

Anthony Hope at the opening of *Peter Pan* 1904

Sugar without the diabetes.

George Jean Nathan

THE BARRYMORES

ETHEL
Miss Barrymore . . . did what came naturally to her; took the stage, filled it, and left the rest of us to stage rear.

Edward G. Robinson *All My Yesterdays*

JOHN
John Barrymore was Icarus, who flew so close to the sun that the wax on his wings melted and he plunged back to earth – from the peak of classical acting to the banalities of show business.

Brooks Atkinson *Broadway* 1970

Barrymore cut through the darkness of the theatre like a sharp, glittering pen-knife.

Brooks Atkinson quoted in Alma Power-Waters, *John Barrymore*

My only regret in the theatre is that I could never sit out front and watch me.

John Barrymore

In some paradoxical fashion, the very manner in which Barrymore seemed almost to revel in his disintegration convinced people who had never seen him in *Hamlet* and *The Jest* that he must have been among the giants.

Gene Fowler *Good Night Sweet Prince* 1942

I always said that I'd like Barrymore's acting till the cows came home. Well, ladies and gentlemen, last night the cows came home.

George Jean Nathan on Barrymore's performance in *My Dear Children* 1940

Conspicuously unclean and smelled highly on many occasions.

David Niven

When I saw what they looked like in daylight my ulcer was cured.

Jack Warner on the notorious Hollywood 'hell-raisers' John Barrymore and Errol Flynn

LIONEL
Of the three Barrymores, Lionel was the one most at odds with the theatre. His attitude towards it amounted to a psychosis. He needed it; he had plenty of talent for it. But he was not a public person. He was happier – though less successful – in private occupations like painting, sculpting, etching, composing music and writing.

Brooks Atkinson *Broadway* 1970

Lionel uses words only to flog them. He makes them suffer.

John Barrymore on his brother

MAURICE
This founder of the house of Barrymore was English – born Herbert Blyth – pre-eminently a man's man, and beyond question a woman's man, of a wit so telling and yet so good hearted that even the objects of his keen satire joined in laughter at their own expense. On the stage he was always a picture – in private an Apollo in a slop suit. Amateur champion middle-weight boxer,

narrator of a thousand stories, quick in resentment of an insult, generous to a foe, burner of candles at both ends, Bedouin of Broadway, this was the Barrymore that I knew.

Otis Skinner *Footlights and Spotlights* 1924

BEAUMONT AND FLETCHER

They lived together on the Banke side, not far from the Playhouse, both batchelors; lay together; had one Wench in the house between them, which they did so admire; the same cloathes and cloake &c. betweene them.

John Aubrey

For ten pounds Beaumont and Fletcher will give you any one of a dozen plays – each indistinguishable from the other.

Caryl Brahms *No Bed for Bacon*

I have never been able to distinguish the presence of Fletcher during the life of Beaumont, nor the absence of Beaumont during the survival of Fletcher.

Samuel Taylor Coleridge *Notes for Lecture on Beaumont and Fletcher*

Dear Edith, you spoil the rhythm by putting in a 'very'. The line is 'On a clear morning you can see Marlow'. On a *very* clear day you can also see both Beaumont and Fletcher.

Noël Coward to **Edith Evans** in rehearsal

Though he [Fletcher] treated love in perfection, yet Honour, Ambition, Revenge, and generally all the stronger Passions he either touch'd not or not masterly. To conclude all; he was a limb of Shakespeare.

John Dryden *Preface to Troilus and Cressida*

The blossoms of Beaumont's imagination draw no sustenance from the soil, but are cut and slightly withered flowers stuck into sand.

T.S. Eliot

How I doe love thee Beaumont, and thy *Muse*.

Ben Jonson 'To Francis Beaumont' *Epigrammes* 1616

The pair wrote a great deal that was pretty disgraceful, but at least they had been educated out of the possibility of writing *Titus Andronicus*.

George Bernard Shaw *Saturday Review* 19 February 1898

BEGINNINGS

There was some gay, provocative dialogue, only one line of which I can recall: 'Crumbs! How exciting.'

Noël Coward (on his stage debut) *Present Indicative* 1937

The boy who took the part of Kate made a fine, bold, black-eyed hussy badly in need of taming. I cannot remember seeing any actress in the part who looked it better.

W.A. Darlington 1922 on **Laurence Olivier**, aged fourteen, in *The Taming of the Shrew*

I got all the schooling any actress needs. That is, I learned to write enough to sign contracts.

Hermione Gingold *How to Grow Old Disgracefully* 1988

A young gentleman by name Mr Gravel has commenced an Actor on Account of his debts, for He is accounted an Extravagant young Fellow. . . . The people in general here rather pity than condemn him: this is the consequence of loose morals and may serve him as a lesson to others.

Contemporary account of American actor **Samuel Greville**'s debut in *Hamlet*, 1767; quoted in Michael Billington, *The Guinness Book of Theatre Facts and Feats* 1982

In Maeterlinck's *The Blue Bird* I played the cat . . . my entrance . . . I made as big as I could, naturally, with the immortal line, 'Mee-ow-you'.

Rex Harrison *Rex* 1974

Actors cannot choose the manner in which they are born – consequently it is the one gesture in their lives completely devoid of self-consciousness.

Helen Hayes *On Reflection* 1968

I had no real ambition about acting, but I knew there had to be something better than the bloody chemist's shop.

Glenda Jackson who started working life at Boot's the Chemist

I thought all acting was making love in tights to pretty women, and I determined to devote my life to it.

Jerome K. Jerome *On the Stage and Off* 1885

There comes a time in everyone's life when he feels he was born to be an actor. . . . This sort of thing generally takes a man when he is about nineteen and lasts till he is nearly twenty. But he doesn't know this at the time.

Ibid.

I know mum and dad do not want me to act and think that I won't. BUT I WILL.

Alec McCowen diary entry, aged 13 *Sunday Times* 19 January 1992

One went to school, one wanted to act, one started to act and one is still acting.

Maggie Smith

The small boy who played Brutus is already a great actor.

Ellen Terry on **Laurence Olivier** diary entry December 1916, after seeing the 9-year-old Olivier in a school play at All Saints School, Marylebone

I learned two things at RADA: first, that I couldn't act; second, that it didn't matter.

Wilfred Hyde White

SARAH BERNHARDT

(ON HERSELF)
I loved many people, many things. But all I can remember now is that I loved the stage. Write of me only that please, young reporter, that I loved the stage.

Sarah Bernhardt quoted in Ben Hecht, *A Child of the Century* 1923

(BY OTHERS)
She is a bit of smoke, a breath of mist – a fugitive vision of delicate features under a shower of hair and a cloud of lace.

Anonymous critic 1868 in H. and D.L. Thomas *Living Biographies of Famous Women*;

quoted in F.S. Pepper *Dictionary of Biographical Quotations* 1985

She has the head of a virgin and the body of a broomstick.

Alexandre Dumas 1865

The most remarkable phenomenon of the 19th century.

Edmond de Goncourt

You are too stupid to be much of an actress, but it will keep you out of mischief.

Julie von Hard, Bernhardt's mother, when Bernhardt started her training

A great actress from the waist down.

Madge Kendal quoted by Brooks Atkinson, *New York Times Book Review* 25 May 1969

She was morbid to the point of artistic passion. She fell deeply in love with an undertaker's assistant but refused to marry him when he would not permit her to be present at an embalming. Between the hours of her rehearsals she visited the cemeteries of Paris and sat among the tombstones like a sister of the departed.

H. and D.L. Thomas *Living Biographies of Famous Women*

It has been said that she died in harness. That expression of a plodder overtaken by death is inadequate for so gallant, so defiantly twinkling an exit. She was a boat that went to the bottom with its orchestra playing gaily.

Alexander Woollcott *Enchanted Aisles* 1924

BILLING

I'm now quite glad my name is Hermione Gingold because it's such a long name that on theatre billboards there isn't room for another name beside it.

Hermione Gingold *How to Grow Old Disgracefully* 1989

BROADWAY

'The Great White Way'

'The Street of the Midnight Sun'

Broadway – a branch of the narcotics world run by actors.

Bertolt Brecht

What a glorious garden of wonders the lights of Broadway

would be to anyone lucky enough to be unable to read.

G.K. Chesterton *What I Saw in America* 1923

When you leave New York you're camping out.

Nat Goodwin

Broadway is like a powerful magnet, with a pull that is overwhelming.

Mary Martin quoted in D. Richards, *The Curtain Rises* 1966

In 42nd Street it is a glowing summer afternoon all night: one might almost wear white trousers and a straw hat.

Paul Morand quoted in B. Atkinson, *Broadway* 1970

I read Shakespeare very well. *Variety* I still cannot read.

Maurice Pagnol commenting on the unique 'showbiz' language of *Variety*

Since Mr [Charles] Dickens' time the pigs of Broadway have changed only in form, having taken on the semblance of humans. You can see them today in the streetcars and subway trains, pushing and grunting their way to seats while women stand clinging to the straps. You can see them wandering along Broadway, old hogs familiar with every sty in the city, and young porkers just learning the ways of swine, their little eyes eagerly watching every passing skirt.

Of an evening they gather in cabarets, wallowing in illicit liquor and shouting through a conversational garbage made up of oaths and filthy stories and scandal.

A pig is a pig even when it wears evening clothes. . . .

Damon Runyan

The hardened artery.

Walter Winchell

As far as Broadway is concerned, a star that is no longer in the ascendant is already extinct.

Walter Winchell

MRS PATRICK CAMPBELL

(ON HERSELF)
I look like a burst paper bag. . . . I must borrow a chair with a high back so that I can hide my chins behind it.

(BY OTHERS)
The Lord Mayor's coach with nothing inside it.

James Agate on Mrs Campbell as Mrs Alving in Ibsen's *Ghosts*

The best tragic or emotional actress in the country. In the sheer acting sense, by which one means the marriage of spirit and the technical means to convey that spirit, Mrs Campbell has no rival on our stage.

James Agate 1928; review of Mrs Patrick Campbell as Ella Rentheim in *John Gabriel Borkman*

Her voice was like Casals' cello and her silences had the emotional significance of Maeterlinck's shadowy speech.

James Agate quoted in *Bernard Shaw and Mrs Patrick Campbell: Their Correspondence* (ed. Alan Dent) 1952

This was an actress who, for twenty years had the world at her feet. She kicked it away, and the ball rolled out of her reach.

Ibid.

On one occasion after a particularly wild 'tantrum' she walked to the footlights and peered out at Yeats, who was pacing up and down the stalls of the Abbey Theatre. 'I'd give anything to know what you're thinking,' shouted Mrs Pat. 'I'm thinking', replied Yeats, 'of the master of a wayside Indian railway station who sent a message to his Company's headquarters saying: "Tigress on the line: wire instructions." '

Gabriel Fallon *Sean O'Casey: The Man I Knew*

As for the final stabbing scene, she might as well have tickled herself with a straw and died o' laughing.

Punch review of Mrs Patrick Campbell as Juliet in *Romeo and Juliet* 1895

It is greatly to Mrs Patrick Campbell's credit that, bad as the play was, her acting was worse.

George Bernard Shaw
reviewing *Fedora* 1895

You will tell me that Mrs Patrick Campbell cannot act. Who said she could? – Who wants her to act? – Who cares tuppence whether she possesses that or any other second-rate accomplishment? On the highest plane one does not act, one *is*. Go and see her move, stand, look, kneel – go and breathe the magic atmosphere that is created by the grace of all those deeds; and then talk to me about acting, forsooth!

George Bernard Shaw *Saturday Review* 7 March 1896

Bah! You have no nerve, you have no brain: you are the caricature of an 18th-century male sentimentalist, a Hedda Gabler titivated with odds and ends from Burne-Jones' rag-bag. You are an owl sickened by two days of my sunshine.

George Bernard Shaw 1913

If only you could write a book entitled WHY, THOUGH I WAS A WONDERFUL ACTRESS, NO MANAGER OR AUTHOR WOULD EVER ENGAGE ME TWICE IF HE COULD POSSIBLY HELP IT, it would be a best-seller. But you couldn't. Besides, you don't know. I do.

George Bernard Shaw letter 19 December 1938; *Bernard Shaw and Mrs Patrick Campbell: Their Correspondence* (ed. Alan Dent) 1952
Shaw and Mrs Patrick Campbell enjoyed a correspondence over many years but the letters ceased after her persistent attempts to persuade him to allow these private letters to be published.

In the acting of women with brains and with natures complex, strange or highly strung she had not her equal on the English stage.

The Times obituary 1940

She was a sinking ship firing upon her rescuers.

Alexander Woollcott *While Rome Burns* 1934

An ego like a raging tooth.

W.B. Yeats quoted in Gabriel Fallon, *Sean O'Casey: The Man I Knew*

CENSORSHIP

Nothing is unacceptable on stage except the breakdown of communication.

Howard Barker quoted in *Contemporary Dramatists* 1977

The result of the rehearsal is that H.M. thinks I had better not call her daughter 'a degraded woman', and I agree! Also she is *not* to say to Sir C. in describing her wooing of Clutterbuck, 'I have nothing to offer as dowry but my virtue', to which C. replies, 'Ah, little enough'.

Arthur Bigge describing some difficulties arising during an amateur production of *L'Homme Blasé* with Princess Louise, daughter of Queen Victoria (H.M.)

I acknowledge Shakespeare to be the world's greatest dramatic poet, but regret that no parent could place the uncorrected book in the hands of his daughter, and therefore I have prepared the Family Shakespeare.

Thomas Bowdler preface to Thomas and Harriet Bowdler's expurgated edition, *The Family Shakespeare* 1818

Nothing is added to the original text, but those words and expressions are omitted which cannot with propriety be read aloud in a family.

Ibid.

I think sex should be done, but unlike justice, not *seen* to be done.

Evelyn Laye quoted in D. Richards, *The Curtain Rises* 1966

Requirement: Jack and Deirdre must sit on the bed as allowed. They may not lie. Jack must be fully clothed, not in *déshabillé*, and Deirdre's slip must be inside her breeches.

The Lord Chamberlain on John Osborne's play *The World of Paul Slickey*; quoted in G. Snell, *The Book of Theatre Quotes* 1982

If the theatre were to be shut up, the stage wholly silenced and suppressed, I believe the world, bad as it is now, would be ten times more wicked.

Antoine Houdar de la Motte

Christians must not lift up their eyes to stage plays, the pleasurable delights of polluted eyes, lest their lusts be inflamed by them.

Origen 3rd century AD

The first condition of progress is the abolition of censorship.

George Bernard Shaw

What matters is not what the censor does to what I have written, but to what I might have written.

Leo Tolstoy

CHARITY GALAS

*We're going to do a Midnight
    Matinée!
We're going to do a Midnight Show!
We're not quite sure
What charity it's for
But probably the Press will know . . .*

Noël Coward *Midnight Matinée* (song); *The Lyrics of Noël Coward* 1965

CHEKHOV

Southern Fried Chekhov.

Cast nickname for *The Wisteria Tree*, Joshua Logan's adaptation of *The Cherry Orchard*, set in the deep South

I *hate* plays that have a stuffed bird sitting on the book-case screaming, 'I'm the title! I'm the title! I'm the title!'

Noël Coward on Chekhov's *The Seagull*

If you were to ask me what *Uncle Vanya* is about, I would say about as much as I can take.

Robert Garland review of *Uncle Vanya* in *Journal American* 1946

I cannot bear Shakespeare, you know, but your plays are even worse.

Leo Tolstoy to Chekhov quoted in M. Gorelick, *New Theatres for Old* 1940

CHILD ACTORS

Two things should be cut – the second Act and that child's throat.

Noël Coward after seeing *Gypsy*

in London with its vivacious child star **Bonnie Langford**

I was grown-up at ten, and first began to grow young at forty.

Madge Kendal quoted in Alfred Miles, *The New Anecdote Book* 1906

CLUBS

The *Players* are all gentlemen who wish they were actors.
The *Lambs* are all actors who wish they were gentlemen.
The *Friars* wish they were both.

19th-century saying on New York's three best-known theatrical clubs

Member of the Garrick after a confrontation: When I joined, all the members were gentlemen.
Herbert Beerbohm Tree: I wonder why they left?

Quoted in Hesketh Pearson, *Beerbohm Tree* 1956

COMEDY

Comedy aims at representing men as worse, and tragedy as better, than in real life.

Aristotle *Poetics* II *c*. 322 BC

Nobody ever died of laughter.

Max Beerbohm

The powerful advantage of our theatrical tradition is that it is profoundly comic. Serious matters can be tackled in the theatre by mucking about and having some fun with what is meant to be unstageable.

Howard Brenton

The most difficult character in comedy is that of a fool, and he must be no simpleton who plays the part.

Cervantes *Don Quixote* 1605

Of all days, the day on which one has not laughed is surely the most wasted.

Chamfort *Maximes et Pensées* 1805

The whole of comedy depends on timing – and if you are really on your toes, you play the audience and you control the laughter.

Noël Coward

All comedians are anarchists.

Ken Dodd

Comedy, like sodomy, is an unnatural act.

Marty Feldman 1969

You may humbug the town as a tragedian, but comedy is a serious thing, my boy, so don't try that just yet.

David Garrick to Jack Bannister; quoted in Laurence Hutton, *Curiosities of the American Stage* 1891

Dying is easy. Comedy is hard.

Edmund Kean

I have noticed that in plays where the characters on stage laugh a great deal, the people out front laugh very little.

Jean Kerr

The debauching of virgins and the *amours* of strumpets are the subject of comedy.

Lactantius *Divinarum Institutionum* VI *c.* 310 AD

A farce or a comedy is best played; a tragedy is best read at home.

Abraham Lincoln to John Hay after seeing Edwin Booth in *The Merchant of Venice* 1863 (Lincoln was assassinated by Booth's brother in 1865.)

A comedian is not an actor. His work bears the same relation to acting as that of a hangman, a midwife, or a divorce lawyer bears to poetry, or that of a bishop to religion.

H.L. Mencken 1929

Comedy is the fountain of sound sense.

George Meredith *The Idea of Comedy* 1877

1. Have I not been heard? 2. Was the line before mine not heard? 3. Was I truthful?

Athene Seyler (checklist after failing to get a laugh in the right place) *The Craft of Comedy* (with Stephen Haggard) 1944

Humour is like a frog – dissect it and it dies.

Mark Twain

Comedy is simply a funny way of being serious.

Peter Ustinov

Comedians; the seond oldest profession which, like the first, has been ruined by amateurs.

Ben Warriss quoted in Simon Brett, *A Comedian Dies* 1979

COSTUME AND MAKE-UP

Mr John Mills wanders around the stage at the St James Theatre looking like a bewildered carrot.

Anonymous critic on John Mills's red wig in *The Uninvited Guest*; quoted in D. Rigg, *No Turn Unstoned* 1982

I am doing it for myself. If I catch sight of my hand it will be the hand of Cleopatra. That will help me.

Sarah Bernhardt explaining her meticulous character make-up to

Mrs Patrick Campbell; quoted in W.G. Robertson, *Life was Worth Living* 1931

It's like looking out of a yak's arse!

Coral Browne on the wig for her part in *The Sea* by Edward Bond

I look like an elderly wasp in an interesting condition.

Mrs Patrick Campbell on the black and yellow costume for her part as an Ancient Egyptian in *False Gods* 1909; quoted in R. May *The Wit of the Theatre* 1969

My attitude to make-up is the same as my attitude to directors – never use them.

Denholm Elliott quoted at the London Theatre Museum exhibition on stage make-up, 1992

Curls, I think (pausing to pat her hair) – yes *curls*.

Edith Evans 1954. After **Christopher Fry** had finished painstakingly reading her the whole of his new play, *The Dark is Light Enough*; recalled by **Noel Davis**

I love the fact that actors always go straight to their appearance. When Bully Bottom is given the part of Pyramus in *A Midsummer Night's Dream*, the first question he asks director Quince is: 'What beard were I best play it in?' There speaks the actor.

Peter Hall *Diaries* 4 July 1972

You hear Macbeth's first line, then Larry's make-up comes on, then Banquo comes on, then Larry comes on.

Vivien Leigh commenting on Olivier's typically heavy stage make-up during the 1937 *Macbeth* at the Old Vic; quoted in A. Holden, *Olivier* 1983

Twenty minutes for character make-up: ninety for a straight and, if you are playing a juvenile, wash your hair and fluff it up, and pinch your cheeks before you go on.

Henry Livings summary of theatre lore on make-up; quoted in R. May, *The Wit of the Theatre* 1969

Oh yes, tired boy stuff, don't you dare remove it with your bloody retouching, old boy.

Laurence Olivier 1937 to theatre photographer Angus McBean. McBean had remarked on his elaborate make-up for Hamlet which included painting the skin under his eyes white.

About wearing period costume; the most important thing is not the dress one wears but what one wears underneath it, and in one's mind.

Athene Seyler *Fans, Trains and Stays* 1947 (reprinted in *The Craft of Comedy* 1958)

Mrs Patrick Campbell's dresses, says the programme, carried out by Mrs Mason of New Burlington Street. I can only say that I wish they had been carried out and buried.

George Bernard Shaw reviewing *Romeo and Juliet* 1895

NOËL COWARD

(ON HIMSELF)
I am determined to travel through life first class.

Noël Coward

My object in *The Vortex* was to write a good play with a whacking good part in it for myself.

Noël Coward television interview (USA) *c.* 1956

I was photographed and interviewed and photographed again. In the street. In the park. In my dressing-room. At my piano. With my dear old mother. Without my dear old mother and on one occasion sitting up in an over-elaborate bed looking like a heavily doped Chinese illusionist.

Noël Coward on the reaction to his play *Easy Virtue* 1926; *Present Indicative* 1937

Why am I always expected to wear a dressing gown, smoke cigarettes in a long holder and say 'Darling, how wonderful'?

Noël Coward

The critics described *Private Lives* variously as 'tenuous, thin, brittle, gossamer, iridescent and delightfully daring'. All of which connotated in the public mind cocktails, repartee, and irreverent allusions to copulation, thereby causing a gratifying number of respectable people to queue up at the box office.

Noël Coward *Present Indicative* 1937

The day I shall begin to worry is when the critics declare, 'This is Noël Coward's greatest play.' But I know they bloody well won't.

Noël Coward

Oh, you know. Jack of all trades, master of none.

Noël Coward *Sunday Mirror*, on the reason for his nick-name *The Master*, quoted in D. Richards, *The Wit of Noël Coward*

A definition of a genius is anyone from England.

Noël Coward quoted by Daniel Massey, BBC television interview 1 March 1992

A lot of people said what a pity that I wasn't more significant. That never worried me because I didn't really particularly wish to be significant. I'd like to be contemporary and bright as a button, but I don't think I was all that keen on being significant.

Noël Coward television interview 1969

I was trained very young as a show-off – and I've continued triumphantly to this moment.

Noël Coward television interview 1969

(BY OTHERS)
A dustbin of a play.

Anonymous critic on Coward's play about drug-abuse, *The Vortex* 1924

Your characters talk like typewriting and you yourself talk like a telegram.

Mrs Patrick Campbell on the first night of *The Vortex* 1924

One can't read any of Noël Coward's plays now, they are written in the most topical and perishable way imaginable, the cream in them turns sour overnight.

Cyril Connolly 1937

Noël Coward is a busy and talented young man, but when it comes to acting I believe he belongs in the will-power class. His notion of acting is to hold his body rigid and bite out cutting remarks.

Don Herold

'I'm richly gifted and highly talented' – that was the phrase he used. It didn't seem arrogant with him, but he used it an awful lot.

Daniel Massey BBC television interview 1 March 1992

Could I write as witty
As Noël Coward
By self-esteem
I should be devoward.

Ogden Nash 'Encyclopedia Britannica', *New Yorker* 23 May 1931

He apparently has nothing any longer to sell us but his own vast personal boredom.

George Jean Nathan
Encyclopaedia of the Theatre 1940

He was his own greatest invention.

John Osborne quoted in William Marchant, *The Pleasure of His Company*

The First Noël.

Dick Richards *The Curtain Rises* 1966

If you wish to see him full-length, you must wait for his cabaret appearances. In these he is benign, though slightly flustered, as a cardinal might be who has been asked to participate in a frenetic tribal rite.

Kenneth Tynan *Persona Grata* 1953

Gracious socially as a royal bastard; tart, vocally, as a hollowed lemon – these are the signs by which we recognise him.

Ibid.

Forty years ago he was Slightly in *Peter Pan*, and you might say he's been wholly in *Peter Pan* ever since.

Kenneth Tynan *Curtains* 1961

If his face suggested an old boot it was unquestionably hand-made.

Kenneth Tynan *The Sound of Two Hands Clapping* 1975

CRITICAL ABUSE

ACTORS
(Listed alphabetically)

MADGE BRINDLEY
Miss Lummins, as Miss Madge Brindley presents her, is straight out of Rowlandson, and she has a deadly aim with her saliva.

Roger Spate reviewing *A Dead Secret* in the *New Statesman* 1957

RICHARD BURTON
You may be as vicious about me as you please. You will only do me justice.

Richard Burton on himself *New York Times* 25 July 1978

CRESTON CLARKE
Last night Mr Creston Clarke played King Lear at the Tabor Grand. All through the five acts of that Shakespearean tragedy he played the King as though under momentary apprehension that someone else was about to play the Ace.

Eugene Field review in *Denver Tribune c.* 1880

CHARLES COCHRAN
Charles B. Cochran played the part of Smart the detective. He certainly must have learned the art of acting in a stable with hungry horses; he did nothing but attempt to chew the paint from the scenery. A more ridiculous chump has never been seen on the stage.

Pennsylvania newspaper reviewing the future impresario

MARION DAVIES

She has two expressions – joy and indigestion.

Dorothy Parker

ELEONORA DUSE

However, it was not the only performance of Hedda Gabler. There was another and, in some ways a better. While Signora Duse walked through her part, the prompter threw himself into it with a will. A more raucous whisper I never heard than that which preceded the Signora's every sentence. It was like the continuous tearing of very thick silk.

Max Beerbohm on Eleonora Duse's *Hedda Gabler* in *Saturday Review*

ROBERT ELLISTON

A wretched Tragedian . . . his attempts at dignity are ludicrous. He is a fine bustling comedian but he bustles in tragedy too.

Henry C. Robinson *Diary* 1811

SAMUEL FOOTE

On a Pseudo Player

Thou Mimic of Cibber – *of Garrick, thou Ape!*
Thou Fop in Othello*! Thou Cypher in Shape!*
Thou Trifle in Person! Thou Puppet in Voice!
Thou Farce of a Player! Thou Rattle for Boys!
Thou Mongrell! Thou dirty face Harlequin Thing!
Thou Puff of bad Paste! Thou Ginger-bread King!

Anonymous poem on the 18th-century actor Samuel Foote; quoted in W.T. Chetwood, *A General History of the Stage*

RUTH GORDON

Ruth Gordon plays Lola Pratt, and anyone who looks like that and acts like that must get off the stage.

Heywood C. Broun

It is a generous role for womanly and impassioned actresses, and many performers have essayed it. I can think of four however, who have not: Totie Edwards, W.C. Fields, Tutankhamen's mummy, and a trained monkey. Not until now that is; Miss Gordon's performance combines elements of all four.

John Simon reviewing Shaw's *Mrs Warren's Profession*

CEDRIC HARDWICKE

He conducted the soul-selling transaction with the thoughtful dignity of a grocer selling a pound of cheese.

Hubert Griffith reviewing Cedric Hardwicke as Marlowe's *Dr Faustus, Sunday Graphic* September 1948; quoted in D. Rigg, *No Turn Unstoned* 1982

HELEN HAYES

Miss Hayes is not, in my minority opinion, one of the world's most gifted performers.

Tennessee Williams on the 'first lady' of American theatre

Fallen archness.

Franklin Pierce Adams on Helen Hayes as Cleopatra in Shaw's *Caesar and Cleopatra* 1925

KATHERINE HEPBURN

She ran the gamut of emotions all the way from A to B.

Dorothy Parker on Hepburn's performance in *The Lake* 1933

MICHAEL HORDERN

Michael Hordern's Cassius has an anxious air. This Cassius watches John Phillips' alarmingly tall Brutus like an insurance agent estimating how much life cover he can offer without insisting on a medical examination.

Sunday Times review of *Julius Caesar* October 1958; quoted in D. Rigg, *No Turn Unstoned* 1982

CHARLES LAUGHTON

Mr Laughton came to Sadlers Wells with all his blushing film vulgarities thick upon him.

James Agate on Charles Laughton in *Henry VIII* 1933

GERTRUDE LAWRENCE

A bad play saved by a bad performance.

George S. Kaufman reviewing Gertrude Lawrence in *Skylark*

MOIRA LISTER

Miss Moira Lister speaks all her lines as if they are written in very faint ink on a tele-prompter slightly too far away to be read with comfort.

Bernard Levin on *The Gazebo* in the *Daily Express* 1960

MONTAGUE LOVE

Mr Love's idea of playing a he-man was to extend his chest three inches and then follow it slowly across the stage.

Heywood C. Broun 1921; quoted in A. Woollcott, *Enchanted Aisles* 1924

FREDERIC MARCH

He came in like a lion and went out like a ham.

Frank Nugent reviewing Frederic March in *The Buccaneer* 1958

RAYMOND MASSEY

Massey won't be satisfied until he's assassinated.

George S. Kaufman 1938; reviewing *Abe Lincoln in Illinois*

GERALDINE McEWAN

Geraldine McEwan, powdered white like a clownish, whey-faced doll, simpered, whined and groaned to such an effect as the Queen, that Edward's homosexuality became both understandable and forgivable.

Milton Shulman reviewing Marlowe's *Edward II* 1968

A.E. MATTHEWS

A.E. Matthews ambled through *This Was a Man* like a charming retriever who has buried a bone and can't remember where.

Noël Coward 1926

GUIDO NADZO

Guido Nadzo is nadzo guido.

George S. Kaufman on a little known American actor

ANNA NEAGLE

Her Victoria made me feel that Albert had married beneath his station.

Noël Coward attrib. after seeing *Victoria Regina*

PETER O'TOOLE

He delivers every line with a monotonous tenor bark as if addressing an audience of deaf eskimos.

Michael Billington on O'Toole's notorious *Macbeth* in *The Guardian* 1980

DENIS QUILLEY

Denis Quilley played the role with all the charm and animation of the leg of a billiard table.

Bernard Levin reviewing *High Spirits*, the musical version of Coward's *Blithe Spirit* 1965

JAY ROBINSON

Mr Robinson was game all right. But what is gameness in a man who is suffering from delusions of adequacy?

Walter Kerr reviewing Jay Robinson (who was also the producer), in *Buy Me Blue Ribbons* 1951

PAUL SCOFIELD

His playing bores the doublet and hose off me.

Bernard Levin on Paul Scofield as Thomas More in Robert Bolt's *A Man for All Seasons* in the *Daily Express* 1960

YORKE STEPHENS

Mr Yorke Stephens fulfills his obligations to Miss Corelli and the audience most scrupulously but with the air of a man who has resolved to shoot himself the moment the curtain has come down.

George Bernard Shaw reviewing *The Sorrows of Satan* by Marie Corelli in the *Saturday Review* 1897

GEOFFREY STEYN

Mr Steyn's performance was the worst to be seen in the contemporary theatre.

Heywood C. Broun on American actor Geoffrey Steyn 1917

Mr Steyn sued Heywood Broun. During the litigation Steyn appeared in another play which prompted the following carefully worded appraisal from Broun: Mr Steyn's performance is not up to his usual standard.

ELIZABETH TAYLOR

Elizabeth Taylor's performance hardly carries into the auditorium. Ambrose Hammer – a critic who loves to heave the harpoon into actors might carry on from there. I merely say that the first night . . . is as grisly as an undertaker's picnic and may be grislier.

Robert Cushman reviewing Elizabeth Taylor's performance in Lillian Hellman's *The Little Foxes* in the *Observer* 1982

EDWARD WOODWARD

As swashbuckling Cyrano, Mr Woodward's performance buckles more often than it swashes.

Kenneth Hurran reviewing

Edward Woodward in Rostand's *Cyrano de Bergerac* in the *Spectator* 1970

MARY ANN YATES
Too much stumping about and too much flumping about.

Kitty Clive quoted in W. Clark Russell, *Representative Actors*

CRITICAL ABUSE – *Plays*

(UN-NAMED PLAYS)
(Listed alphabetically by reviewer)

Rainstorm in Galveston, lasted twenty minutes. Hail storm in Beaumont, ten minutes. Wind storm in Langtry, two days. Barn storm in Opera house, one night.

Anonymous review of a touring show in local paper, Waco, Texas quoted in *The Wit and Humour of the Stage* 1909

Methought this was addressed to me. Metook the hint.

James Agate reviewing a play in which the line 'Methinks you did wrong to come' occurs

It opened at 8.40 sharp and closed at 10.40 dull.

Heywood C. Broun attrib.

The Messrs. Shubert seem to forget that the female knee is a joint and not an evening's entertainment.

Percy Hammond

I have knocked everything in this play except the chorus girls' knees, and there God has anticipated me.

Percy Hammond

Of the acting of Miss Berger's company one may not speak candidly unless one is in a trench.

Percy Hammond

I saw the play at a disadvantage – the curtain was up.

George S. Kaufman attrib. remark quoted in H. Teichmann, *George S. Kaufman: An Intimate Portrait* 1972; (also attributed to Groucho Marx)

In Boston the test of a play is simple. If the play is bad the pigeons snarl at you as you walk across the common.

George S. Kaufman quoted in H. Teichmann, *George S. Kaufman: An Intimate Portrait* 1972

There was laughter at the back of the theatre, leading to the belief that someone was telling jokes back there.

George S. Kaufman

The costumes looked as though they had been selected by Helen Keller.

George Jean Nathan on a 1920s Revue

The Greeks had a word for it – so did the Hebrews – lousy.

Dorothy Parker

The best play I ever slept through.

Oscar Wilde

I've seen more excitement at the opening of an umbrella.

Earl Wilson

The scenery was beautiful but the actors got in front of it.

Alexander Woollcott

(NAMED PLAYS)
(Listed alphabetically by reviewer)

It is dramatized stench.

Anonymous review of Shaw's *Mrs Warren's Profession* 1898; (Mrs Warren operates a chain of brothels in Europe)

There were fifty in the cast and ten real bloodhounds. The dogs gave an excellent performance but received little support from the rest of the company.

Review of ***Uncle Tom's Cabin*** 1907; quoted in J. Aye, *Humour in the Theatre* 1932

Globe Theatre. ***Mr Symkin***. Good God. What piffle.

Ibid.

When Mr Wilbur calls his play ***Halfway to Hell*** he underestimates the distance.

Brooks Atkinson 1934

There's less to this than meets the eye.

Tallulah Bankhead on ***The Burgomaster of Stilemonde*** by Belgian symbolist Maeterlinck; *Tallulah* 1952

The sort of show that gives pornography a bad name.

Clive Barnes on **Kenneth Tynan's** erotic revue *Oh! Calcutta* 1970

One of those plays in which all of the actors unfortunately enunciated very clearly.

Robert Benchley on *Perfectly Scandalous* 1931

Hebrews 13:8

Robert Benchley on the highly sentimental and long running Broadway hit *Abie's Irish Rose*, which he loathed. The Biblical reference reads 'Jesus Christ, the same yesterday, and today, and forever.'

Designed by Cleon Throckmorton from sketches by Santiago Ontanon of an old Spanish intestinal tract.

Robert Benchley on *Bitter Oleander* 1937

So cheap and offensive that it might serve to unite all the races of the world in a common hymn of hate.

Heywood C. Broun on *Abie's Irish Rose* 1927 (Robert Benchley's *bête noire*)

It is enough to make your flesh crawl – right out of the Ethel Barrymore Theatre.

John Chapman on *Last Stop* in *New York Daily News* 1944

Very good – but a month in the wrong country.

Noël Coward 1956; after an Actors' Studio production of Turgenev's *A Month in the Country*

It was very close to the real thing – but it seemed to last twice as long and be just as noisy.

Noël Coward to **Lionel Bart** after the opening of Bart's musical *Blitz* 1962

Twice as long as *Parsifal* and half as funny.

Noël Coward on the musical *Camelot* 1960

There's nothing wrong with that show that shoving the child up the horse's arse won't cure.

Noël Coward on the musical version of *Gone With the Wind* at

Drury Lane, starring 3-year-old **Bonnie Langford**. During the performance one of the horses had defecated heavily on the stage.

I didn't pay £3.50 just to see half-a-dozen acorns and a chipolata.

Noël Coward 1972; after seeing David Storey's ***The Changing Room*** in which most of the actors appear unclothed.

Good Fielding. No Hit.

Kyle Crichton on a stage version of Fielding's ***Tom Jones***

It is the kind of play . . . that one might enjoy more at a second hearing if only the first time through hadn't left one such a strong feeling that once is enough.

W.H. Darlington on ***Rosencrantz and Guildenstern are Dead*** by Tom Stoppard in the *Daily Telegraph* April 1967

It is curious how incest, impotence, nymphomania, religious mania and real estate speculation can be so dull.

Richard Findlater on ***Toys in the Attic*** by Lillian Hellman in *Time and Tide* 1960

More like a Henderson Seed Co. catalogue than an honest to living drama.

Gilbert W. Gabriel on ***Bitter Oleander*** in *The World* 1935

Odets, where is they sting?

Robert Garland on Clifford Odets' play, ***Clash by Night*** 1941

Marks the beginning of the Sodom and Begorra school.

Lionel Hale on the Irish playwright Lady Longford's play about homosexuality, ***Anything but the Truth*** 1937

Boston liked ***Follow the Girls***. Boston also likes baked beans.

Irving Hoffman *Hollywood Reporter* 1944

We're sorry but it's not our cup of tee-hee.

Irving Hoffman reviewing ***Mrs January and Mr Ex*** in *Hollywood Reporter* 1944

Last night a play called *Pure as Snow* was produced at the Broad Street Theatre. It was not as pure as snow.

H.J. Jennings quoted in J. Aye *Humour in the Theatre* 1932

Hook 'n' Ladder is the sort of play that gives failure a bad name.

Walter Kerr 1952

I think they've made a mistake. They've left the show in Detroit, or wherever it was last warming up, and brought in the publicity stills.

Walter Kerr reviewing *Ilya Darling* 1967

I saw this show under adverse circumstances – my seat was facing the stage.

John David Klein on *Three Guys Naked from the Waist Down* 1985

A woman's magazine romance that goes backwards until it disappears up its own pauses.

Herbert Kretzmer on Harold Pinter's *Betrayal* in the *Daily Express* 1978

A dirty-minded little girl's essay on the Russian Empress, played like a chatelaine of an old time 'maison de joie'.

Louis Kronenburger on Mae West's *Catherine Was Great* 1944

I'm afraid *The Intelligent Woman's Guide* I shall have to leave to the intelligent woman: it is too boring for the intelligent man, if I am any sample. Too much gas-bag.

D.H. Lawrence on Shaw's *The Intelligent Woman's Guide* 1928

A lot of Chinese junk. . . . In wise old Lee Vin's opinion, if you want more of China than wide sleeves, and more of a play than romantic twaddle, to pay it a visit would be to enter the world of choosy wrong.

Bernard Levin on *The World of Suzie Wong* in the *Daily Express* 1959

I think *The Amorous Prawn* is perhaps the most grisly, glassy eyed thing I have encountered in the theatre for a very long time, and even outside the theatre its like is rarely met except on fishmongers' slabs, and now I feel very ill indeed, and would like to lie down. Before doing so I should like to say that *The Amorous Prawn* is a farce made out of cobwebs and mothballs, my old socks, empty beer bottles, copies of the *Strand Magazine*, dust, holes, mildew and Mr Ben Travers' discarded typewriter ribbons.

Bernard Levin on *The Amorous Prawn* in the *Daily Express* 1959

Strictly speaking I cannot swear that being kicked in the stomach by a horse would be an experience preferable to seeing this play by Signor Giuseppe Marotti because I have never been kicked in the stomach by a horse. But I have seen this play, and I can certainly say that if a kick in the stomach by a horse would be worse, I do not wish to be kicked in the stomach by a horse.

And I can certainly add that, unpleasant though the prospect of being kicked in the stomach by a horse may be, I would certainly

rather be kicked in the stomach by a horse than see the play again.

Bernard Levin on *Dazzling Prospect* in the *Daily Express* 1961

I think I'll go by boat.

Bernard Levin on Marc Camoletti's *Boeing Boeing* in the *Daily Express* 1963

Why should I pay ten dollars to see something I can see in the bathroom for nothing?

Groucho Marx on *Hair* 1968

No worse than a bad cold.

Harpo Marx on the saccharine sweet play *Abie's Irish Rose* *c.* 1929

The hills are alive with the sound of clichés.

Sheridan Morley on *Mistress of Novices* in *Punch* 1973

There is a number of possible explanations for the presence of *Il Campiello* in the repertoire of the National Theatre at the Olivier. The one I like best is that it represents a complete and never-to-be-repeated mental, physical and theatrical breakdown on the part of all concerned.

Sheridan Morley *Punch* 1973

The majority of mystery plays, with their disappointing solutions, are like sitting nervously around for two hours waiting for a telephone call from one's best girl and then at long length suddenly hearing the bell ring, jumping up eagerly to answer it, and finding that it is her mother! This was no exception.

George Jean Nathan on *The Cat Screams* 1942

Very well then: I say Never.

George Jean Nathan on *Tonight or Never* 1930

Bosh sprinkled with mystic cologne.

George Jean Nathan on T.S. Eliot's *The Cocktail Party* 1950

The frocks were charming.

Review of *Fresh Fields* by Ivor Novello 1933; quoted in D. Rigg, *No Turn Unstoned* 1982

It isn't what you might call sunny. I went into the Plymouth Theatre a comparatively young woman and I staggered out of it three hours later, twenty years older, haggard and broken with suffering.

Dorothy Parker on Tolstoy's *Redemption* in *Vanity Fair* 1928

The House Beautiful is the play lousy.

Dorothy Parker *Life* 1931

Now that you've got me right down to it, the only thing I didn't like about *The Barretts of Wimpole Street* was the play.

Dorothy Parker *New Yorker* 1931

This is a play for people who wash every day.

Billy Rose on Shaw's *Heartbreak House*

Two minutes of *Biarritz* would reconcile a Trappist monk to his monastery for life.

George Bernard Shaw on *Biarritz* by Jerome K. Jerome 1896

NO!

Hannan Swaffer reviewing *Yes and No* 1938

I left the show feeling very keen to get home to the washing up.

Irving Wardle reviewing *What's Got into You* in *The Times* 1981

If this play lasts overnight it should not only be considered a long run but a revival as well.

Alexander Woollcott on *The Lake* (starring Katherine Hepburn)

CRITICISM

Only two roles of dramatic criticism matter. One. Decide what the playwright was trying to do, and pronounce how well he has done it. Two. Determine whether the well-done thing was worth doing at all.

James Agate *Ego 8* 1945

Dramatic criticism has three functions. The first is to let the world know what the previous night's play has been about. There's no reason why a report of this kind should not be written by the same man who describes how in the afternoon he saw a man knocked down in Oxford Street trying to stop a runaway horse. The second function is to tell the

public whether the new play is good, bad or indifferent. This means the critic must know his job. That is if you hold with my dictionary, which defines criticism as 'The art of judging with knowledge and propriety of the beauties and faults of art.' The third is to report the theatre in terms of the art of writing.

James Agate *Ego 9* 1946

I find that when I dislike what I see on stage then I can be vastly amusing, but when I write about something I like, I find I am appallingly dull.

Max Beerbohm

To many people dramatic criticism must seem like an attempt to tattoo soap bubbles.

John Mason Brown quoted in Frank Muir, *The Frank Muir Book*

I love criticism, just so long as it is unqualified praise.

Noël Coward

I know how good I am but I do not know how bad I am.

W.S. Gilbert (the reason he preferred hostile criticism to fulsome praise)

Venom from contented rattlesnakes.

Percy Hammond (definition of dramatic criticism)

You may scold a carpenter who has made you a bad table, though you cannot make a table.

Samuel Johnson

Berating someone for failing to achieve what they never set out to do is one of the most elementary gambits of criticism.

John Osborne *Almost a Gentleman* 1991

It does not follow that the right to criticize Shakespeare involves the power of writing better plays.

George Bernard Shaw

Reviewing has one advantage over suicide; in suicide you take it out on yourself; in reviewing you take it out on other people.

George Bernard Shaw

Ideal dramatic criticism is unqualified appreciation.

Oscar Wilde

CRITICS

When a play is crashingly dull the critic has only two resources. One is sleep, in justification whereof I shall quote William Archer's dictum that the first qualification for a dramatic critic is the capacity to sleep while sitting bolt upright.

James Agate 1932

If Attila the Hun were alive today, he'd be a dramatic critic.

Edward Albee 1983

One of the first and most important things for a critic to learn is how to sleep undetected in the theatre.

William Archer

The dramatic critic is like the clergyman – he stands in a favoured position, and however hard he may hit, the recipient of his blows is, for the most part, unable to strike back.

John Aye *Humour in the Theatre* 1932

Critics are like eunuchs in a harem. They're there every night, they see it done every night, they see how it should be done every night, but they can't do it themselves.

Brendan Behan

Critics should be searched for certain adjectives at the door of the theatre. Irreverent, probing and (above all) satirical. I would have all such adjectives left with their coats in the foyer, only to be redeemed when their notices are written.

Alan Bennett

The critic cannot do his work without hurting; he resembles the dentist.

Eric Bentley *What is Theatre* 1956

At any London first night you'll see the critics creeping off to the pub half-way through Act III. Of course they pretend they have to catch the early editions.

Basil Boothroyd

There are nowadays a sort of persons they call critics that, egad, have no more wit in them than so many hobby horses.

George Villiers, 2nd Duke of Buckingham *The Rehearsal* 1671

To poison plays I see some where they sit,
Scattered like ratsbane, up and down the pit.

William Congreve 1697

Critics never worry me unless they are right – but that does not often occur.

Noël Coward

It's so unwise of critics to predict. One said he would eat his hat if it (*Nude With Violin*) ran in the West End. It is still running. Of course I will not stand over him while he masticates the hat.

Noël Coward *Daily Mail* interview 1957

Who notices when they meet a critic whose face is tense with pain? It is one of the marks of the profession.

Robertson Davies *Murther and Walking Spirits* 1991

There are very few critics who when given an egg of talent in their hands can resist crushing it.

Peter Hall *Diaries* 14 July 1974

The critic is often an unsuccessful author, almost always an inferior one.

Leigh Hunt

Reviewers must normally function as huff-and-puff artists blowing laggard theatre-goers stageward.

A.A. Milne

The dramatic critic who is without prejudice is on the same plane with the General who does not believe in taking life.

George Jean Nathan *Comedians All*

The better and more honest a critic you are, the fewer friends will eventually send flowers up to the funeral parlour.

George Jean Nathan

Critics: those who would send Hedda Gabler to the Marriage Guidance Council.

John Osborne *A Better Class of Person* 1981

A critic is a legless man who teaches running.

Channing Pollock

A drama critic is a man who leaves no turn unstoned.

George Bernard Shaw *New York Times* 1950

As for the little puny critics, who scatter their peevish strictures in private circles, and scribble at every author who has the eminence of being un-connected with them, as they are usually spleen-swoln from a vain idea of increasing their consequence, there will always be found a petulance and illiberality in their remarks which should place them as far beneath the notice of a gentleman, as their original dullness had sunk them from the level of the most unsuccessful author.

Richard Brinsley Sheridan preface to *The Rivals* 1775

You will not easily persuade me that there is no credit or importance in being at the head of a band of critics, who take upon them to decide for the whole town, whose opinion and patronage all writers solicit, and whose recommendation no manager dares refuse. (Mr Dangle)

Richard Brinsley Sheridan *The Critic* 1779

A man who knows the way but can't drive the car.

Kenneth Tynan (definition of a critic) quoted in *New York Times Magazine* 9 January 1966

A good drama critic is one who perceives what is happening in the theatre of his time. A great drama critic is one who perceives what is not happening.

Kenneth Tynan

They search for ages for the wrong word which, to give them credit, they eventually find.

Peter Ustinov

The critic leaves at curtain fall
To find in starting to review it,
He scarcely saw the play at all
For watching his reaction to it.

E.B. White *Critic*

A newspaperman, whose sweetheart ran away with an actor.

Walter Winchell (definition of a critic)

Has anybody seen a dramatic critic in the day-time? Of course not. They come out after dark, up to no good.

P.G. Wodehouse *New York Mirror* 1955

CRITICS –
Personalities

CLIVE BARNES
It seems to me that giving Clive Barnes his CBE for services to the theatre is like giving Goering the DFC for services to the RAF.

Alan Bennett

If I decide to stay around Broadway beyond the current season, it will be for the pleasure of throwing his fat, limey posterior out in the street.

David Merrick

MAX BEERBOHM
The gods bestowed on Max the gift of perpetual old age.

Oscar Wilde

ROBERT BENCHLEY
(ON HIMSELF)
I do most of my work sitting down; that's where I shine.

It took me fifteen years to discover I had no talent for writing, but I couldn't give it up because by that time I was too famous.

HAZLITT
Hazlitt . . . had perhaps the most uninteresting mind of all our distinguished critics.

T.S. Eliot *Essays: Dryden*

GEORGE JEAN NATHAN
(ON HIMSELF)
There are two kinds of dramatic critics: destructive and constructive. I am destructive. There are two kinds of guns: Krupp and pop.

The World in False Face 1923

I hit upon dramatic criticism as a way to live luxuriously without too much brain exercise.

Encyclopaedia of the Theatre 1940

DOROTHY PARKER
(ON HERSELF)
Ducking for apples – change a letter and it's the story of my life.

I was the toast of two continents: Greenland and Australia.

Quoted in J. Keats *You Might As Well Live: Life and Times of Dorothy Parker* 1970

(BY OTHERS)
Discussing a job with a prospective employer Mrs Parker explained 'Salary is no object. I only want enough to keep body and soul apart.'

Robert E. Brennan *Wits End*

You see, she is so odd a blend of Little Nell and Lady Macbeth. It is not so much the familiar phenomenon of a hand of steel in a velvet glove as a lacy sleeve with a bottle of vitriol concealed in its folds.

Alexander Woollcott *While Rome Burns* 1934

KENNETH TYNAN

The sheer complexity of writing a play always had dazzled me. In an effort to understand it, I became a critic.

On himself *New York Mirror* 1963

Quite dreadful, he would not get a chance in a village hall unless he were related to the vicar.

Beverley Baxter on Tynan as First Player in the Alec Guinness *Hamlet* 1951

He understood the buzz of actors' energy with a good text.

William Dudley December 1991

ALEXANDER WOOLLCOTT
(ON HIMSELF)
All the things I really like to do are either immoral, illegal or fattening.
(Woollcott was the originator of this widely quoted remark.)

The thing's a terrible insult and I've decided to swallow it.

On George S. Kaufman's thinly disguised portrayal of him in *The Man Who Came to Dinner* 1939

(BY OTHERS)
He was vindictive, shockingly petty, in a feminine fashion, given to excesses when expressing his preferences or his prejudices.

Tallulah Bankhead *Tallulah* 1952

His entrances down the aisles of New York theatres were more dramatic than most of the shows he reviewed.

John Mason Brown *The Portable Woollcott* 1946

His life was what the marquees describe as a 'continuous performance'.

Ibid.

Alexander Woollcott, in a rage, has all the tenderness and restraint of a newly caged cobra.

Noël Coward

The New Jersey Nero who mistakes his pinafore for a toga.

Edna Ferber attrib. *c.* 1934

A striking combination of hero-worshipper and Madame Defarge.

Margaret Case Harriman *The Vicious Circle* 1951

I blame Alexander Woollcott and Robert Benchley and Dorothy Parker for parenting the cutesy and cruel critics who carve up the theatre we know now.

Mercedes McCambridge

No-one writing about the theatre in his time was as provocative, or brought as much gusto and excitement to his subject. His emotions overrode his judgement, making his hates and enthusiasms superlative.

Brock Pemberton quoted in Samuel H. Adams, *A. Woollcott; His Life and His World* 1945

The clowning blunder of my life.

Carr Van Anda on hiring Woollcott as drama critic of the *New York Times* quoted in S.H. Adams, *A. Woollcott; His Life and His World* 1945

He always praises the first show of the season, being reluctant to stone the first cast.

Walter Winchell quoted in S.H. Adams, *A. Woollcott; His Life and His World* 1945

DEDICATION

Always a man to keep everything in proportion so long as the theatre was on top, Mr Langner remarked after the Armistice (1918) that he was glad the war was over because he wanted to organise another theatre.

Brooks Atkinson on **Lawrence Langner** in *Broadway* 1970

This lady was so very natural an actress, and was so powerfully affected by her feelings, that she seldom retired from any great tragic part without being in some degree affected by a stomachic complaint.

William Cook on 18th-century actress **Hannah Pritchard** in *Memoirs of Samuel Foote* 1805

I hate this new solemnity in the theatre. If anybody says to me 'She's a dedicated actress' I'd like to strangle her. What is she dedicated about?

Noël Coward

Why must the show go on?
The rule is surely not immutable,
It might be wiser and more suitable
Just to close
If you are in the throes
Of personal grief and private woes.

Noël Coward *Why Must the Show Go On?* (song); *The Lyrics of Noël Coward* 1965

Never at any time have I gone on the stage without longing for the moment when the curtain would come down on the last act.

Sir Johnstone Forbes-Robertson (who would rather have been a painter); quoted in Hesketh Pearson, *The Last Actor-Managers* 1950

Actors playing with her these days whispered that as she gave her final death shriek in the part [Meg Merrilees], she pounded her breast, which was known to be on fire with cancer, so as to make her cry one of real agony.

Eleanor Ruggles on **Charlotte Cushman** in *Prince of Players: Edwin Booth*

I want to retire to a faraway desert island, a beautiful desert island, with a stretch of sea and sand and moonlight – just enough to read *Variety* by.

Lilian Tashman quoted in Maurice Zolotov, *No People Like Show People* 1951

When I'm acting I sometimes want to get my performance, put it through the mincer, chuck it down the sink and start all over again.

Billie Whitelaw *Daily Mail* 13 June 1992

DIRECTORS

Theatre director . . . a person engaged by the management to conceal the fact that the players cannot act.

James Agate *Sunday Times*

Theatre consists of two great arts: acting and playwriting; and there is no third art necessary to co-ordinate them.

James Agate quoted in W. Redfield, *Letters from an Actor* 1967

A director has but one task: to make each rehearsal so amusing that the actors will look forward to the next one.

Martin Esslin quoted in P. Hay, *Theatrical Anecdotes* 1987

All you can do with Shaw is to fan the actors out in a semi-circle, put the speaker at the top, and hope for the best.

Tyrone Guthrie quoted in A. Ross, *Astonish Us in the Morning: Tyrone Guthrie Remembered* 1977

It is almost impossible to make any form of art without totalitarian behaviour.

Peter Hall *Diaries* 28 April 1978

In the theatre the director is God – but unfortunately the actors are atheists.

Zarco Petan *The Times* 15 June 1977

The only time he [the director] is of any use to me is if I've left my script in the car, and he volunteers to fetch it.

Wilfred Hyde White quoted in R. May, *The Wit of the Theatre* 1969

DIRECTORS – *Individuals*

PETER BROOK
I can take any empty space and call it a bare stage.

On himself *The Empty Space* 1968

When we talk in Britain these days of a director as a creative genius . . . we are almost invariably talking of a foreigner . . . Peter Brook is the only British man of the theatre for whom such a claim can confidently be made . . . Brook is someone prepared to take risks, fail and then try again, succeed and then try again: a genius, and a creative one.

Benedict Nightingale *The Times Literary Supplement*

GEORGE DEVINE
He suffered talent gladly.

John Osborne quoted in R. Findlater, *At The Royal Court* 1981

PETER HALL
(ON HIMSELF)
I really work for the author and a good rehearsal – something which extends the actors and myself.

Diaries 18 June 1972

There is nothing worse for a director than the first day. Much worse than the first night.

Diaries 2 January 1974

(BY OTHERS)
The trouble with God is he thinks he's Peter Hall.

Graffito on the walls of the National Theatre, 1970s

I do wish he'd stop pretending to be so bloody nice, when he's really a dictator.

Glenda Jackson quoted in *The Times* 20 June 1992

See also: Herbert Beerbohm Tree

DRESSING ROOM TALK

No matter how bad this is, I'm going to tell the poor boy I like it.

Playwright **Robert Anderson's** father at the opening of *Silent Night, Lonely Night* New York 1959

Gushing visitor who had just seen John Barrymore play Hamlet: Oh Master! I enjoyed your performance so much.
John Barrymore: Not half as much as I'm enjoying yours.

Boy were you on that stage!

Diahann Carroll catch-all phrase for those embarrassing moments when you have to find something positive to say about the performance you have just witnessed

OTHER USEFUL EXCLAMATIONS INCLUDE:

My dear, unbelievable!

Noël Coward

My dear chap! Good isn't the word!

W.S. Gilbert

And *what* about *you* then?

George Hall (recalled by **Selina Cadell**)

Well, nobody got hurt.

Richard Maney quoted in W. Redfield, *Letters from an Actor*

ELEONORA DUSE

Her features have the placidity of long grief; so many storms have broken over them that nothing can disturb again this sea of calm distress.

James Agate

She acted from the head down, not from the feet up. Her body was eloquent because her legs had less to do with manipulating it and guiding it than her brain. . .

George Jean Nathan *Materia Critica* 1924

The extended right arm of Eleonora Duse had in it all the tears of *Tristan and Isolde*.

Ibid.

No physical charm is noble as well as beautiful unless it is the expression of a moral charm; and it is because Duse's range includes these high moral notes that her compass, extending from the depths of a mere predatory creature like Claude's wife up to Marguerite Gautier at her kindest or Magda at her bravest, so dwarfs the poor little octave and a half on which Sarah Bernhardt plays such pretty canzonets and stirring marches.

George Bernard Shaw quoted in M. Billington, *The Guinness Book of Theatre Facts and Feats* 1982

EPILOGUES

If it be true that good wine needs no bush,
'Tis true that a good play needs no epilogue.

William Shakespeare Epilogue of *As You Like It*

Catherine had three hundred lovers. I did the best I could in a couple of hours.

Mae West curtain speech of her play *Catherine Was Great* 1944

EPITAPHS

Her name cut clear upon this marble cross,
Shines as it shone when she was still on earth,
While tenderly the mild, agreeable moss
Obscures the figures of her date of birth.

Dorothy Parker tombstone of an actress from *Tombstones in the Starlight*

Good my lord, will you see the players well bestowed? Do you hear, let them be well used; for they are the abstract and brief chronicles of the time: after your death you were better have a bad epitaph than their ill report while you live.

William Shakespeare *Hamlet*, Act III, Scene 2

EPITAPHS – *Individuals*

LIONEL BARRYMORE
He played everything but a harp.

Lionel Barrymore suggestion for his own epitaph

GEORGINA DREW BARRYMORE
It's a cruel loss and I shall never get over it. But I must say they've given the old girl some damn good notices.

Maurice Barrymore on the obituaries for his wife, 1893

DION BOUCICAULT
His First Holiday.

Dion Boucicault suggestion for his tombstone

RICHARD BURBAGE
Exit Burbage. 1619.

Tombstone inscription St Leonard's church, Shoreditch, East London

No more young Hamlett, old Heironymoe.
King Leer, the grieved Moore and more beside,
That lived in him, have now for ever dy'de.

John Fletcher attrib. From *An elegie on the death of the famous actor Rich: Burbage*

SAMUEL FOOTE
Foote from his earthly stage, alas! is hurled;
Death took him off, who took off all the world.

Samuel Foote was famous as a mimic; quoted in R. Ryan, *Dramatic Table Talk* 1825

DAVID GARRICK

I am disappointed by that stroke of death which has eclipsed the gaiety of nations and impoverished the public stock of harmless pleasure.

Samuel Johnson *Epitaph on Garrick* 1779

WILLIAM S. GILBERT

His foe was folly and his weapon wit.

Anthony Hope inscription on Gilbert's memorial tablet, Victoria Embankment

OLIVER GOLDSMITH

*Here lies Nolly Goldsmith, for
    shortness called Noll,
Who wrote like an angel, but talked
    like poor poll.*

David Garrick 1774

*Poet, naturalist, and historian,
Who left scarcely any style of writing
    untouched,
And touched none that he did not
    adorn.*

Samuel Johnson *Epitaph on Goldsmith* 1776

BEN JONSON

O, rare Ben Jonson!

John Young epitaph for Ben Jonson in Westminster Abbey. Possibly this should have read *Orare per* Ben Jonson (Pray for Ben Jonson) but was altered by the stone-cutter

GEORGE S. KAUFMAN

Over my dead body.

George S. Kaufman when asked to write his own epitaph

DAN LENO

So little and frail a lantern could not long harbour so big a flame.

Max Beerbohm on the early death, aged 44, of the popular comic Leno, who was a mere 5 foot tall. Obituary, *Saturday Review* 1904.

MARIE LLOYD

*Tired she was, and she wouldn't show
    it.
Suffering she was, and hoped we
    didn't know it.
But He who loved her knew, and,
    understanding all,
Prescribed long rest, and gave the final
    call.*

Inscription on her tombstone in Fortune Green Cemetery.

DOROTHY PARKER

Excuse my dust.

Dorothy Parker suggested epitaph for herself

FAILURE

DOUGLAS QUAYLE
Douglas Quayle
Actor
'Resting'

Gravestone inscription

WILLIAM SHAKESPEARE
Good friends, for Jesus' sake forbear,
To dig the dust enclosed here.
Blest be the man that spares these
stones.
And curst be he that moves my bones.

William Shakespeare inscription
on his tombstone at Stratford-
upon-Avon

GEORGE BERNARD SHAW
Hic jacet
Bernard Shaw.
Who the devil was he?

George Bernard Shaw
suggested epitaph for himself
supplied at the request of the
London Evening News

There is much to be said for
failure. It is more interesting than
success.

Max Beerbohm

There is nothing the British like
more than a bloke who comes
from nowhere, makes it, and then
gets clobbered.

Melvyn Bragg *Rich* (a biography
of Richard Burton)

Sing a lament for the plays that fail –
A dirge for the shows that fold.
A tear on the bier of the flop of the
year
And the tickets that couldn't be sold.

Howard Dietz 'Lament for
Failures' from *The Night was
Unruly*

Fifth Column, sixth draft, seventh
producer, eighth refusal.

Ernest Hemingway on the
disastrous history of his one and
only play; quoted in M. Zolotow,
No People Like Show People 1951

Even a Hungarian can make a
mistake.

Alexander Korda who refused a
film contract for Vivien Leigh

weeks before she became a
sensation in *The Mask of Virtue*
1936

As a rule, the Flop Obvious, is
caused by a single moment of
delirium, the first point of
deviation from sense, a wild
snatch at flitting fashion.
Managements cannot afford to be
running footmen at fashion's
capricious heels.

J.C. Trewin quoted in D.
Richards, *The Curtain Rises* 1966

Little except punch drunk
optimism can explain an obvious
flop.

Ibid.

When you are down and out
something always turns up – and it
is usually the noses of your friends.

Orson Welles

FAME

I like to be introduced as
America's foremost actor. It saves
the necessity of further effort.

John Barrymore

None of your Dames for me! I
don't want to go about the
country labelled and be charged
double for everything.

Lilian Baylis

A sign of a celebrity is that his
name is often worth more than his
services.

Daniel J. Boorstin

Once you're a star actor people
start asking you questions about
politics, astronomy, archaeology
and birth control.

Marlon Brando

The despised star system, to true
followers of the drama, may
appear to be a shameful
compromise, but to a hard-
working playwright, believe me, it
is frequently a very great comfort.

Noël Coward

Theatre people are always pining
and agonizing because they're
afraid that they'll be forgotten.

And in America they're quite right. They will be.

Agnes De Mille

The painter dead, yet still he charms the eye,
While England lives his fame can never die.
But he who struts his hour upon the stage
Can scarce extend his fame for half an age.
No pen nor pencil can the actor save;
The art and artist share one common grave.

David Garrick quoted in Edgar Pemberton, 'The Marvel of Mary Anderson', *Munsey's Magazine* 1904–5

An actress's life is so transitory – suddenly you're a building.

Helen Hayes 1955 on hearing a New York theatre was to be named after her

Oh, it's great to be a theatre again!

Helen Hayes 1983 (The first theatre had been demolished and a new one had just been named after her.)

It is the fate of actors to be judged by echoes which are altogether delusive – when they have passed out of immediate ken, and some

fifty years hence some old fool will be saying: 'There never was an actor like Irving.'

Henry Irving letter 1891

It is just as cold in Westminster Abbey as it is in the village churchyard. I don't want to die.

Laurence Olivier interviewed by Gawn Grainger, quoted in A. Holden, *Olivier* 1988

It is difficult to live up to one's posters . . . when I pass my name in such large letters I blush, but at the same time instinctively raise my hat.

Herbert Beerbohm Tree
Hesketh Pearson, *Beerbohm Tree* 1956

FANS

Enthusiastic fan to **Tallulah Bankhead** in mid-performance: I really want to f... you!

Tallulah Bankhead: And so you shall – after the show – you sweet old-fashioned thing. (Attrib.)

I lost my nerve in the theatre because of the perfectly sweet fans who came and would break the place up; I hated that, not being in control.

Dirk Bogarde *By Myself*, Channel 4 TV January 1992

Split me if I'd not a hundred times rather be spoken to by Mr Garrick than His Majesty, God Bless him!

Charlotte Burney

A fan club is a group of people who tell an actor he's not alone in the way he feels about himself.

Jack Carson

Get away, dear! I don't need you any more!

Norma Talmadge when approached by a fan a few years after her retirement in 1930

FILM AND TELEVISON

It doesn't matter how 'big' you are as long as you fill it from the inside.

Alan Badel 1965; when asked on the set of *Man and Superman* whether a stage performance

might seem too 'big' for the television screen; recalled by **Martin Jarvis**

How often stage and screen, dividing the loyalties of talented actors, have played havoc with their sense of direction and crippled their potentialities in consequence.

John Gielgud *Distinguished Company*

A great actor wants to act, which he has more freedom to do on the stage. He doesn't want to worry about mechanical things, as he has to do in the film studios.

Peter Glenville 1962 quoted in *Olivier* (ed. L. Gourlay) 1973

I think Charles Laughton did lack technique; when inspiration failed, as fail it often must, he had very little resource either of voice or movement. This often happens when actors, even actors of the greatest talent, whose experience has chiefly been in films, attempt great parts on the stage.

Tyrone Guthrie on Laughton's Macbeth at the Old Vic 1934; quoted in *A Life in the Theatre* 1959

God felt sorry for actors, so he gave them a place in the sun and a swimming-pool; all they had to sacrifice was their talent.

Cedric Hardwicke on Hollywood quoted in S. Morley, *Tales from the Hollywood Raj* 1983

In the movies you keep everything in. In the theatre you let everything out.

Richard Johnson *Sunday Times* 28 June 1992

over the other actors, and hired a van to pick up your wages. Fabulous.

Ian McShane on working in the TV soap *Dallas* quoted in the *Daily Mail* 28 April 1990

Films are where you sell what you've learned on the stage.

Ralph Richardson quoted in A. Holden, *Olivier* 1988

Don't come too close, you'll see through my talent.

Ralph Richardson attrib. to the lighting cameraman on the set of *The Charge of the Light Brigade*

FINANCE

Acting in films is . . . retirement acting – you just give an exhibition of your former skills.

Walter Matthau 1979 quoted in J. Green, *A Dictionary of Contemporary Quotations* 1982

Like working in a factory, it was great. You clocked in, said your lines, made sure you didn't fall

In merry old England it once was a rule,
The king had his poet and also his fool,
But now we're so frugal, I'd have you to know it,
Poor Cibber must serve both for fool and for poet.

Anonymous on the actor/dramatist **Colley Cibber** who was made Poet Laureate in 1730

His cuffs are frayed – offer him £5.00 less.

Anonymous producer after an actor had successfully auditioned for him

I enjoy my little part. As to salary, well, the truth is there isn't much, but there's a real pudding in the second act.

Anonymous actor quoted in J. Aye, *Humour in the Theatre* 1932

There'll be an awful lot of windows to clean.

Squire Bancroft on being shown rival manager Beerbohm Tree's extravagant new theatre, Her Majesty's

It is one of the tragic ironies of the theatre that only one man in it can count on steady work – the night watchman.

Tallulah Bankhead

Every crowd has a silver lining.

Phineas T. Barnum

Dear God, send me a good Hamlet – but make him cheap.

Lilian Baylis attrib.

Your excellency, I am accustomed, when I bring an attraction to town, to spend $400 on advertising. As you have done half the advertising for me, I herewith enclose $200 for your parish.

Sarah Bernhardt letter to the Bishop of Chicago who had loudly denounced her 'unsuitable' choice of plays

I can spin out these rough and tumble dramas (*The Poor of New York*) as a hen lays eggs. It's a degrading occupation, but more money has been made out of guano than out of poetry.

Dion Boucicault

To keep up morale in my staff and to fool rival producers and theatrical reporters, I always instructed managers of my road companies to add $300 to their nightly reports of box-office receipts. The system worked fine until one of them wired, 'Only theatre in town burned to ground this afternoon No performance. Receipts $300.'

William A. Brady

When an actor has money he doesn't send letters, but telegrams.

Anton Chekhov

I discover that I have not been paid for some time and have decided to withdraw my services. If I'm not paid I don't appear.

Albert Finney quitting *Reflected Glory* June 1992

Civil servants, treasury officials and cabinet ministers still believe one should work in the arts for honour.

Peter Hall *Diaries* 27 March 1972

With respect to the extravagance of actors, as a traditional character, it is not to be wondered at. They live from hand to mouth: they plunge from want into luxury; they have no means of making money breed, and all professions that do not live by turning money into money, or have not a certainty of accumulating it in the

end by parsimony, spend it. Uncertain of the future, they make sure of the present moment. This is not unwise.

William Hazlitt *On Actors and Acting*

I can speak with authority on the subject of being hard up. I have been a provincial actor.

Jerome K. Jerome *On the Stage and Off* 1885

Is it a stale remark to say that I have constantly found the interest excited at a playhouse to bear an exact inverse proportion to the price paid for admission?

Charles Lamb

No one ever went broke underestimating the taste of the American Public.

H.L. Mencken

Never give a sucker an even break.

Walter Mizner

What, ask for a salary when blackberries are ripe!

John S. Potter actor-manager, when asked by one of his company for a small part of the money owed him

A guy who likes to wear a black hat and meet blondes.

Billy Rose (definition of a theatrical 'angel', who puts up the production money)

Never invest your money in anything that eats or needs repairing.

Billy Rose

The trouble with him is that he is in love with his wife and an actor can only afford to be in love with himself.

George Bernard Shaw

The trouble, Mr Goldwyn, is that you are only interested in art and I am only interested in money.

George Bernard Shaw when Samuel Goldwyn offered to buy the film rights of his plays

I am dying as I have lived – beyond my means.

Oscar Wilde on learning the cost of his medical treatment, 1900

Angels with checkbooks rush in where even fools fear to tread.

Walter Winchell

FIRST NIGHTS

A first night in London of a Tallulah Bankhead play is a wild orgy of emotion.

1920s London theatre critic quoted in Maurice Zolotow, *No People Like Show People* 1951

Dear God, please don't let me make a fool of myself tonight.

Tallulah Bankhead ritual prayer before an opening night – followed by a glass of champagne; quoted in Maurice Zolotow, *No People Like Show People* 1951

I made the usual ritualistic phone calls that I make after a first night. Never mind, never mind, I said.

Peter Hall *Diaries* 3 May 1974 (after the first night of *Next of Kin* by John Hopkins)

Audience – a gathering of optimists who want to enjoy themselves and hope for the best. Audience, First Night – a gathering of optimists who want to enjoy themselves and hope for the worst.

Ronald Jeans quoted in R. May, *The Wit of the Theatre* 1969

Opening night is the night before the play is ready to open.

George Jean Nathan

A hand on your opening and may your parts grow bigger.

Dorothy Parker first night telegram to Uta Hagen; quoted in R. Huggett, *The Curse of Macbeth* 1981

I think that first nights should come near the end of a play's run – as indeed they often do.

Peter Ustinov

DAVID GARRICK

Garrick was pure gold beat out into thin leaf.

James Boswell

I never saw in my life such brilliant piercing eyes as Mr Garrick's are. In looking at him, when I have chanced to meet them, I have really not been able to bear their lustre.

Fanny Burney *Diary* 1771

He contradicted the proverb that one cannot make bricks without straw, by doing what is infinitely more difficult, making actors and actresses without genius.

Kitty Clive *c.* 1747

But when . . . I first beheld Garrick, young and light and alive in every muscle and feature, what a transition! It seemed as if a whole century had been stepped over in the transition of a single scene; old things were done away, and a new order at once brought forward, bright and luminous and clearly destined to dispel the barbarism and bigotry of a tasteless age, too long attached to the prejudices of custom, and superstitiously devoted to the illusions of imposing declamation.

Richard Cumberland *Memoirs* 1806–7

*Our Garrick's a salad; for in him we
see*
Oil, vinegar, sugar and saltness agree.

*Though equal to all things, for all
things unfit;*
*Too nice for a statesman, too proud for
a wit.*

*On the stage he was natural, simple,
affecting;*
*'Twas only that when he was off he
was acting.*

*He cast off his friends as a huntsman
his pack.*
*For he knew when he pleas'd he could
whistle them back.*

*Of praise a mere glutton, he
swallowed what came,*
*And the puff of a dunce he mistook it
for fame.*

Oliver Goldsmith *Retaliation* 19
April 1774

David, madame, looks much older
than he is for his face has had
double the business of any other
man's: it is never at rest. . . . I
don't believe he even has the same
look for half an hour together in
the whole course of his life; and
such an eternal, restless, fatiguing
play of the muscles must certainly
wear out a man's face before its
real time.

Samuel Johnson quoted by
Fanny Burney, *Diary* 1778

Garrick, Madam, was no
disclaimer; there was not one of
his own scene-shifters who could
not have spoken 'To be, or not to
be' better than he did; yet he was
the only actor I ever saw who I
could call a master both in
comedy and tragedy.

Samuel Johnson to Mrs Siddons;
quoted in J. Boswell, *The Life of
Samuel Johnson* 1791

That young man never had his
equal and never will have a rival.

Alexander Pope

Garrick . . . made himself a slave
to his reputation. . . . It was
difficult to get him, and when you
had him, as difficult to keep him.
He never came into company but
with a plot how to get out of it.
He was for ever receiving
messages of his being wanted in
another place. . . . Being used to
exhibit himself at a theatre or a
large table he did not consider an
individual as worth powder and
shot.

Joshua Reynolds *Notes on
Garrick*

Jack Bannister told me he was
behind the scenes one night when
Garrick was playing Lear; and that
the tones in which Garrick uttered

the words 'O fool! I shall go mad!' absolutely thrilled him.

Samuel Rogers *Table Talk* 1856

JOHN GIELGUD

(ON HIMSELF)
What I'd like to do is die on stage in the middle of a good performance and with a full house.

*Director **Peter Brook** was some weeks into rehearsals for **Oedipus** and things were still at the introspective discussion stage, with very little progress on the practical front. As part of the road to self-knowledge each of the cast was asked to think of the most terrifying thing imaginable. When it came to **Gielgud**'s turn his response was simple:*

We open next Tuesday!

(BY OTHERS)
It is a matter of theatrical history that Mr John Gielgud has lost ground during the last three years before the tempestuous onslaught of Mr Laurence Olivier.

Beverley Baxter 1947

Mr Gielgud has the most meaningless legs imaginable.

Ivor Brown reviewing Gielgud as Romeo, May 1924; quoted in D. Rigg, *No Turn Unstoned* 1982

His tactless remarks, over the decades, have joined the ranks of the happiest theatre legend of our time and, apart from their sheer funniness, they have always been entirely forgivable because they spring spontaneously from the heart, without a glimmer of malice.

Alec Guinness *Blessings in Disguise* 1985

Sir John Gielgud is the finest actor in the world from the neck up.

Kenneth Tynan 1959

GREEK DRAMA

You know Electra? Well, Electra is like one day in my daughter's life.

Sarah Adler on her actress daughter Celia; quoted in L. Rosenfeld, *Bright Star of Exile* 1977

Well, that's put the theatre back two and a half thousand years!

Noel Davies on emerging from Peter Hall's acclaimed production of *The Oresteia* 1981

In Aristophanic comedy there was no limit, in word or action, to obscenity. Living men were not only ridiculed, but grossly slandered. Aristophanes seems to have been free to bring any accusations, however monstrous, or cruel, or indecent, against anybody.

Kenneth Dover *The Greek World* (ed. H. Lloyd-Jones) 1962

How did the Greeks stand marble benches in their theatres?

Aldous Huxley

The Graces, seeking to possess some sacred enclosure which should never fail, found the soul of Aristophanes.

Plato attrib. inscription for Aristophanes' tomb; quoted by Lord Neaves, *The Greek Anthology* 1897

IBSEN

These Ibsen creatures are 'neither men nor women, they are ghouls', vile, unlovable, unnatural, morbid monsters and it were well indeed for society if all such went and drowned themselves at once.

Review of the first English production of *Rosmersholm* in *The Gentlewoman* 1891

A crazy fanatic . . . a crazy cranky being . . . not only consistently dirty but deplorably dull.

Review of Ibsen's *Ghosts* 1892 (*Ghosts* deals with the subject of venereal disease)

'*Peer Gynt*' – written by a mad poet. One goes crazy oneself if reading this book.

Hans Christian Andersen 1870

In his bones he is a moralist, in practice an artist.

James Huneker

It was as though someone had dramatized the cooking of a Sunday dinner.

Clement Scott reviewing *The Doll's House* for *Sporting and Dramatic News* 1889

An open drain, a loathsome sore, an abominable piece, a repulsive and degrading work.

Clement Scott review of the first London production of *Ghosts* in the *Daily Telegraph* 1892

There is no need to enter into the details of so commonplace and suburban a story. In essence it is trivial.

Clement Scott reviewing Ibsen's *The Wild Duck* in the *Daily Telegraph* 1894

A reformer who calls you to crawl with him into a sewer, merely to see and breathe its feculence.

William Winter

INSULTS

Rachel, French tragedienne, savouring an opening night triumph: 'When I made my entrance the audience sat there completely open-mouthed.'
Anonymous fellow actress: 'Nonsense. They never all yawn at exactly the same time.'

If you really want to help the American theatre darling, be an audience.

Tallulah Bankhead to a young actress

Darling, they've absolutely ruined your perfectly dreadful play.

Tallulah Bankhead to **Tennessee Williams** after seeing the film of *Orpheus Descending*

The abilities of a young actress were being defended by one of her admirers: 'You must admit she has some wonderful moments.'
Sarah Bernhardt: 'Oh yes, but some terrible half hours.'

It's still the same dear little face we all loved so in *Candlelight* (pause) – but there's another face round it.

Lilian Braithwaite on French actress **Yvonne Arnaud**

The Comtesse de Brémont presents her compliments to Mr W.S. Gilbert and in reply to his answer to her request for an interview for *St. Paul's*, in which he states his terms as twenty guineas for that privilege, begs to say that she anticipates the pleasure of writing his obituary for nothing.

Comtesse de Brémont quoted in G. Snell, *The Book of Theatre Quotes* 1982

She comes on stage as if she'd been sent for to sew rings on the new curtains.

Mrs Patrick Campbell on **Lillian Gish**

But it's *sooo* long Mr Jones, even *without* the H's.

Mrs Patrick Campbell to **Henry Arthur Jones** who had been reading aloud to her, in his strong cockney accent, his seemingly interminable new play *Michael and His Lost Angel*

Wm. Wheatleigh Esq.,
Manager,
New York City.

Dear Sir,

This will introduce the eminent tragedian Mr McKean Buchanen. He wants to play in New York. I have seen him play Macbeth, Richelieu and poker. He plays the latter best.

C.W. Couldock quoted in Milton Nobles, *Shop Talk* 19th century

Who could take that scruffy, arrogant buffoon seriously?

Eddie Fisher on **Richard Burton** (who had taken Fisher's wife, Elizabeth Taylor)

Tallulah Bankhead to Lynn Fontanne: How lucky you are to be married to Alfred Lunt, darling. His directing, his acting, his theatre sense. Where would you be without it?'
Lynn Fontanne: 'Probably playing *your* parts.'

Oh to be in England now that June's here.

Judy Garland on the Broadway debut of English actress **Lady June Inverclyde**

I only have a misleading lady.

W.S. Gilbert on a disappointing piece of casting quoted in J. Aye *Humour in the Theatre* 1932

You – effeminate guys of the theatre, what do you know about real war!

Ernest Hemingway

She knows when she should come on, and she knows when she should go off – it's the bit in the middle that foxes her.

Hugh Hunt on an unnamed actress

She has made an acting style out of post-nasal drip.

Pauline Kael on Sandy Dennis

Tallulah who?

Beatrice Lillie

Pauline Kael has aptly observed that Miss Dennis 'has made an acting style out of post-nasal drip'. It should be added that she balanced her post-nasal condition with something like a pre-frontal lobotomy, so that when she is not a walking catarrh she is a blithering imbecile.

John Simon reviewing *The Fox* 1968

Diana Rigg is built like a brick mausoleum with insufficient flying buttresses.

John Simon 1970 (Miss Rigg had appeared naked in *Abelard and Heloise*)

Ah . . . (pause). Your *father* was a great actor.

Constantin Stanislavski to Joseph Schildkraut after seeing him in *Peer Gynt* 1923. Schildkraut's father was the renowned Viennese actor Rudolf Schildkraut.

Among the select group of plays written for eminent husband and wife teams in coronation years, it ranks very high.

Kenneth Tynan 1953, on Terence Rattigan's *The Sleeping Prince*, written for Laurence Olivier and Vivien Leigh

Miss Ilona Massey, the blonde film actress who is making her Broadway debut in this production is doubtless very good in films.

Willela Waldorf review in the *New York Post*

If I can't go to their openings I'll wait three days and go to their closings.

Walter Winchell *c.* 1920; on the Shubert brothers, who had banned the critic from their theatres

Alexander Woollcott to **Peggy Wood**: I don't think you would make a good Lady Macbeth. Do you?
Peggy Wood to **Alexander Woollcott**: No. But you would!

HENRY IRVING

(ON HIMSELF)
For an actor who can't walk, can't talk and has no face to speak of, I've done pretty well.

Henry Irving to **Ellen Terry**

(BY OTHERS)
He danced, he did not merely walk – he sang, he by no means merely spoke. He was essentially artificial, in distinction to being merely natural.

Edward Gordon Craig *Henry Irving* 1931

I go to the pantomime only at Christmas.

W.S. Gilbert when asked if he had seen Irving as Faust

Of what the French call diction – of the art of delivery – he has apparently not a suspicion. This forms three fourths of an actor's obligations and in Mr Irving's acting these three fourths are simply cancelled.

Henry James *Scenic Art*

He achieved the celebrated feat of performing *Hamlet* with the part of Hamlet omitted and all other parts as well, substituting for it and for them the fascinating figure of Henry Irving, which for many years did not pall on his audience and never palled on himself.

George Bernard Shaw preface to *Ellen Terry and Bernard Shaw* (ed. C. St. John) 1931

He does not merely cut plays; he disembowels them.

George Bernard Shaw 'Blaming the Bard', *Saturday Review*, September 1896

He has an ugly ear! Large, flabby, ill-cut, and pasty looking, pale and lumpy.

Ellen Terry *Notes on Irving*

The hero, though a mannerist of the Macready type, acted wonderfully. . . . The way in which Irving acted his own dream, and describes the way in which he carried out the murder, is wonderful and ghastly, as well as the scene at his death . . . it was a most successful performance.

Queen Victoria on Irving's command performance of *The Bells* at Windsor Castle, 1889

I am very, very pleased.

Queen Victoria to Irving when she dubbed him the first ever theatrical Knight in 1895

Irving's legs are dinstinctly *precious*, but his left leg is a *poem*.

Oscar Wilde

EDMUND KEAN

(ON HIMSELF)
Fight for me, I have no resources in myself; mind is gone and the body is hopeless. God knows my heart. I would do but cannot. Memory, the first of goddesses, has forsaken me, and I am left without a hope but from those old resources that the public and myself are tired of. Damn God, damn ambition. The soul leaps, the body falls.

Letter to W.H. Halpin 1830; quoted in Peter Hall, *Diaries* 1982

(BY OTHERS)
With . . . Byron to a private pit box to see Mr Kean in *Richard III*. He was extremely happy: and is a very short man with a piercing black eye. 'Off with his head; so much for Buckingham', was given thus; The instant he received the news of Buckingham being prisoner he said quickly, 'Off with his head', and then, advancing to the front of the stage, added with a savage smile, 'So much for Buckingham.'

Lord Broughton *Recollections of a Long Life* 1865

Kean is original; but he copies from himself.

Samuel Taylor Coleridge 27 April 1823; quoted in *Table Talk and Omniana* (ed. T. Ashe) 1884

To see him act is like reading Shakespeare by flashes of lightning.

Ibid.

There is in Mr Kean an infinite variety of talent, with a certain monotony of genius.

William Hazlitt – 'Mr Kean's Duke Aranza', *The Examiner* 10 December 1815

You cannot say that Kean has style. You can only judge his performance by the number of electrical shocks in it.

William Hazlitt

If he was irregular and unartist-like in his performance so is Niagara compared with the waterworks of Versailles.

Fanny Kemble quoted in M. Billington, *The Guinness Book of Theatre Facts and Feats* 1982

No Sir, I did not see Mr Kean. I saw Othello; and further, I shall not act the part again.

John Philip Kemble on being asked by a friend if he had seen the 'little man Kean' on stage the night before

I went to see Mr Kean and was thoroughly disgusted. This monarch of the stage is a little, insignificant man, slightly deformed, strongly ungraceful, seldom pleasing to the eye, still seldomer satisfying to the ear – with a voice between grunting and croaking, a perpetual hoarseness which suffocates his words and a vulgarity of manner which his admirers are pleased to call mature.

Mary Russell Mitford *Letter* 3 July 1814

Kean! Ah Kean! I saw him once. He was a splendid Gipsy.

Arthur Wing Pinero *Trelawney of the Wells* 1898

Edmund Kean, the great flamboyant 19th-century actor, is said to have varied his diet according to the part he had to play. For tyrants he would eat roast pork. For murderers, raw beef. For lovers, boiled mutton. There is no record of the roles he played when he ate ham.

Dick Richards *The Curtain Rises* 1966

KITCHEN SINK

What does he show? Lentils boiling in a pot while six men march up and down. Is this entertainment?

Noël Coward attrib. on the plays of Arnold Wesker

Since the war a terrible pall of significance has fallen over plays.

Noël Coward to James Dow on the theatre of the 1950s; quoted in D. Richards, *The Wit of Noël Coward*

Contemporary English drama is the measuring out of life in tepid teacups.

The Times 1965

VIVIEN LEIGH

By Jove, she's a clinker!

Winston Churchill

She was often underrated because she was so beautiful.

George Cukor quoted in Gavin Lambert, *On Cukor*

Everyone talks about the lovely place Vivien had in London. Well, it always smelled like kitty litter, which she kept in the hall.

Joan Fontaine quoted in *Celebrity Gossip*

She made life hell for everyone near her, unless they did everything she wished, as she wished and when she wished.

Wolfe Kaufman

I only saw Vivien Leigh once in my life in person. That was at the Ritz-Carlton Hotel in Boston. I got into the elevator and she was there. And I got goose pimples. I got off on the third floor, like a fool. The goose pimples remained for ten minutes which, I am told, is a medical phenomenon.

Walter Matthau

She had big hands and packed a hefty slap.

Alec McCowen (who was slapped nightly by Miss Leigh in the 1952 *Antony and Cleopatra*) *Sunday Times* 19 January 1992

She wanted us to be like brother and sister. But, fortunately, occasional incest was allowed.

Laurence Olivier

You are the Mrs Pat Campbell of the age.

George Bernard Shaw 1942

She had the misfortune to be one of the most physically beautiful actresses of her period.

J.C. Trewin quoted in Vivien Leigh's obituary in the *Observer* 1967

She picks at the part with the daintiness of a debutante called upon to dismember a stag.

Kenneth Tynan on Vivien Leigh in *Antony and Cleopatra* 1951

When she takes the stage she commands it as if she had first arrived there suspended from the bill of a stork.

Tennessee Williams quoted in A. Walker, *Vivien* 1987

OSCAR LEVANT

(ON HIMSELF)
I'm a controversial figure: my friends either dislike me or hate me.

Quoted by Walter Winchell in *Winchell Exclusive* 1975

(BY OTHERS)
Oscar was a man of principle. He never sponged off anybody he didn't admire.

Harpo Marx

When Oscar comes on stage he weaves on like a drunk trying to find the rest room.

Jack Paar

Oscar has mellowed – like an old pistol.

Billy Rose

There's nothing wrong with Oscar Levant – nothing that a miracle couldn't fix.

Alexander Woollcott attrib.

To autograph seekers he has only three words: 'Go to Hell'.

Maurice Zolotov

LIFE

A quarrel in the theatrical world usually ends in one actor taking another's part.

John Aye *Humour in the Theatre* 1932

But men must know, that in this theatre of man's life it is reserved only for Gods and angels to be lookers-on.

Francis Bacon *The Advancement of Learning* Bk. II, Ch. 20

Life – with a capital F!

Lilian Baylis

Life begets life. Energy creates energy. It is by spending oneself that one becomes rich.

Sarah Bernhardt

To others we are not ourselves but a performer in their lives cast for a part we do not even know we are playing.

Elizabeth Bibesco *Haven* 1951

An actress without talent, forty years old, ate a partridge for dinner, and I felt sorry for the partridge, for it occurred to me that in its life it had been more talented, more sensible, and more honest than the actress.

Anton Chekhov *Notebooks* 1892–94

The trouble with Freud is that he never played the Glasgow Empire Saturday night.

Ken Dodd *The Times* 1965; quoted in J. Green, *A Dictionary of Contemporary Quotations* 1982

For, Heaven be thanked, we live in
*   such an age,*
When no man dies for love, but on
*   the stage.*

John Dryden *Mithridates*

Everybody has his own theatre, in which he is manager, actor, prompter, playwright, scene-shifter, boxkeeper, doorkeeper, all in one, and audience into the bargain.

Julius and Augustus Hare *Guesses at Truth* 1827

Life used to be full of third acts, bringing everything nicely to a comforting close, with a satisfying solution. But life isn't like that any longer. There is no solution. You can't send people back to their homes any more with their problems solved. If you did solve their problems, they just wouldn't believe it.

Laurence Olivier quoted in A. Holden, *Olivier* 1988

All the world's a stage,
And all the men and women merely
players:
They have their exits and their
entrances;
And one man in his time plays many
parts,
His acts being seven ages.

William Shakespeare *As You Like It* Act II, Scene 7

When we are born we cry that we are
come
To this great stage of fools.

William Shakespeare *King Lear* Act IV, Scene 6

Life's but a walking shadow, a poor
player,
That struts and frets his hour upon the
stage,
And then is heard no more:

William Shakespeare *Macbeth* Act V, Scene 5

I hold the world but as the world,
Gratiano;
A stage, where every man must play a
part,
And mine a sad one.

William Shakespeare *The Merchant of Venice* Act I, Scene 1

THE LUNTS

(ON THEMSELVES)
We can be bought but we can't be bored.

Alfred Lunt and **Lynn Fontanne** quoted in Alfred Lunt's obituary 1977

(BY OTHERS)
They are deeply concerned with only three things – themselves, the theatre (in so far as it concerns themselves), and food – good, hot food.

Noël Coward *Diaries* 17 September 1953

Alfred Lunt has his head in the clouds and his feet in the box office.

Noël Coward

If you want a play to run many a munt,
Get Lynn Fontanne and Alfred Lunt.

Robert Sherwood quoted in S. N. Behrman, *People in a Diary* 1972

Their attitude can most clearly be expressed by a child's copybook maxim, about duty; doing their duty towards the play, the dramatist, the audience, according to their own high standards.

G.B. Stern

MELODRAMA

Listen to me, Your Lordship. You have broken up my business, you have ruined my home, you have sent my son to prison and my wife to a dishonoured grave, and you have seduced my only daughter. But, have a care, Lord Fitz Wallop, I am a man of quick temper. Do not try me too far.

Horace Wyndham melodrama epitomized; quoted in J. Aye, *Humour in the Theatre* 1932

METHOD ACTING

A man of the theatre died last night: – It will take a hundred years before the harm that man has done to the art of acting can be corrected.

Stella Adler on learning of the death of Lee Strasberg 1982

I should like you to convey when you are acting it that the man you portray has a brother in Shropshire who drinks port.

J.M. Barrie to an anxious actor seeking help in interpreting his part

He had two rules for playing with Method actors: 1. Let them improvise to their hearts' content and just wait for your cue; and 2. Don't ever play an eating scene with them, because they spit all over you.

Humphrey Bogart recalled by Nathaniel Benchley in *Celebrity Gossip* 1984

Mr Strasberg went off into a long dissertation on the art of acting, most of which was pretentious balls.

Noël Coward *Diaries* 25 May 1958

If you must have motivation think of your pay packet on Friday.

Noël Coward 1926; quoted in Sheridan Morley, *A Talent to Amuse* 1985

Well I have a bash at it, and if it doesn't go, I have another bash at it.

Wendy Hiller when asked about her 'method' by an American reporter; quoted in P. Hay, *Broadway Anecdotes* 1989

I don't want any of that Stanislavski shit from you.

Charles Laughton to Eli Wallach before rehearsals for *Major Barbara*; quoted in D. Garfield, *The Actor's Studio* 1980

It is a simple common sense approach to releasing and bringing in to play the creative powers that all actors have in them by virtue of themselves being living human beings.

Clifford Odets quoted in *Acting – A Handbook of the Stanislavski Method* (ed. T. Cole) 1947

It teaches not how to play this or that part but how to create organically.

Lee Strasberg quoted in *Acting – A Handbook of the Stanislavski Method*

The connection between role and soul.

Lee Strasberg attrib.

The Method as practised by the *New York Actors' Studio* under Lee Strasberg not only sank the actor into his part, it completely lost him. And that is the basic difference between Stanislavski and The Method.

Michael R. Turner *Bluff Your Way in the Theatre* 1967

MOTIVATION

The whole motivation for any performer: 'Look at me, Ma!'

Lenny Bruce

I've done the most awful rubbish in order to have somewhere to go in the morning.

Richard Burton

Actors are like racehorses. You just rein them in or whip them on and make sure you give them a lump of sugar if they do well.

Terry Hands quoted in M. Billington, *The Guinness Book of Theatre Facts and Feats* 1982

Now that we have a surplus female population it is clear that all women cannot marry, they cannot enlist, nor yet go out to the colonies and become domestic servants. So they sigh after the stage.

George Moore 1886

The more intelligent of my young colleagues, in ceaseless talks seeking some rationalization of our lives, agree that their choice of *métier* was to satisfy an urgent need to express themselves. . . . I have to confess, rather shamefacedly, that I have never been conscious of any need other than to show off.

Laurence Olivier *Confessions of an Actor* 1982

All the inspiration I ever needed was a telephone call from a producer.

Cole Porter

You don't act to earn your living. You act to lie, to lie to yourself, to be what you cannot be and because you're fed up with what you are. You act so as not to know yourself, and because you know yourself too well. You act because you're a liar from birth. You act because you'd go mad if you didn't.

Jean-Paul Sartre *Kean* 1954 (translated by Frank Hauser)

MUSIC HALL/ VAUDEVILLE

She had a heart as big as Waterloo station.

James Agate about music hall star Marie Lloyd

The aim of the music-hall is, in fact, to cheer the lower classes up by showing them a life uglier and more sordid than their own.

Max Beerbohm

With the collapse of vaudeville new talent has no place to sink.

George Burns

Vaudeville is a species of entertainment derived from the dregs of drama and musical comedy, assembled in such wise that they shall appeal to the dregs of the drama and musical comedy audiences.

George Jean Nathan *American Mercury* 1929

The domestic back parlour of music hall itself.

John Osborne on theatrical digs in *A Better Class of Person* 1981

Every performance given by Marie Lloyd is a Command Performance by order of the British Public.

Poster for Marie Lloyd's performance at the Pavilion Theatre, 1912. She had been left out of the Royal Command performance on the same night because her three marriages and two divorces were considered too scandalous for George V and Queen Mary.

MUSICALS

I must say Bernard Shaw is greatly improved by music.

T.S. Eliot on *My Fair Lady* 1958

The trouble with nude dancing is that not everything stops when the music stops.

Robert Helpmann after seeing *Oh! Calcutta* 1969

Musicals – a series of catastrophes ending with a floor show.

Oscar Levant

An American musical so bad that at times I longed for the boy-meets-tractor theme of Soviet drama.

Bernard Levin on *Flower Drum Song* in the *Daily Express* 1960

Definition of a musical – disorderly conduct occasionally interrupted by talk.

L.L. Levinson

These shows are to the theatres what wines are to a substantial dinner.

George Jean Nathan quoted in M. Billington, *The Guinness Book of Theatre Facts and Feats* 1982

It seems that the moment anyone gets hold of an exclamation mark these days, he promptly writes a musical show around it.

George Jean Nathan

There will be a quick rash of hairy American filth, but it shouldn't threaten the existence of decent, serious British filth.

John Osborne writing in *Time* magazine after the London opening of the American musical *Hair*

As synthetic and padded as the transvestite's cleavage.

Frank Rich on *La Cage aux Folles* in the *New York Times* 1983

I had to hit myself on the head afterwards with a small hammer to get that stupid *Tomorrow* song out of my head.

Ian Shoales on *Annie* 1977

Musicals – millions of pounds riding on a piece of piffle.

Mark Steyn Channel 4 TV 10 March 1992

LAURENCE OLIVIER

(ON HIMSELF)
I believe I was born to be an actor.

Sunday Times 3 November 1963

An actor is a sitting duck in any case, but an actor who is a Lord is a duck flying straight towards you, a figure of fun.

(After becoming the first actor to receive a peerage, 1970)

I am an actor because that is all I am qualified to do. I shall go on acting until a couple more illnesses cause me to drop. And then I shall write that dreaded book.

Los Angeles Times 26 February 1978

I am far from sure when I am acting and when I am not. Or, more frankly, when I am lying and when I am not. For what is good acting but convincing lying?

Confessions of an Actor 1982

I may be rather feminine but I am not effeminate.

Quoted by M. Billington in *Olivier: In Celebration* (ed. G. O'Connor) 1988

I don't enjoy acting, but I can't live without it. I'm like a sort of carthorse with a collar round its neck: if you take it off, it starts whinnying for it.

Quoted in A. Holden, *Olivier* 1988

(BY OTHERS)
A comedian by instinct and a tragedian by art.

James Agate quoted in A. Walker, *Vivien* 1987

No actor before him has ever triumphed in such a wide diversity of roles or created so much history.

Michael Billington *The Guinness Book of Theatre Facts and Feats* 1982

Gulping down his lines as if they were so many bad oysters.

John Mason Brown reviewing the New York production of *Romeo and Juliet* in the *Post* 1940

This Oedipus is one of those performances in which blood and electricity are somehow mixed. It pulls down lightning from the sky. It is as awesome, dwarfing and appalling as one of nature's angriest displays.

John Mason Brown on *Oedipus Rex*, New York 1946 in *Seeing Things* 1946

He came on smelling a rose, laughing softly with a private delight; barefooted, ankleted, black.

Ronald Bryden on Olivier's *Othello* at the Old Vic, 1964

Olivier brandished his technique like a kind of stylistic alibi. In catching the eye he frequently disengaged the brain.

Russell Davies Channel 4 TV 3 March 1992

Olivier is a great impersonator. I am always myself.

John Gielgud quoted in A. Holden *Olivier* 1988

He handicapped himself by wearing a beard and mane so stupendous that his voice came to me as though he were talking through a tree.

Hubert Griffith *Sunday Graphic* review of Olivier's *King Lear*, 1946

Offstage he was not notably handsome or striking, but with make-up he could achieve a flashing Italianate, rather saturnine, but fascinating appearance. The voice already had a marvellous ringing baritone brilliance at the top; he spoke with a beautiful and aristocratic accent, with keen intelligence and a strong sense of rhythm. He moved with catlike agility. He had, if anything, too strong an instinct for the sort of theatrical effect which is striking and memorable. From the first moment of the first rehearsal it was evident that here was no ordinary actor, not everyone's cup of tea – no very strong personality can be that; not necessarily well-cast for Hamlet, but inevitably destined for the very top of the tree.

Tyrone Guthrie 1937 *A Life in the Theatre* 1959

Acting is not imitation but revelation of the inner self. This is not what Larry does or sets out to do. He is a performer.

Peter Hall quoted in A. Holden, *Olivier* 1988

The theatre is his form of Church – a temple to man's knowledge of man, a place where people gather together and somebody talks to them and they are moved.

Joan Plowright (wife) quoted in A. Holden, *Olivier* 1988

The very boldness of Larry's personality, his natural drive and his pragmatism make him unsuitable to play an introspective, wavering character like Hamlet.

Michael Redgrave *In My Mind's Eye* 1983

He will spend 30 seconds sizing you up, decide what kind of person you want him to be, and then he will turn into that person.

Kenneth Tynan

He is our model Richard III and his Hotspur is unique, but he has no intrinsic majesty; he always fights shy of pathos; and he cannot play old men without letting his jaw sag and his eyes wander archly in magpie fashion – in short, without becoming funny.

Kenneth Tynan after seeing Olivier's Lear 1946

I had been told this was the last flourish of romantic acting. It's nothing of the sort. It's an anthology of everything that has been discovered about acting in the last three centuries.

Franco Zeffirelli on Olivier's Othello 1964 in K. Tynan, *The Sound of Two Hands Clapping* 1975

OPPROBRIUM

Stage plays are the most petulant, the most impure, impudent, wicked, unclean, the most shameful and detestable atonements of filthy devil-gods.

St. Augustine of Hippo

The Theatres – those Cages of Uncleanness, and public schools of Debauchery.

St. Augustine of Hippo

What need I comment on the lewdness of those spectacles, and give a detailed description? For what is to be met with there but lewd laughing, and smut, ranting and buffoonery? In a word it is all Scandal and Confusion.

St. John Chrysostom

Spending time in theatres, produces fornication, intemperance, and every kind of impurity.

St. John Chrysostom

He diverts the ladies with the charming rhetoric of *snotty-nose*, filthy *vermin in the beard*, *nitty jerkin*, *louse-snapper*, and *letter in the chamber pot*; and with an abusive description of a countess, and a rude story of a certain lady with some other varieties of this kind too coarse to mention. . . . There is more physic than comedy in such sentences as these. *Crocus metallorum* will scarce turn the stomach more effectively.

Jeremy Collier *A Short View of the Immorality and Profaneness of the English Stage*, 1698. Collier was commenting on Thomas

D'Urfey's *Don Quixote* which typified the lewdness of the period.

I am persuaded that Satan hath not a more speedy way and fitter school to work and teach his desire, to bring men and women into his share of concupiscence and filthy lusts of wicked whoredom, than those plays and theatres.

John Northbrooke *Spiritus est Vicarius Christi in Terra* 1579

Stage plays . . . are sinfull, heathenish, lewde, ungodly Spectacles, and most pernicious Corruptions, condemned in all ages, as intolerable Mischiefs to Churches, to Republickes, to the manners, mindes and soules of men. And . . . the profession of Play-poets, of Stage-players; together with the penning, acting, and frequenting of Stage-playes, are unlawful, infamous and misbeseeming Christians.

William Prynne *Histrio-Mastix: The Players Scourge or Actors Tragedie* 1633

Do they [plays] not maintain bawdry, insinuate foolery, and renew the remembrance of heathen idolatry? Do they not induce whoredom and uncleanness? Nay, are they not rather plain devourers of maidenly virginity and chastity?

Philip Stubbes *Anatomie of Abuses* 1583

There is a total extinction of all taste; our authors are vulgar, illiberal: the theatre swarms with wretched translations, and ballad operas, and we have nothing new but improving abuse.

Horace Walpole

I understand they [plays] are now forbidden because of the plague. I like the policy well if it hold still, for a disease is but lodged or patched up that is not cured in the cause, and the cause of plagues is sin, if you look to it well; and the causes of sin are plays; therefore the cause of plagues are plays.

Thomas White

Nudity on stage? I think it's disgusting. But if I were 22 with a great body, it would be artistic, tasteful, patriotic and a progressive religious experience.

Shelley Winters

PANTOMIME

The smell of wee-wee and oranges.

Tommy Trinder definition of pantomime

PLAYS

Aristotle
Took another swig from the bottle,
And remarked to a friend:
'A play must have a beginning,
A middle and an end.'

Anon. quoted in G. Snell, *The Book of Theatre Quotes* 1982

Very few plays are any good and *no* first plays are any good.

George Abbot *Saturday Evening Post* 1955

The greater the play the less production it will need.

James Agate

I don't see why people need new plays all the time. What would happen to concerts if people wanted new music all the time?

Clive Barnes

Plays are not written, they are re-written.

Dion Boucicault a playwright, famous for his 'adaptations'

A play is like a cigar. If it is a failure, no amount of puffing will make it draw. If it is a success everybody wants a box.

Henry J. Byron

If a gun is hanging on the wall in the first act it must fire in the last.

Anton Chekhov

The most important ingredients of a play are life, death, food, sex and money, but not necessarily in that order.

Noël Coward

If the critics unanimously take exception to one particular scene it is advisable to move that scene to a more conspicuous place in the programme.

Noël Coward

When they told me the day of the well-made play was over, all I could think was, thank God the day of the well-made aeroplane isn't over.

Noël Coward quoted in R. May, *The Wit of the Theatre* 1969

The stage play is a trial, not a deed of violence. The soul is opened, like the combination of a safe, by means of a word. You don't require an acetylene torch.

Jean Giraudoux

I believe that the theatre begins with the word. In the beginning there is the word. Absolutely!

Peter Hall

One begins with two people on a stage and one of them had better say something pretty damn quick.

Moss Hart *Contemporary Dramatists* 1977

I believe that plays that are successful are usually more entertaining than plays that fail. This will come as a revolutionary idea only to those who allow themselves to be intimidated by small critics who work for small quarterlies.

Jean Kerr quoted in D. Richards, *The Curtain Rises* 1966

Good dialogue is like the most charming interior of a house, but it is of little use if the foundations are insecure and the drains don't work.

Somerset Maugham to **Noël Coward** quoted in M. Billington, *The Guinness Book of Theatre Facts and Feats* 1982

The most exciting form of writing is the writing of plays.

A.A. Milne *It's Too Late Now* 1939

The only rule I have found to have any meaning in writing is to try and not bore yourself.

John Mortimer *Five Plays* (Introduction) 1971

Much of the contemporary English polite comedy writing suggests a highly polished and very smooth billiard table with all the necessary brightly polished cues but without balls.

George Jean Nathan *Encyclopaedia of the Theatre* 1940

American playwriting by and large enjoys all the attributes of a violin, save only its melodiousness. The necessary guts are there, but the bow lacks the gift of evoking poetic song from them.

Ibid.

Five surefire indications the play will be terrible:
1. When, as the curtain goes up, you hear the newsboys shouting, 'Extra! Extra!"
2. As soon as you hear the line, 'If a man kills a man, that's murder. Why isn't it then also murder if a man in uniform does the same thing? War is murder!'
3. Any mystery in which, at the very start, someone remarks that the nearest house is two miles away.
4. The moment anyone puts something into a drawer with a furtive look.
5. Any translation from the Hungarian in which the heroine is called Countess Katinka.

Ibid.

We English are more violent than we allow ourselves to know. That is why we have the greatest body of dramatic literature in the world.

John Osborne

My own view is that a play that is susceptible to crucial rewriting in rehearsal should never have reached that stage.

John Osborne *Almost a Gentleman* 1991

> *The play's the thing*
> *Wherein I'll catch the conscience of the*
> *king.*

William Shakespeare *Hamlet*
Act II, Scene 2

> *Is there no play,*
> *To ease the anguish of a torturing*
> *hour?*

William Shakespeare *A*
Midsummer Night's Dream Act V,
Scene 1

There must be something radically
wrong with a play if it pleases
everybody.

George Bernard Shaw 1914;
after the success of *Pygmalion*

> *Through all the drama – whether*
> *damn'd or not –*
> *Love gilds the scene, and women guide*
> *the plot.*

Richard Brinsley Sheridan *The*
Rivals 1775

It is a received point among poets,
that where history gives you a
good heroic outline for a play,
you may fill up with a little love at
your own discretion. (Mr Puff)

Richard Brinsley Sheridan *The*
Critic 1779

Ever while you live have two
plots to your tragedy. The grand
point in managing them is only to
let your underplot have as little
connexion with your main plot as
possible. (Mr Puff)

Ibid.

A good many inconveniences
attend playgoing in any large city,
but the greatest of them all is
usually the play itself.

Kenneth Tynan *New York Herald*
Tribune 1957

There can be no great drama
without a noble national life, and
the commercial spirit of England
has killed that.

Oscar Wilde *The English*
Renaissance of Art (lecture) 1882

PLAYWRIGHTS

There are no dull subjects, only
dull playwrights.

Robert Anderson

Dramatist – one who adapts plays from the French.

Ambrose Bierce *The Devil's Dictionary*

I always think the poor playwright is the most scurvily-treated being in the theatre.

Denys Blakelock *Advice to a Player* 1958

You've got to love the real world if you're a dramatist, and if the real world is not as you like it, then that's got to be the stuff of your drama, or you end up with windy, hollow, romantic writing.

Howard Brenton *The Times* 13 April 1992

Our poets make us laugh at Tragedy. And with their Comedies they make us cry.

George Villiers 2nd Duke of Buckingham

Poor man. He's completely unspoiled by failure.

Noël Coward attrib. on a successful but over-rated playwright

Wise beginners of playwrights will, of course, after a little while compare their press notices with

their royalties and decide that they still have a great deal to learn.

Noël Coward

What is there in your play that is so deep? Apart from the plot, which is completely submerged after the first four pages.

Noël Coward

Any dramatist finds that his plays fall into two categories: those for which he had some hopes but which went wrong either in the writing or in the production; and those for which he had none, and which surprised him by achieving public approval.

Ronald Duncan *Collected Plays* 1971

Conflict is the force that drives a theatrical writer.

Dario Fo *The Independent* 1 April 1992

We have given a comedy of M. Viennet in order not to be obliged to play one of his tragedies.

Arsène Houssaye *Behind the Scenes at the Comédie Française* 1889

I think paradise will be regained on 44th Street when young playwrights understand that they must try not to write plays that will cause nice ordinary people from Riverdale to wish they were dead.

Jean Kerr quoted in D. Richards, *The Curtain Rises* 1966

There are three primal urges in human beings: food, sex, and re-writing someone else's play.

Romulus Linney quoted in P. Hay, *Theatrical Anecdotes* 1987

The only truth which is demanded from the dramatist is truth to character. Subject to this truth he is required to present in the refracting mirror of the stage such distortion of real life as will best reflect his meaning.

A.A. Milne *It's Too Late Now* 1939

I've left a trail of richer but sadder authors after me.

Robert Morley quoted in his obituary, *The Times* 4 June 1992

An actor without a playwright is like a hole without a doughnut.

George Jean Nathan quoted in M. Billington, *The Guinness Book of Theatrical Facts and Feats* 1982

Agents and managers like their popular models to be annually unchanged. If the new Ayckbourn or Stoppard is too unlike the last one there will be complaints from those who had got such reliable mileage from previous makes.

John Osborne *A Better Class of Person* 1981

Most playwrights should observe the same constitutional rights as the Queen: to be consulted, to advise and to warn.

John Osborne *Almost a Gentleman* 1991

If you can't write a play without being taught – don't.

George Bernard Shaw

Writing a play is like smashing that [glass] ashtray, filming it in slow motion, and then running the film in reverse, so that the fragments of rubble seem to fly together. You start – or at least I start – with the rubble.

Tom Stoppard quoted in K. Tynan, *Show People* 1980

A playwright is a lay preacher peddling the ideas of his time in popular form.

August Strindberg

My Dear Sir,

    I have read your play. Oh, my dear Sir!

        Yours faithfully etc.

Herbert Beerbohm Tree reply to an aspiring playwright

Show me a congenital eavesdropper with the instincts of a Peeping Tom and I will show you the makings of a dramatist.

Kenneth Tynan *Pausing on the Stairs* 1957

The first rule for a young playwright to follow is not to write like Henry Arthur Jones . . . The second and third rules are the same.

Oscar Wilde

An incinerator is a writer's best friend.

Thornton Wilder *New York Times* 6 November 1961

PLAYWRIGHTS
– *Individuals*

SAMUEL BECKETT

It was an expression, symbolic in order to avoid all personal error, by an author who expected each member of his audience to draw his own conclusions, make his own errors. It asked nothing in point, it forced no dramatized moral on the viewer, it held out no specific hope. . . . We're still waiting for Godot, and shall continue to wait. When the scenery gets too drab and the action too slow, we'll call each other names and swear to part forever – but then, there's no place to go.

Review of a production of *Waiting for Godot* in San Quentin prison, *San Quentin News*, 28 November 1957; quoted in M. Esslin, *The Theatre of the Absurd* 1962

You either like Samuel Beckett's plays or you think they are a heap of twaddle. They remind me of something John Betjeman might do if you filled him up with Benzedrine and then force fed him intravenously with Guinness.

Tom Davies *Observer* 17 June 1979; quoted in F.S. Pepper, *The Dictionary of Biographical Quotations* 1985

Beckett's *Waiting for Godot* . . . arrived in London ten years ago like a sword burying itself in an over-upholstered sofa.

Penelope Gilliatt review in the *Observer* quoted in M. Billington,

The Guinness Book of Theatre Facts and Feats 1982

A play in which nothing happens twice.

Vivian Mercier on *Waiting for Godot* quoted in G. Snell, *The Book of Theatre Quotes* 1982

I suspect that Beckett is a confidence trick perpetrated on the twentieth century by a theatre-hating God. He remains the only playwright in my experience capable of making forty minutes seem like an eternity and the wrong kind of eternity at that.

Sheridan Morley *Punch* 1973

The suggestion that something is being said about the human predicament won't hold water any more than Beckett's incontinent heroes can.

Spectator 1959; quoted in C. Jarman, *The Guinness Dictionary of Poisonous Quotes* 1991

APHRA BEHN
With Dryden she vied in indecency and was not overcome.

Dr John Doran

All women together ought to let flowers fall upon the tomb of Aphra Behn, for it was she who

earned them the right to speak their minds.

Virginia Woolf

BERTOLT BRECHT
I don't regard Brecht as a man of iron-grey purpose and intellect, I think he is a theatrical whore of the first quality.

Peter Hall quoted in F. Muir, *The Frank Muir Book*

For me the two playwrights to be avoided at all costs are Brecht and Anouilh

Robert Morley

I admit that, like Wagner, he is a great man: but I can't stand him at any cost.

Peter Ustinov

GEORGE VILLIERS, 2ND DUKE OF BUCKINGHAM
A man so various that he seemed to be,
Not one, but all mankind's epitome.

John Dryden *Absalom and Achitophel* 1681

WILLIAM CONGREVE
Wickedness is no subject for comedy: to forget this was

Congreve's greatest error, and almost peculiar to him.

Samuel Taylor Coleridge

Mirabel, the fine gentleman of *Way of the World* is, I believe, not far distant from the real character of Congreve.

Thomas Davies *Dramatic Miscellanies* 1785

William Congreve is the only sophisticated playwright England has produced; and like Shaw, Sheridan and Wilde, his nearest rivals, he was brought up in Ireland.

Kenneth Tynan *Curtains* 1961

He spoke of his works as trifles that were beneath him, and hinted to me at our first conversation that I should visit him upon no other foot than that of a gentleman who led a life of plainness and simplicity. I answered that had he been so unfortunate as to be a mere gentleman, I should never have come to visit him, and I was very much disgusted at so unseasonable a piece of vanity.

Voltaire *Letters Concerning the English Nation* 1733

CORNEILLE
Corneille is to Shakespeare as a clipped hedge is to a forest.

Samuel Johnson *Rambler* No. 60

JOHN DRYDEN
His mind was of a slovenly character – fond of splendour, but indifferent to neatness. Hence most of his writings exhibit the sluttish magnificence of a Russian noble, all vermin and diamonds, dirty linen and inestimable sables.

Thomas B. Macaulay 'John Dryden', *Edinburgh Review* January 1828

EURIPIDES
A cliché anthologist and maker of ragamuffin manikins.

Aristophanes

GEORGES FEYDEAU
Without the right timing Feydeau falls flat on his face.

Alexander Woollcott

LADY GREGORY
Now that the Abbey Players are world-renowned, I begin to realise that with such an audience and such actors an author is hardly needed. Good acting covers a multitude of defects. It explains the success of Lady Gregory's plays.

Oliver St. John Gogarty

LILLIAN HELLMAN
She writes like an angel, but she's a dreary bore as spinach is a dreary bore. I say she's spinach and the hellman with her.

Tallulah Bankhead (Hellman had refused to join Bankhead in suppporting the cause of Finland against Stalin during World War II.)

VICTOR HUGO
The lighthouse in a sea of absurdity.

Friedrich Nietzsche *The Twilight of the Idols* 1899

EUGENE IONESCO
For me the theatre is most often a confession. The admissions I make are incomprehensible to the deaf; but what else can I do.

On himself

BEN JONSON
He killed Mr Marlow, the poet, on Bunhill, coming from the Green-Curtain play-house.

John Aubrey *Brief Lives*

A great lover and praiser of himself, a contemner and scorner of others, given rather to lose a friend than a jest, jealous of every word and action of those about him.

William Drummond *Conversations with Jonson* pub. 1842

He was not only a professed imitator of Horace, but a learned plagiary of all the others; you track him everywhere in their snow.

John Dryden Essay *Of Dramatick Poesie*

I can't read Ben Jonson, especially his comedies. To me he appears to move in a wide sea of glue.

Alfred Tennyson quoted in *Alfred Lord Tennyson, A Memoir by His Son* 1897

Every half quarter of an hour a glass of Sack must be sent into his Guts, to tell his Brains they must come up quickly, and help out with a line.

Robert Wilde *The Benefice*

GEORGE S. KAUFMAN
It was not his own but the pottiness of the world that begloomed him, that gave the Kaufman pompadour the look of the first plume of the hearse. What can a witty man do but hang his head in a land that has resolutely turned its back on wit, that is ready to cry sabotage to satire, that has traded in its once famous slapstick for a global sceptre.

Ben Hecht 'Kaufman', *The Bedside Phoenix Nest* (ed. M. Levin) 1965

A morning glory climbing a pole.

Alexander Woollcott attrib. quoted in H. Teichmann, *George S. Kaufman* 1972

CLARE BOOTHE LUCE

No woman of our time has gone further with less mental equipment.

Clifton Fadiman

MAURICE MAETERLINCK

The joy of every parodist.

George Bernard Shaw

DAVID MAMET

Mamet has a miraculous ear for the heightened music of American dialect – it makes poetry out of common usage.

New York Post 1991

CHRISTOPHER MARLOWE

Marlowe . . . was perhaps good enough to make it possible to believe that if he had been born thirty years ago, he might now be a tolerable imitator of Mr Rudyard Kipling.

George Bernard Shaw *Saturday Review* 25 May 1895

He is the true Elizabethan blank-verse beast, itching to frighten other people with the superstitious terrors and cruelties in which he does not himself believe, and wallowing in blood, violence, muscularity of expression, and strenuous animal passion as only literary men do when they become thoroughly depraved by solitary work, sedentary cowardice, and starvation of the sympathetic centres. It is not surprising to learn that Marlowe was killed in a tavern brawl: what would be utterly unbelievable would be his having succeeded in stabbing anyone else.

George Bernard Shaw 'The Spacious Times' July 1896; *Dramatic Opinions and Essays* Vol. II 1909

The first English poet whose powers can be called sublime was Christopher Marlowe.

Algernon Swinburne *The Age of Shakespeare* 1879

It so happened that at Deptford, a little village about three miles distant from London, as he went to stab with his poynard one named Ingram, that had invited him thither to a feast, and was then playing at tables, he quickly perceyving it, so avoyded the thrust, that withal drawing out his dagger for his defence, he stabbed this Marlowe in the eye, in such sort, that his braines comming out at the dagger's point, hee shortly after dyed.

William Vaughan *Golden Grove* 1600

MUSTAPHA MATURA

What makes Mustapha Matura our finest dramatist of West Indian origin? A wry humour, a warmth of feeling, a knack for observing human oddity and for embodying it in quirky, unpredictable dialogue, and the fundamental seriousness with which he writes of people who, like himself, have in some sense become severed from their roots.

Benedict Nightingale *The Times*

SOMERSET MAUGHAM

(ON HIMSELF)
My world popularity is the most interesting thing about me.

Quoted in T. Morgan, *Somerset Maugham* 1980

(BY OTHERS)
Willie Maugham has a stop-watch by his side and, on completion of the day's quota, goes to the terrace and prepares for the elaborate ritual of the dry martini.

Cecil Beaton *The Strenuous Years*

Somerset Maugham hated people more easily than he loved them; I

love people more easily than I hate them. That is the difference between me and Somerset Maugham.

Noël Coward

Two fundamental failings rob him of greatness. His works do not suggest those 'mysteries' which, as Proust puts it, 'have their explanation probably only in other worlds and a presentiment of which is precisely what moves us most in life and art'. His other fault is the fear of appearing old-fashioned.

William Gerhardie *Memoirs of a Polyglot* 1925

He was offered a knighthood but when I asked him why he had not accepted he replied: 'They knight jockeys now'.

Godfrey Winn quoted in D. Richards *The Curtain Rises* 1966

ARTHUR MILLER

I always preferred *This is Your Life* as a television show.

Noël Coward to Claudette Colbert at the Broadway first night of *After the Fall*

MOLIÈRE

Of all dramatists, ancient and modern, Molière is perhaps that one who has borne most constantly in mind the theory that the stage is a lay pulpit, and that its end is not merely amusement, but the reformation of manners by means of amusing spectacles.

George Saintsbury *A Short History of French Literature* 1882

Molière had cruel enemies, especially among the inferior writers of the day and their cliques. He also aroused the opposition of the pious, who accused him of writing scandalous books. He was charged with having exposed the characters of powerful persons in the characters of his plays, whereas he had done nothing but hold up views in general for the reprobation of mankind. He would have suffered punishment as a result of these accusations had not Louis XIV, who had encouraged and supported Racine and Despreaux, likewise protected him.

Voltaire *Life of Molière*

He had ambitions to play tragedy, but in this field was not successful. He was exceedingly voluble in speech and had a sort of hiccough which was quite unsuitable to serious roles. This, however, only served to make his acting in comedy more enjoyable.

Ibid.

TOM MURPHY

It has been possible for Tom Murphy to do things which are of enormous significance to theatre as a whole; to write tragedy when many argued that tragedy can no longer be written; to restore a religious sense . . . to move beyond absurdity . . . and to produce theatrical images of transformation at a time when the world seems all too fixed and inescapable. . . . It is this which makes him a great playwright.

Fintan O'Toole

EUGENE O'NEILL

Though he possesses the tragic vision, he cannot claim the tragic tongue.

John Mason Brown

He'll probably never write a good play again.

George Bernard Shaw on hearing that O'Neill had given up drinking; quoted in A. and B. Gelb, *O'Neill*

O'Neill gave birth to the American theatre and died for it.

Tennessee Williams quoted in A. and B. Gelb, *O'Neill*

JOHN OSBORNE

No leader of thought or ideas. A conceited, calculating young man blowing a little trumpet.

Noël Coward *Diaries* 5 May 1959

ARTHUR WING PINERO

His eyebrows look like the skins of some small mammal just not large enough to be used as mats.

Max Beerbohm

HAROLD PINTER

The meaningfulness of a Pinter play is not in its conclusion but in its journey – each pause is a halt on the way to darkness.

Gareth Lloyd Evans quoted in D. Richards, *The Curtain Rises* 1966

LUIGI PIRANDELLO

The relentless pessimism that pervades his work was best

articulated by a character in the short story *The Deathwatch*: 'I'm not suffering on my account, or on your account. I'm suffering because life is what it is.'

William Rose Benét *Reader's Encyclopaedia* 1948

JEAN-PAUL SARTRE

He is his decade's foremost theatrical confidence man, which in view of the competition is no mean achievement. . . . His fecundity in such directions as philosophy, politics, sociology, the novel, the short story, the cinema and the drama is that of a rabbit, yet he seems to operate under the delusion that his reproductions are not rabbits but lions and tigers, whereas even the rabbits he factually delivers himself of are of the mechanical toy variety, stuffed with the sawdust of borrowed ideas.

George Jean Nathan *The World of George Jean Nathan* (ed. C. Angoff) 1952

FRIEDRICH SCHILLER

He razed mental Bastilles.

Heinrich Heine *The Romantic School* 1836

TOM STOPPARD
(ON HIMSELF)
For me it is such a relief to get an idea!

I write plays because dialogue is the most respectable way of contradicting myself.

JOHN VANBRUGH

The general opinion is that he is as sprightly in his Writings as he is heavy in his Buildings.

Voltaire *Letters Concerning the English Nation* (Vanbrugh was an architect as well as a dramatist.)

ORSON WELLES

There but for the grace of God goes God.

Herman J. Mankiewicz (Mankiewicz was co-writer of *Citizen Kane* but Welles tried to get his name taken off the credits.)

THORNTON WILDER

(ON HIMSELF)

I would love to be the poet laureate of Coney island. I would feel enormous satisfaction in being regarded as the voice of the average American.

Quoted in *New York Journal* 11 November 1955

(BY OTHERS)

A strange mixture of poet, prophet, hummingbird and gadfly.

Alexander Woollcott *c.* 1933; quoted in S.H. Adams, *A. Woollcott: His Life and His World* 1945

WILLIAM WYCHERLEY

In truth Wycherley's indecency is protected against the critics as a skunk is protected against the hunters. It is safe because it is too filthy to handle, and too noisesome even to approach.

Thomas Macaulay *Critical and Historical Essays: On the Comic Dramatists of the Restoration* 1843

He appears to have led, during a long course of years, that most wretched life, the life of a vicious old boy about town.

Ibid.

As King Charles was extremely fond of him upon account of his wit, some of the Royal Mistresses set no less value upon Those Parts in him, of which they were more proper judges.

Major Richardson Pack 1719

See also: Beaumont and Fletcher, Chekhov, Noël Coward, Ibsen, Shakespeare, George Bernard Shaw, Oscar Wilde, Tennessee Williams.

PREJUDICE

No man, being forbidden to do so, shall converse with the wife of another man. But this shall not apply to the wives of actors.

The Code of Manu, VIII; *c.* AD 100

Concerning players, we have thought fit to excommunicate them so long as they continue to act.

Decree of the First Council of Arles AD 314

All bearwards, common players of interludes, counterfeit Egyptians etc., shall be taken, adjudged and deemed rogues, vagabonds and sturdy beggars.

Act of Parliament 1597

All stage-players and players of interludes and common plays are hereby declared to be, and are, and shall be taken to be rogues . . . whether they be wanderers or no, and notwithstanding any licence whatsoever from the king or any person or persons to that purpose.

Ordinance of Parliament 9 February 1647

No actors, or dogs, or Jews.

Notice outside Hollywood in the early years of the 20th century

Critics are forever discovering homosexual references in my plays where they don't exist.

Edward Albee 1983

'Tis as hard a matter for a pretty woman to keep herself honest in a theatre, as 'tis for an apothecary to keep his treacle from the flies in hot weather; for every libertine in the audience will be buzzing about her honey-pot.

Thomas Brown quoted in J.H. Wilson, *All the King's Ladies* 1958

One should never take one's daughter to a theatre. Not only are plays immoral; the house itself is immoral.

Alexander Dumas *fils*

THE PRESS

Some are born great, some achieve greatness, and some hire public relations officers.

Anonymous

I don't care what you say about me, as long as you say *something* about me, and as long as you spell my name right.

George M. Cohan

Don't ever believe anyone who says a bad press doesn't really hurt. You just have to find ways of coping with it.

Peter Hall *Diaries* (Foreword) pub. 1982

No one ever won an interview.

Laurence Olivier quoted in J. Osborne, *Almost a Gentleman* 1991

If you just say nothing there is no way they can make you talk.

Twiggy

Every actor in his heart believes everything bad that's printed about him.

Orson Welles

There is much to be said in favour of modern journalism. By giving us the opinions of the uneducated, it keeps us in touch with the ignorance of the community.

Oscar Wilde

There is only one thing in the world worse than being talked about, and that is not being talked about.

Oscar Wilde *The Picture of Dorian Grey* 1891

PRODUCERS

The only way a producer can make an actress great is to marry her.

Traditional saying

Impresario – a promoter with a cape.

L.L. Levinson

The theatre will only triumph when all producers are dead!

Joan Littlewood quoted in T. Cole and H. Chinoy, *Directors on Directing*, 1976

PRODUCERS
– *Individuals*

GEORGE M. COHAN
He was the boy owner of the American flag, and throughout his life he was the Yankee Doodle Boy.

Ward Morehouse *George M. Cohan* 1943

JED HARRIS
A strange, paradoxical creature, fated to destroy everything he loves, including himself.

Edna Ferber

When I die, I want to be cremated and have my ashes thrown in Jed Harris's face.

George S. Kaufman

DAVID MERRICK

He displayed a sneaky knack for extending the life of a production beyond the reasonable expectations of the playwright's mother.

Walter Kerr

If there is any serious doubt that David Merrick is one of the greatest showmen in Broadway history, it can be dispelled by the fact that his flops are as fabled as his hits.

Frank Rich *New York Times* 1960

BILLY ROSE

Without his name in the paper, Billy felt nude.

Ben Hecht *A Child of the Century* Vol. V 1954

FLORENZ ZIEGFELD

He introduced into the American theatre an era of lavishness and glamour that has never been surpassed.

Eddie Cantor *Take My Life* 1957

He was the kind of fellow who made people feel honoured to have him owe them money.

Buddy De Sylva quoted in Eddie Cantor, *Take My Life* 1957

Do a good show every night because Ziegfeld may be out front.

Broadway saying, still used long after Ziegfeld's death

PROLOGUES

Prologues precede the piece in mournful
  verse,
As undertakers walk before the hearse.

David Garrick Prologue to *The Apprentice*

The drama's laws the drama's patrons
  give.
For we that live to please must please
  to live.

Samuel Johnson Prologue for the opening of Drury Lane Theatre 1747

PROMPTS

The players conne not their parts without book, but are prompted by one called the Ordinary, who followeth at their back with the book in his hand, and telleth them softly what they must pronounce aloud.

Richard Carew *The Survey of Cornwall* 1602

PURPOSE

The theatre, like the plague, is a crisis which is resolved either in death or in the return to complete health.

Antonin Artaud

Theatre is the first serum that man invented to protect himself against the sickness of despair.

Jean-Louis Barrault *Nouvelle Réflexions sur le Théâtre*

I'm not a postman. . . . I don't deliver messages.

Brendan Behan when interviewed on BBC televison about the meaning of his plays; quoted in G. Snell, *The Book of Theatre Quotes* 1982

All art is a challenge to despair.

E.C. Bentley *The Life of the Drama* 1965

The purpose is to take you beyond day-to-day ambitions and remind you of your potential.

Steven Berkoff *Sunday Express Magazine* 9 August 1992

All arts contribute to the greatest art of all: Lebenskunst – the art of getting through life.

Bertolt Brecht

Hard political people don't like the theatre, because they think plays get muzzy and ideologically unsound.

Howard Brenton *The Times* 13 April 1992

The theatre should be necessary – like a bank or a grocer's shop. It should provide something that people cannot get anywhere else.

Peter Brook *Observer* 1970

The business of plays is to recommend virtue, and discountenance vice.

Jeremy Collier *A Short View of the Immorality and Profaneness of the English Stage* 1698

A play should give you something to think about. When I see a play and I understand it for the first time, then I know it can't be much good.

T.S. Eliot *New York Post* 1963

I am weary up to retirement of seeing plays which deal with the mentally sick and the spiritually infirm. I'm sick and tired of being scolded and told I have no compassion.

Helen Hayes

The actor in his turn scatters blessings. He passes the benediction on. He is part of the healing fraternity.

Bernard Miles quoted in D. Richards, *The Curtain Rises* 1966

The office of drama is to exercise, possibly to exhaust, human emotions. The purpose of comedy is to tickle those emotions into an expression of light relief; of tragedy, to wound them and bring the relief of tears.

Laurence Olivier *Reflections of an Actor* 1984

A play is not to show occurrences that happen every day, but things just so strange, that though they never *did*, they might happen.

Richard Brinsley Sheridan *The Critic* 1779

I don't think any writer has much purpose back of him unless he feels bitterly the iniquities of the society he lives in.

Tennessee Williams

If there is any one thing for all the cast to remember it is the primary aim of the play: the making of 'poetic reality' in which everything occurs with the ease and spontaneity of occurrences in life, no matter how long and carefully the play has been planned and written with that objective in mind.

Tennessee Williams letter to **Bette Davis** about *Night of the Iguana* 1961

QUICK THINKING

Mr Wood seems rather thin skinned about his Bottom.

Newspaper comment on an actor's reaction to criticism of his acting in *A Midsummer Night's Dream* quoted in J. Aye, *Humour in the Theatre* 1932

It's no good looking up your entrance – you missed it!

Robert Atkins directing *A Midsummer Night's Dream* at Regent's Park Open Air Theatre, to a 'fairy' he found sitting with her head between her knees when she should have been on stage

Madge Kendal complained that Sarah Bernhardt's roles were often too 'passionate' for her to bring her daughter to see.
Sarah Bernhardt: Madame, had it not been for passion you would have no daughter to bring.

James Agate to **Lilian Braithwaite:** For a long time I have wanted to tell you I regard you as the second-best actress in London.
Lilian Braithwaite: I'm so flattered to hear that – from the second-best drama critic in London.

No one I know darling.

Coral Browne on seeing the 10-foot high golden phallus designed for the National Theatre production of *Oedipus* 1968

It [Olivier's sword] flew straight into **Lilian Baylis**'s stage box, nearly killing one of the governors. Everybody was trying to contain their laughter, but the problem was that the stage fight could not continue without the sword. I crawled offstage and hid behind the box, hoping for it to be handed to me, but the governor was too stunned to retrieve it. After what seemed like an eternity, I heard Miss Baylis say, 'Oh give them back the sword, so they can finish and we can all go home'.

Stuart Burge on an incident during *Hamlet* at the Old Vic 1937

Lady Diana Cooper (who starred as a non-speaking statue in the religious drama *The Miracle*) to **Noël Coward**: Didn't you write *Private Lives*? Not very funny.
Noël Coward: Weren't you in *The Miracle*? Very funny indeed.

Then lead the way, good Father,
And Heavens so shine,
I can't remember another blessed line.

Mrs Guinness, exiting after drying while playing Olivia in

Twelfth Night quoted in C. Benson, *Mainly Players* 1926 (Also attributed to **Julia Marlowe**)

Arrogant Actor: Last night I was a sensation. I had the audience glued to their seats.
George Jessel: How clever of you to think of it.

I'm going to fall back on the casting couch.

Maureen Lipman when asked for her contingency plans if she failed as an actress

Ladies and gentlemen, if you will allow me to finish the play, I will go home and learn how to act.

Edward Sothern 1852, after being booed during the Boston production of *The Heir at Law*

Madam, if you are invited to play golf you do not take your tennis racquet.

Donald Wolfit response to being asked how he did not mix up his many Shakespearean roles; quoted in R. Harwood, *Donald Wolfit* 1971

REALISM

Realistic? But the stage is art. Kramskoy has a picture on which the faces are painted beautifully. What would happen if one cut out the nose of one of the faces and substituted a real one for it? The nose would be realistic. But the picture would be ruined.

Anton Chekhov quoted in M. Billington, *The Guinness Book of Theatre Facts and Feats* 1982

RECOGNITION

Photographer at the reception for Noël Coward's play, *Pacific 1860*: Could you please tell me your name?
Noël Coward: I recommend you to *Who's Who* – and hell.

Quoted in D. Richards, *The Wit of Noël Coward*

It is time that some official recognition were shown of his achievement in keeping the British flag flying over Ruritania.

Evening Standard 1951; comment after the death of **Ivor Novello**

REHEARSALS

There was the usual actors' fussing – like dogs walking round and round a place where they going to sleep.

Peter Hall *Diaries* 19 November 1974

Most playwrights at rehearsals are as much use as a father, all masked-up and sterilized, at the delivery of a child.

John Osborne *Almost a Gentleman* 1991

REPUTATION

Hard by the Mall lives a wench call'd Nell,
King Charles the Second he kept her.
She hath got a trick to handle his pr...,
But never lays hands on his sceptre.

Anonymous poem on actress **Nell Gwynne**, mistress of Charles II

This agreeable actress (**Peg Woffington**) in the part of *Sir Harry* coming into the Greenroom said pleasantly, In my conscience, I believe half the men in the House take me for one of their own sex. Another actress reply'd, It may be so, but in my conscience, the other half can convince them to the contrary.

W.R. Chetwood *A General History of the Stage* 1749

Discretion contributed not a little to make her the Cara, the Darling of the Theatre; for it will be no extravagant thing to say, scarce an audience saw her that were less than half of them lovers, without a suspected favourite among them.

Colley Cibber on **Anne Bracegirdle** 'The Romantick Virgin', in *Apology for the Life of Colley Cibber, Comedian* 1740

RESTING

Don't be depressed . . . you are only gathering strength for the next spring.

Harley Granville Barker quoted in D. Blakelock, *Advice to a Player* 1958

RESTORATION THEATRE

Restoration theatre gives me the overwhelming impression of a sex-orientated, fashionable club: the Playboy Club of the day.

Peter Hall *Diaries* 20 August 1977

RALPH RICHARDSON

(ON HIMSELF)
Has anyone seen a talent? Not a very big one, but I seem to have mislaid it.

Ralph Richardson to his fellow actors after reading the vicious reviews of his 1952 *Hamlet*

(BY OTHERS)
Nature . . . has unkindly refused him any tragic facilities whatever. His voice has not a tragic note in its whole gamut. . . . He cannot blaze. He saws away at his nether lip with the enthusiasm of a Queen's Hall fiddler or a maniac reducing a torso to its minimum.

James Agate 1938 on Richardson's Othello; quoted in G. O'Connor, *Ralph Richardson: An Actor's Life* 1982

A year or two ago Richardson had the habit of acting all his parts with his buttocks.

James Agate *Ego 1* 1935

I don't know his name but he's got a face like half a teapot.

George VI

SCENERY AND LIGHTING

Irving of course stuck to gaslight, subtler and more magical than the electric; it restricted the painter's palette but was *alive* and imperceptibly a-quiver; it interposed a film of waving air between actor and spectator.

William Bridges–Adams quoted in R. Speaight, *A Bridges-Adams Letter book* 1971

One evening at Althorp when Garrick was about to exhibit some particular stage-effect of which they had been talking, a young man got up and placed candles on the floor, that the light be thrown on his face as from the lamps in the theatre. Garrick, displeased at this officiousness, immediately sat down again.

Samuel Rogers on a visit by

Garrick to Lord Spencer at Althorp; quoted in *Table Talk* 1856

What child is here, that coming to a play and seeing Thebes written in great letters on an old door, doth believe that it is Thebes?

Sir Philip Sidney quoted in D. Cook, *A Book of the Play* 1876

SHAKESPEARE

(ON HIMSELF)
Alas! 'tis true I have gone here and
*   there,*
And made myself a motley to the
*   view,*
Gored mine own thoughts, sold cheap
*   what is most dear,*
Made old offenses of affections new.

Sonnet CX 1609

(BY OTHERS)
Whaur's yer Wully Shakespeare noo?

Anonymous Scottish theatre-goer on the first night of the Scottish play *Douglas*, by John Home 1756

Shakespeare, Madam, is obscene, and, thank God we are sufficiently advanced to have found it out.

Anonymous American quoted by Frances Trollope in *Domestic Manners of the Americans* 1832

I keep saying, Shakespeare, Shakespeare, you are as obscure as life is.

Matthew Arnold letter to A.H. Clough, December 1847

Mr William Shakespeare was born at Stratford-on-Avon in the county of Warwick. His father was a Butcher, and I have been told heretofor by some of the neighbours, that when he was a boy he exercised his father's Trade, but when he killed a Calfe he would do it in high style, and make a speech.

John Aubrey *Brief Lives*

His Comedies will remaine witt as long as the English tongue is understood, for that he handles *mores hominum* (the ways of mankind).

Ibid.

Shakespeare is in the singularly fortunate position of being, to all intents and purposes, anonymous.

W.H. Auden *Forewords and Afterwords*

The only tribute a French translator can pay Shakespeare is not to translate him.

Max Beerbohm 'Hamlet, Princess of Denmark' (on Bernhardt's Hamlet), *Around Theatres* Vol. I 1924

It will, I believe, be universally acknowledged, that few authors are so instructive as Shakespeare; but his warmest admirers must confess that his plays contain much that is vulgar, and much that is indelicate. . .

It is hoped that the present publication will be approved by those who wish to make the young reader acquainted with the various beauties of this writer unmixed with anything that can raise a blush on the cheek of modesty.

Thomas and **Harriet Bowdler** preface to their expurgated (bowdlerised) edition, *The Family Shakespeare* 1818

Shake was a dramatist of note;
He lived by writing things to quote.

Henry C. Bunner *Shake, Mulleary and Go-ethe c.* 1884

I have tried lately to read Shakespeare, and found it so intolerably dull that it nauseated me.

Charles Darwin

Shakespeare, who (taught by none)
did first impart,
To Fletcher wit, to labouring Jonson
art:
He, Monarch-like, gave those his
subjects law,
And is that Nature which they paint
and draw.

John Dryden Prologue to his version of *The Tempest* 1667

Those who accuse him to have wanted learning, give him the greater commendation: He was naturally learned; he needed not the spectacles of books to read nature; he looked inwards, and found her there.

John Dryden *An Essay of Dramatic Poesy* 1668

I hear a great deal about Shakespeare, but I cannot read him, he is such a bombast fellow.

King George II

Was there ever such sad stuff as a great part of Shakespeare? Only one must not say so! What! What!

King George III quoted by Fanny Burney, *Diary*

The remarkable thing about Shakespeare is that he really is very good, in spite of all the people who say he is very good.

Robert Graves

There is an upstart crow, beautified with our feathers, that with his Tiger's heart wrapped in a player's hide, supposes he is well able to bombast out a blank verse as the best of you; and being an absolute *Johannes factotum*, is in his own conceit the only Shake-scene in a country.

Robert Greene *A Groatsworth of Wit bought with a Million of Repentance* 1592 (Greene believed Shakespeare had plagiarized his plots.)

I don't really approve in my Puritan soul of moving Shakespeare into a modern period in order to illuminate him. You merely illuminate some things and obscure others.

Peter Hall *Diaries* 22 November 1973

Homosexuality? No, I know nothing of the joys of homosexuality. My friend Oscar can no doubt tell you all about that. But I must say that if *Shakespeare* asked me, I would have to submit.

Frank Harris attrib.

If we wish to know the force of human genius we should read Shakespeare. If we wish to see the insignificance of human learning we may study his commentators.

William Hazlitt *Table Talk* 1821–22

The genius of *Shakespeare* was not to be depressed by the weight of poverty, nor limited by the narrow conversation to which men in want are inevitably condemned; the incumbrances of his fortune were shaken from his mind, *as dewdrops from a lion's mane.*

Samuel Johnson preface to *The Plays of William Shakespeare* (Johnson himself had been through periods of poverty and deep depression.)

The stream of Time, which is continually washing the fabrics of other poets, passes without injury by the adamant of Shakespeare.

Ibid.

Shakespeare never had six lines together without a fault. Perhaps you may find seven but this does not refute my general assertion.

Samuel Johnson J. Boswell, *The Life of Samuel Johnson* 1791

I remember, the players have often mentioned it as an honour to Shakespeare, that in his writing, whatsoever he penn'd, he never blotted out a line. My answer hath been, would he had blotted out a thousand.

Ben Jonson *Timber or Discoverie Made Upon Man and Matter* 1640

Sweet Swan of Avon.

Ben Jonson *To the Memory of My beloved, the Author, William Shakespeare* 1628

He was not of an age but for all time.

Ibid.

The trouble with Shakespeare is that you never get to sit down unless you're a king.

George S. Kaufman quoted in H. Teichmann, *G.S. Kaufman; An Intimate Portrait* 1972

Shakespeare is not our poet – but the world's.

W.S. Landor *To Robert Browning*

When I read Shakespeare I am struck with wonder
That such trivial people should muse and thunder
In such lovely language.

D.H. Lawrence *When I Read Shakespeare* 1929

What there was in the world to be done in Shakespearean has largely been done by Shakespeare.

Georg Lichtenberg *Aphorisms* 1764–99

It matters not to me whether Shakespeare be well or ill acted; with him the thought suffices.

Abraham Lincoln quoted in *Revue des Deux Mondes*

The most important thing to remember about Shakespeare is that he was a writer, working on commission. . . . I like to think that if the Bard were alive today he'd be out at the beach in Beverley Hills tapping out 'High Concept' Movies of the Week on his Wang word processor, up to his ruff in cocaine.

Maureen Lipman *How Was It For You?* 1985

Shakespeare made his heroes foreigners and his clowns English.

H.L. Mencken

I don't think I should want to know Shakespeare. I know him as well as I want by knowing his plays.

Jonathan Miller

Or sweetest Shakespeare, Fancy's child
Warble his native wood-notes wild.

John Milton *L'Allegro* 1632

What needs my Shakespeare for his honoured bones
The labour of an age in piled stones?
Or that his hallowed reliques should be hid
Under a starry-pointing pyramid?
Dear son of memory, great heir of fame,
What need'st thou such weak witness of thy name?
Thou in our wonder and astonishment
Has built thyself a live long monument.

John Milton *An Epitaph on the Admirable Dramatic Poet W. Shakespeare*

He seems to have known the world by intuition, to have looked through nature at one glance.

Alexander Pope *Preface to the Works of Shakespeare*

Brush up your Shakespeare,
Start quoting him now.
Brush up your Shakespeare,
And the women you will wow.

Cole Porter song lyric from *Kiss Me Kate* 1948

With the single exception of Homer, there is no eminent writer, not even Sir Walter Scott, whom I despise so entirely as I despise Shakespeare, when I measure my mind against his plays.

George Bernard Shaw *Dramatic Opinion and Essays*, Vol. II 1909

Crude, immoral, vulgar and senseless.

Leo Tolstoy

Shakespeare's hideous stage clowns were the maggots in his apple.

Peter Ustinov

Shakespeare is a savage with sparks of genius which shine in a dreadful darkness of night.

Voltaire

This enormous dunghill.

Voltaire

Now we sit through Shakespeare in order to recognize the quotations.

Orson Welles attrib.

He had read Shakespeare and found him weak in chemistry.

H.G. Wells *Lord of the Dynamos*

If the copyright had not expired the royalties from Shakespeare's works would have paid off the National Debt.

Ted Willis House of Lords 22 November 1978; quoted in F.S. Pepper, *A Dictionary of Biographical Quotations* 1985

SHAKESPEARE'S PLAYS

You give them all you've got and the author says to you: 'You've given all you've got? Good. Now, more. Good. Now more. More, damn you. More, more! *More! More!*' Until your heart and guts and brain are pulp and the part feeds on you, eating you. Acting great parts devours you. It's a dangerous game.

Laurence Olivier *Observer* 9 February 1969; quoted in A. Holden, *Olivier* 1988

ANTONY AND CLEOPATRA

It was a pleasing prospect. Only I was vile.

Tallulah Bankhead on the 1937 American production

Tallulah Bankhead barged down the aisle last night as Cleopatra and sank.

John Mason Brown 1937

Miss Bankhead played the Queen of the Nil.

George Jean Nathan 1937

AS YOU LIKE IT

A nice little girl in a wood.

James Agate review of **Peggy Ashcroft** as Rosalind 1933

You can't play Rosalind without a hat and a tree.

Peggy Ashcroft to **Eileen Atkins**

CYMBELINE

Cymbeline is an unrewarding part, but surely he is more than a testy Father Christmas in cricket pads.

Felix Barker reviewing **Richard Harris** as Cymbeline; *Evening News* 1957

HAMLET

Ophelia said I deplore
That young Hamlet's becoming a
    bore.
He just talks to himself,
I'll be left on the shelf —
Or dead by the end of Act Four.

Anonymous

I have lately been told by a gentleman who has frequently seen Mr Betterton perform this part of Hamlet, that he observ'd his Countenance (which was naturally ruddy and sanguine) in this scene of the fourth act where his Father's Ghost appears, thro' the violent and sudden Emotions of Amazement and Horror, turn instantly on the Sight of his Father's Spirit, as pale as his Neckcloth, when every Article of his Body seem'd to be affected with a tremor inexpressible; so that, had his Father's Ghost actually risen before him, he could not have been seized with more real agonies; and this was felt so strongly by the audience, that the blood seem'd to shudder in their veins likewise, and they in some Measure partook of the Astonishment and Horror, with which they saw this excellent actor affected.

Anonymous account of
Thomas Betterton in *Hamlet*
quoted in *Laureat* 1740

I have no hesitation in saying that it is the high water mark of English Shakespearian acting in our time.

James Agate on **John Gielgud**'s
Hamlet 1929

Mr Olivier's Hamlet is the best performance of Hotspur this generation has seen.

James Agate 1937

As Ophelia Miss Cherry Cottrell strikes me as being unripe.

James Agate 1937

Richard Burton once drank a quart of brandy during his performance of *Hamlet* on Broadway. The only visible effect was that he played the last two acts as a homosexual.

James Bacon

The goddamndest bore in literature, that pompous ass the ghost.

John Barrymore

A hoop through which every very eminent actor must sooner or later jump.

Max Beerbohm

In the matter of soliloquies we cannot accept Hamlet as an unbiased authority. We merely find in him the possible origin of the belief that talking to oneself is a bad sign.

Max Beerbohm

From first to last no-one smiled. . . . One laugh in that dangerous atmosphere, and the whole structure of polite solemnity would have toppled down, burying beneath it the national reputation for good manners.

Max Beerbohm on **Sarah Bernhardt** as Hamlet; 'Hamlet, Princess of Denmark', *Around Theatres*, Vol. I 1924

Imagine this: one night in a dream, the Bard of Avon hits on his finest so far and wakes himself up and supposes himself to be quilling down the necessary notes of the vision. Next morning he reads what he has written:
CASTLE
SCANDINAVIA
BLOKE IN TIGHTS

Ken Campbell *Furtive Nudist* 1992

He burst forth with the fury of the thunderstorm, making everything give way to his tremendous touches.

John Cole on **Edmund Kean** as Hamlet

John Barrymore to **Jimmy Durante**: 'You know Jimmy, some day you ought to play Hamlet.'
Jimmy Durante: 'To hell with 'em small towns. New York's the only place for me.'

I saw *Hamlet Pr. of Denmark* played: but now the old playe began to disgust this refined age; since his Majestie being so long abroad:

John Evelyn *Diary* 26 November 1661

'Indeed Mrs Partridge,' says Mrs Miller, 'you are not of the same opinion with the town; for they are all agreed that Hamlet is acted by the best player who ever was on the stage.'

'He the best player!' cries Partridge with a contemptuous sneer. 'Why, I could act as well as he myself. I am sure if I had seen a ghost, I should have looked in the very same manner, and done just as he did. And then, to be sure, in that scene, as you called it, between him and his mother, where you told me he acted so fine, why, Lord help me! any man, that is, any good man, that had such a mother, would have done exactly the same.'

Henry Fielding discussion of **Garrick**'s Hamlet in the novel *Tom Jones* 1749

Larry, it's one of the finest performances I've ever seen, but it's still my part.

John Gielgud to **Laurence Olivier** after Olivier's 1937 debut in *Hamlet*; quoted in William Redfield, *Letters from an Actor* 1967

My dear fellow, I never saw anything so funny in my life, and yet it was not in the least vulgar.

W.S. Gilbert when asked by **Sir Herbert Beerbohm Tree** for an opinion of his performance as Hamlet

A pert, ill-mannered, spoiled, bad-tempered boy with little sense and a theatrical temperament.

Norman Hapgood after **Sarah Bernhardt**'s first Broadway performace as Hamlet, January 1901; quoted in Brooks Atkinson, *Broadway* 1970

More of a *Spamlet* really.

Jason Hillgate on **Albert Finney**'s Hamlet at the National Theatre in *Theatre* 1975

The best thing about Ian McKellen's Hamlet is his curtain call.

Harold Hobson *Sunday Times* 1971 quoted in D. Rigg, *No Turn Unstoned* 1982

I confess myself utterly unable to appreciate that celebrated soliloquy in *Hamlet* beginning 'To be or not to be', and tell whether it be good, bad or indifferent, it has been handled and pawed about by declamatory boys and men, and torn so inhumanly from its living place and principle of continuity in the play, till it has become to me a perfect dead number.

Charles Lamb 1811

The tragedy of tackling a family problem too soon after college.

Tom Masson

This evening I am engaged to spend with a foreigner. He is a Dane, unjustly deprived of his father's fortune by his mother's marrying a second time. I have never yet seen him, but I hear that all the world will be there, which I think is a little unfeeling, as he is a little low-spirited sometimes almost to madness. For my part, from what I have heard, I do not think the poor young man will live out the night.

Hannah More letter to her family 1776

In Leslie Howard's he was the Duke of Windsor out to get Stanley Baldwin and wife, with

Winston Churchill playing both
Rosencrantz and Guildenstern. In
John Gielgud's he was Lord Alfred
Douglas having an exciting,
melodramatic cup of tea with
Beverley Nichols.

George Jean Nathan on two
20th-century interpretations of
Hamlet

A leering milk roundsman of
Denmark Hill.

John Osborne on his Hamlet at
Hayling Island, 1951 in *A Better
Class of Person* 1981

Ralph (Richardson) chatted about
Hamlet, telling me it was like the
most amazing train and all Albert
(Finney) had to do was to get on
it and rush along through cuttings,
through stations, through tunnels
until finally he reached his
destination. He must not get off at
any of the stations on the way.

Ralph Richardson quoted by
Peter Hall, *Diaries* 13 October
1975

*Prince Hamlet thought Uncle a traitor
For having it off with his Mater;
Revenge Dad or not?
That's the gist of the plot,
And he did – nine soliloquies later.*

Stanley J. Sharpless in the *New
Statesman*; quoted in F. Metcalf,
*Penguin Dictionary of Humorous
Quotations* 1986

The Tragedy of Hamlet is a
coarse, barbarous piece, which
would not be tolerated by the
basest rabble in France or Italy . . .
one would think that this work
was the fruit of the imagination of
a drunken savage.

Voltaire

The central problem in *Hamlet* is
whether the critics are mad, or
only pretending to be mad.

Oscar Wilde

HENRY V
Do you know why you're so
good in this part? Because you are
England!

Charles Laughton to **Laurence
Olivier** 1937

KING LEAR
A strange, horrible business, but I
suppose good enough for
Shakespeare's day.

Queen Victoria

MACBETH
To mankind in general, Macbeth
and Lady Macbeth stand out as the
supreme type of all that a host and
hostess should not be.

Max Beerbohm

Simone Signoret's Lady Macbeth,
a conical, bell-tented matron who

moves on wheels like a draped Dalek surmounted by a beautiful Medusa head, speaks with a monotonous French accent punctuated by American vowels.

Alan Brien *Sunday Teleg.aph* 1966

I could never bring myself to play the part of someone with such curious notions of hospitality.

Edith Evans quoted in Richard Huggett, *The Curse of Macbeth* 1981

Saw Macbeth which, though I saw it lately, yet appears a most excellent play in all respects, but especially in divertisement, though it be deep tragedy: which is strange perfection in tragedy, it being most proper here, and suitable.

Samuel Pepys *Diary* 8 January 1667

Her Lady Macbeth is more niminy-piminy than thundery blundery, more viper than anaconda, but still quite competent in its small way.

Kenneth Tynan on **Vivien Leigh** in *Macbeth* with Laurence Olivier 1955

Judging from the banquet, Lady Macbeth seems an economical housekeeper and evidently

patronised local industries for her husband's clothes and the servants' liveries, but she takes care to do her own shopping in Byzantium.

Oscar Wilde on **Ellen Terry** as Lady Macbeth in Irving's production, 29 December 1888 (The Sargent portrait of Ellen Terry in her Byzantine costume hangs in the National Portrait Gallery, London.)

THE MERCHANT OF VENICE
Any fan of Walt Disney comics could see that he had modelled his appearance on Scrooge McDuck.

Clive James reviewing **Laurence Olivier** as Shylock, 1974

THE MERRY WIVES OF WINDSOR
In the first act alone of *The Merry Wives of Windsor* there is more life and movement than in all German literature.

Karl Marx

A MIDSUMMER NIGHT'S DREAM
To the King's Theatre, where we saw *Midsummer Night's Dream*, which I had never seen before, nor shall ever again, for it is the

most insipid, ridiculous play that ever I saw in my life.

Samuel Pepys *Diary* 29 September 1662

OTHELLO

[Ralph] Richardson killed himself from the start with a disastrous make-up; no man looking like a golliwog can persuade us that he is talking like a god.

Harold Hobson 1938

I think Shakespeare and Richard Burbage got drunk together one night and Burbage said, 'I can play anything you write, anything at all.' And Shakespeare said, 'Right, I'll fix you, boy!' And then he wrote *Othello*.

Laurence Olivier quoted in A. Holden, *Olivier* 1988

Why was not this called 'The Tragedy of the Handkerchief'? Had it been Desdemona's garter, the sagacious Moor might have smelt a rat; but the handkerchief is so remote a trifle, no Booby, on this side of Mauretania, could make any consequence from it.

Thomas Rymer *The Tragedies of the Last Age Considered* 1678

RICHARD III

In the evening went to see Larry (Olivier) in *Richard III*. A

tremendous evening. I think the greatest male performance I have ever seen in the theatre. Came out moved and highly exhilarated. He is far and away the greatest actor we have.

Noël Coward *Diaries* 21 September 1944

You have to use every sound in your voice for Hamlet. In *Richard III* I only used three notes. I based it on imitations I'd heard people do of Irving.

Laurence Olivier on his 1944 Richard III; quoted in J. Mortimer, *In Character* 1983

ROMEO AND JULIET

Mr Olivier plays Romeo as if he were riding a motor-bike.

Review of **Laurence Olivier** in the 1935 London production; quoted in A. Holden, *Olivier* 1988

She won all hearts with flower-like, passionate Juliet.

John Gielgud on **Peggy Ashcroft** 1935

Romeo and Juliet is a play, of itself, the worst that ever I heard in my life, and worse acted that ever I saw these people do.

Samuel Pepys *Diary* 1 March 1662

A rotationary movement of the hand, as if describing the revolution of a spinning jenny; multiplied slaps upon his forehead, and manual elevation of his fall hair; repeated knocking upon his own breast and occasional rapping at the chests of others; the opening of his ruffles, like a schoolboy run riot from the playground, and a strange, indistinct groping inside of his shirt, as if in search of something uncommonly minute, filled up the round of his action, while a voice most unmusical, exerted to a harsh and painful screech, afforded the finishing touch to a Romeo decidedly the worst we have ever witnessed on the London boards.

The Sun 1815 review of **Edmund Kean** in *Romeo and Juliet*

THE TEMPEST
He looked like a coal miner with a tail coming up from the coal face.

Sunday Express 1954; review of **Richard Burton** as Caliban

Last Tuesday, at the request of Lady S–, who patronized a poor actor, we all went to the play – which was Dryden's *Tempest* – and a worse performance have I seldom seen. Shakespeare's *Tempest*, which for fancy, invention, and originality, is at the head of beautiful improbabilities, is rendered by the addition of Dryden a childish chaos of absurdity and obscenity; and the grossness and awkwardness of these poor unskilful actors rendered all that ought to have been obscure so shockingly glaring, that there was no attending to them without disgust. All that afforded me any entertainment was looking at Mr Thrale, who turned up his nose with an expression of contempt at the beginning of the performance, and never suffered it to return to its usual place till it was ended!

Fanny Burney on **Dryden**'s reworking of *The Tempest* in *Diary* 20 October 1779

TWELFTH NIGHT
Claire Bloom played Viola like a wistful little Peter Pan who is worried to death about Tinkerbell.

Time and Tide 1953

I cannot learn it, and if I cannot learn it, Shakespeare did not write it!

Donald Wolfit on Act IV, Scene 2 in *Twelfth Night* where Feste, as Sir Topaz, mercilessly taunts Malvolio; quoted in R. Harwood, *Donald Wolfit* 1971

GEORGE BERNARD SHAW

(ON HIMSELF)

I'm too important to be in an anthology.

People must not be forced to adopt me as their favourite author, even for their own good.

I am like a dentist, there is so much that is wounding about my work.

Arms and the Man was so completely misunderstood that it made my reputation as a playwright.

My only policy is to profess evil and do good.

I lay an eternal curse on anyone who shall now or at any time hereafter, make schoolbooks of my work and make me hated as Shakespeare is hated. My plays were not designed as instruments of torture.

It is an instinct with me personally to attack every idea which has been full grown for ten years, especially if it claims to be the foundation of human society.

Review January 1896 *Dramatic Opinions and Essays* Vol. I 1896

My capers are part of a bigger design than you think: Shakespeare is one of the Towers of the Bastille, and down he must come.

Letter to **Ellen Terry** 27 January 1897

For ten years past, with an unprecedented pertinacity and obstination, I have been dinning into the public head that I am an extraordinarily witty, brilliant and clever man. That is now part of the public opinion of England; and no power in heaven or on earth will ever change it. I may dodder and dote; I may potboil and platitudinize; I may become the butt and chopping block of all the bright, original spirits of the rising generation; but my reputation shall not suffer: it is built up fast and solid, like Shakespeare's, on an impregnable basis of dogmatic re-iteration.

'Valedictory', 21 May 1898, *Dramatic Opinions and Essays* Vol. II 1909

I cannot guarantee myself as the greatest living hokum merchant, but I am certainly one of the best ten.

Quoted in Frank Harris, *Bernard Shaw* 1931

The fact is, I write my plays mostly on the tops of buses.

Quoted in Hesketh Pearson, *Bernard Shaw* 1942

(BY OTHERS)
You invite Shaw down to your place because you think he will entertain your friends with brilliant conversation. But before you know where you are he has chosen a school for your son, made your will for you, regulated your diet and assumed all the privileges of your family solicitor, your housekeeper, your clergyman, your doctor and your dressmaker. When he has finished with everyone else he incites the children to rebellion. And when he can find nothing more to do he

goes away and forgets all about you.

Anonymous hostess. B. Cerf, *Shake Well Before Using* 1948; quoted in F.S. Pepper, *Dictionary of Biographical Quotations* 1985

There was a young man of Moose
  Jaw,
Who wanted to meet Bernard Shaw;
When they questioned him, 'Why?'
He made no reply,
But sharpened an axe and a saw.

Anonymous *c.* 1918

Shaw's plays are the price we pay for Shaw's prefaces.

James Agate

Shaw was charming with one person, fidgety with two, and stood on his head with four.

Stanley Baldwin quoted by G.W. Lyttelton, *The Lyttelton – Hart-Davis Letters* 18 July 1956

He uses the English language like a truncheon.

Max Beerbohm

Wells was a cad who didn't pretend to be anything but a cad. Bennett was a cad pretending to be a gentleman. Shaw was a gentleman pretending to be a cad.

Hilaire Belloc quoted in J.B. Priestley, *Thoughts in the Wilderness*

It is all very well to believe, as Shaw did, that all criticism is prejudiced, but, with Shaw's dramatic criticism, the prejudice is more important than anything else.

Eric Bentley

Oh dear me – it's too late to do anything but *accept* you and *love* you – but when you were quite a little boy somebody ought to have said 'hush' just once.

Mrs Patrick Campbell letter to George Bernard Shaw, 1 November 1912

Shaw, someday you'll eat a beefsteak and then no woman in London will be safe.

Mrs Patrick Campbell attrib. (Shaw was a vegetarian.)

Few are more capable of having the best of everything both ways. His spiritual home is no doubt in Russia; his native land is the Irish Free State; but he lives in comfortable England. . . . He derides the marriage vow and even at times the sentiment of love itself; yet no-one is more happily or wisely married. . . . He is at once an acquisitive capitalist and a sincere Communist. He makes his characters talk blithely about killing men for the sake of an idea; but would take great trouble not to hurt a fly.

Winston Churchill *Great Contemporaries* 1937

An Irish smut dealer.

Anthony Comstock

Shaw's relations with women have always been gallant, coy even. The number he has surrendered to physically have been few – perhaps not half a dozen in all – the first man to have cut a swathe through the theatre and left it strewn with virgins.

Frank Harris *Bernard Shaw* 1931

A freakish homunculus germinated outside lawful procreation.

Henry Arthur Jones (rival playwright)

George Bernard Shaw, most poisonous of all the poisonous haters of England, despiser, distorter and denier of the plain truths whereby men live; topsy turvey perverter of all human relationships, menace to ordered social thought and ordered social life; irresponsible braggart, blaring self-trumpeter; idol of opaque intellectuals and thwarted females; calculus of contrariwise; flibbertygibbet pope of chaos;

portent and epitome of this generation's moral and spiritual disorder.

Henry Arthur Jones

Shaw's works make me admire the magnificent tolerance and broadmindedness of the English.

James Joyce quoted in G. Griffin, *The Wild Geese*

He is a good man fallen among Fabians.

Lenin

That noisiest of all old cocks.

Percy Wyndham Lewis *Blasting and Bombardiering* 1937

He writes like a Pakistani who has learned English when he was twelve years old in order to become a chartered accountant.

John Osborne letter in the *Manchester Guardian* 1977

Shaw was a good and brilliant man . . . had he created Mr Osborne, he would have relieved his heavy dullness with something lovable.

(Prof) Bert G. Hornback letter in the *Manchester Guardian* in response to John Osborne

Shaw avoided passion almost as prudently as Coward. Frigidity and caution demand an evasive style and they both perfected one.

John Osborne *A Better Class of Person* 1981

He had goat's eyebrows . . . and wintry blue eyes, which reminded me of a dead chicken.

Lilli Palmer quoted in *Celebrity Gossip* 1984

A dessiccated bourgeois . . . a fossilized chauvinist, a self-satisfied Englishman.

Pravda 1924

As an iconoclast he was admirable, but as an icon rather less so.

Bertrand Russell 'George Bernard Shaw', *Portraits From Memory* 1956

I think Shaw on the whole is more bounder than genius.

Bertand Russell review of *Man and Superman* 1904

Sherard Blaw, the dramatist who had discovered himself, and who had given so ungrudgingly of his discovery to the world.

Saki

George Too Shaw To Be Good.

Dylan Thomas letter to Pamela Hansford Johnson, October 1933

The more I think you over the more it comes home to me what an unmitigated Middle Victorian ass you are.

H.G. Wells

An excellent man: he has no enemies and none of his friends like him.

Oscar Wilde quoted by Shaw in a letter, 25 September 1896

The way Bernard Shaw believes in himself is very refreshing in these atheistic days when so many people believe in no God at all.

Israel Zangwill

RICHARD BRINSLEY SHERIDAN

(ON HIMSELF)
When I say an ill-natured thing 'tis out of pure good humour.

Attrib.

When I write in a Hurry I always feel to be not worth reading, and what I try to take Pains with, I am sure never to finish. . . .

Letter to David Garrick, 10 January 1778

A man may surely be allowed to take a glass of wine *by his own fireside.*

To a friend who remarked on the calm way he sat in the Piazza Coffee House while his theatre was burning to the ground, 1809; quoted in T. Moore, *Memoirs of the Life of R.B. Sheridan*

(BY OTHERS)
Whatever Sheridan has done or chosen to do has been *par excellence*

the *best* of its kind. He has written the best comedy (*The School for Scandal*), the best opera (*The Duenna*), the best farce (*The Critic*), and the best address (The Monologue on Garrick) and to crown all, delivered the best oration (the famous Begum speech) ever conceived or heard in this country.

Lord Byron quoted in M. Billington, *The Guinness Book of Theatre Facts and Feats* 1982

Every man has his element: Sheridan's is hot water.

Lord Eldon quoted in Lord Broughton, *Recollections of a Long Life* 1865

He *could* not make enemies. If anyone came to request the repayment of a loan from him, he borrowed more. A cordial shake of his hand was a recipt in full for all demands. He could 'coin his smile with drachmas', cancelled bonds with *bons mots*, and gave jokes in discharge of a bill.

William Hazlitt 'On the Spirit of Obligations', *New Monthly Magazine* 24 January 1824

Sheridan wrote for the actor as Handel wrote for the singer, setting him a combination of strokes which, however difficult some of them may be to execute finely, are familiar to all practised actors as the strokes which experience has shown to be proper to the nature and capacity of the stage-player as a dramatic instrument.

George Bernard Shaw in *Saturday Review* 27 June 1896

SHOW BUSINESS

There's no business,
Like show business
Like no business I know.

Irving Berlin song lyric from *Annie Get Your Gun* 1946

That's what show business is – sincere insincerity.

Benny Hill *Observer* 1977; quoted in J. Green, *The Cynic's Lexicon* 1984

In show business you're a fruit picker. You go where the work is.

Orson Welles *Newsweek* 27 February 1967

SARAH SIDDONS

(ON HERSELF)
Alas, after I became celebrated none of my sisters loved me as they did before.

Quoted in S. Rogers, *Table Talk* 1856

(BY OTHERS)
She is sparing in her action because English nature does not act much.

James Boaden *Memoirs of Mrs Siddons* 1827

I found her the Heroine of a Tragedy – sublime, elevated and solemn. In face and person truly noble, and commanding; in manners quiet and stiff; in voice, deep and dragging; and in conversation, formal, sententious, calm and dry.

Fanny Burney *Diary* 1787

As a stranger, I must have admired her noble appearance and beautiful countenance, and have regretted that nothing in her conversation kept pace with her promise; and as a celebrated actress, I had still only to do the same.

Ibid.

A sort of radiance comes round her in scenes where strong heroic virtues are displayed.

Ibid.

The beau ideal of acting . . . nothing ever was, or can be, like her.

Lord Byron quoted in R. Manvell, *Sarah Siddons* 1970

I should as soon think of going to bed with the Archbishop of Canterbury as Mrs Siddons.

Lord Byron attrib.

Damn it, Madame, there is no end to your nose.

Thomas Gainsborough while painting Mrs Siddons's portrait

She was Tragedy personified. She was the stateliest ornament of the public mind. She was not only the idol of the people, she not only hushed the tumultuous shouts of the pit in breathless expectation, and quenched the blaze of surrounding beauty in silent tears but to the retired and lonely student, through long years of solitude, her face has shone as if an eye had appeared from heaven.

William Hazlitt

Madam, you who so often occasion a want of seats to other

people, will the more easily excuse the want of one yourself.

Samuel Johnson when unable to find an unoccupied chair during a visit from Mrs Siddons, 1783; quoted in J. Boswell, *The Life of Samuel Johnson* 1791

I smelt blood. I swear that I smelt blood.

J. Sheridan Knowles on Mrs Siddons as Lady Macbeth

Her voice appeared to have lost its brilliancy (like a beautiful face through a veil).

Henry Crabb Robinson *Diary* 21 April 1812

Sex was out of the question. Although the face and form were majestically beautiful, it was the *mind* that 'burned within her' that gave the charm to the Pythoness.

William Robson *The Old Playgoer* 1846

From the moment she assumed the dress she became the character; she never chatted or coquetted by the green-room fire but placed herself where no word of the play could escape her, or the illusion for a moment be destroyed.

Ibid.

She is too grand a thing for me.

William Siddons (husband)

Were a Wild Indian to ask me, what was like a queen, I would have bade him look at Mrs Siddons.

Tate Wilkinson *The Wandering Patentee* Vol. IV 1795

SLIPS OF THE TONGUE

Boiled, rolled Caesar, I present thee with my sword.

Anonymous actor intending to address 'Royal, bold Caesar'; quoted in J. De Morgan, *In Lighter Vein* 1907

You potted snake with ham and tongue.

Anonymous actress muddling the line from *A Midsummer Night's Dream*, 'You spotted snake with double tongue.' quoted in J. Aye, *Humour in the Theatre* 1932

Now children, because you have all been so good today, Mr Thorkelson will read to you from *The Sale of Two Titties*.

Marie Christiansen in *I Remember Mama* quoted in P. Hay *Theatrical Anecdotes* 1987

Shall I lay surgery upon my Poll?

Charles Kemble intending to say 'Shall I lay perjury upon my soul?' quoted in J. Aye, *Humour in the Theatre* 1932

Let us retire and seek a nosy cook.

Lillie Langtry to a stage lover; quoted in J. De Morgan, *In Lighter Vein*, 1907

STAGE FRIGHT

I used to play always to the exit light or Gents or Ladies, but I never looked at the audience. I found it too frightening.

Dirk Bogarde *By Myself*, Channel 4 TV, January 1992

They say when the lights hit you the pain and the fear go – it's a goddam lie – they don't.

Judy Garland quoted by **Dirk Bogarde** in *By Myself*, Channel 4 TV, 1992

It's as though you have crossed Niagara on a tightrope 250 times and, on the 251st crossing – vertigo. You are convinced you can't move across the stage without falling over. You go rigid from the knees down. You

suddenly wonder, why am I doing this?

Derek Jacobi *Sunday Times* 24 May 1992

STAGE MANAGEMENT

It required a bland, conscientious temperament that expected abuse and never admiration. The best stage-managers are usually women, who bear indignity for the historical necessity of continuity itself.

John Osborne *A Better Class of Person* 1981

STAR QUALITY

Madame, it will be eight o'clock when it suits you.

Besotted callboy to **Sarah Bernhardt**

A star is a person who works hard all his life to become well-known and then wears dark glasses to avoid being recognized.

Fred Allen quoted in *The Wit's Dictionary*

The great ones have a little something extra. To love of the theatre, to intelligence and willingness to work, they bring a personal incandescence that cannot be acquired or imitated.

Brooks Atkinson (on **Katherine Cornell**) in *Broadway* 1970

Trains, dear? We had them stopped on matinée days, naturally.

Gladys Cooper when asked by Dirk Bogarde how she coped with the noise of trains thundering over Hungerford Bridge above the Playhouse Theatre

People are stars in the theatre in direct ratio with how many people want to go to bed with them.

Noël Coward quoted by Daniel Massey on BBC Television, 1 March 1992

When she walks on screen and says 'Hello' people ask, 'Who wrote that wonderful line of dialogue?'

Leo McCarey probably about **Ingrid Bergman**

He doesn't displace air.

Michèal MacLiammoir on the difference between a good actor and a great actor

Those whom God has touched on the shoulder.

Laurence Olivier quoted in A. Walker, *Vivien* 1987

Star quality is danger and vulnerability in equal measures.

Eric Portman recalled by Noel Davis

> As in a theatre, the eyes of men,
> After a well-grac'd actor leaves the
>   stage,
> Are idly bent on him that enters next,
> Thinking his prattle to be tedious.

William Shakespeare *Richard II* Act V, Scene 2

And when do you want me to do that little something for which you are paying me so much money?

Ellen Terry to Dion Boucicault (son of the playwright and one of the first theatre directors), after patiently listening to his endless production notes

SUCCESS

For an actress to be a success she must have the face of Venus, the brains of Minerva, the grace of Terpsichore, the memory of

Macaulay, the figure of Juno and the hide of a rhinoceros.

Ethel Barrymore quoted in George Jean Nathan, *The Theatre in the Fifties* 1953

The toughest thing about success is that you've got to keep on being a success.

Irving Berlin

My definition of success is control.

Kenneth Branagh 1987

Three theatrical Dames,
Eminent and respectable,
Our accents are undetectable
And though we've achieved our aims
If they knew what we'd done
In Eighteen Ninety One
They certainly wouldn't have made us
  Dames.

Noël Coward *The Lyrics of Noël Coward* 1965

The only thing that prevents Celia Johnson from becoming the greatest actress of her time is her monotonous habit of having babies.

Noël Coward

He has so many irons in the fire that he was never able to forge

any single one into a weapon with which to conquer the world.

Curtis Dahl on playwright, novelist and Professor of Medicine, **Robert Montgomery Bird**

Becoming a Dame hasn't helped my insecurities; a title doesn't ensure you're going to get another job.

Judi Dench *Daily Mail* 21 January 1992

I may never have been pretty but I was jolly larky and that's what counts in the theatre.

Edith Evans *Radio Times* 14–20 August 1976

I am not an agricultural labourer, but I have this in common with a certain type of ploughman who in bygone days was awarded by the squire with a pair of corduroy breeches and a crown piece in each pocket, in consideration of his having brought up a family of fifteen children without extraneous assistance. I have been rewarded for having brought up a family of sixty-three plays without ever having to apply to the relieving officer for parochial assistance. This knighthood I take to be sort of commuted old-age pension.

W.S. Gilbert on receiving his knighthood, 1907. (His partner Arthur Sullivan had received his knighthood 27 years earlier.)

For an actor success is simply delayed failure.

Graham Greene quoted in J. Green, *A Dictionary of Contemporary Quotations* 1982

Strange how yesterday's commercial plays and films become undisputed artworks of today. A lesson for the over-serious – particularly the over-serious critic who naturally suspects the successful.

Peter Hall *Diaries* 21 March 1973

The morning after an opening the reek of success is as immediately detectable as the reek of failure, with no word said. I remember Larry saying success smelt like Brighton.

Peter Hall *Diaries* 27 January 1977

The fate of a play is decided by knitting. When the lady at the box office is knitting, the play is a flop. But when the prompter can get on undisturbed with knitting her pullover during the performance, then the piece is sure to be a great success.

Ferenc Molnár quoted in P. Hay, *Theatrical Anecdotes* 1987

Anyone can sympathize with the sufferings of a friend, but it requires a fine nature to sympathize with a friend's success.

Oscar Wilde

TALENT

There is no such thing as a great talent without great will-power.

Honoré de Balzac *La Muse du Département* 1843

Always get a good actress – the beautiful girl won't be noticed beyond the third row.

Tyrone Guthrie during rehearsals for Sidney Sheldon's *Roman Candle*, 1960

She's O.K. if you like talent.

Ethel Merman on **Mary Martin** 1958

We used to have actresses trying to become stars. Now we have stars trying to become actresses.

Laurence Olivier

TECHNIQUE

'My dear Mr Barrymore, we are extras, not character actresses.'

Female extras (hired by John Barrymore to carry Ophelia's body during his *Hamlet*), when urged to look less like chorus girls and more like the virgins they were supposed to portray

Text? Text? I've never heard of it. What the hell is text? All I want laddie, is first the bizness, then the cues, and I bet my last bob I get a bread and butter notice.

Jobbing actor in the 1880s recalled by **Frank Benson**, *My Memoirs*

It took me a long time to discover that the key thing in acting is honesty. Once you know how to fake that, you've got it made.

Anonymous actor quoted in Edmund Carpenter, *Oh, What a Blow That Phantom Gave Me!* 1973

Now, dears, all we can do is go on our knees and pray for lust.

Lilian Baylis aiming to achieve the required sexuality for *Measure for Measure*; quoted in F. Barker, *The Oliviers* 1953

The artist's personality must be left in his dressing room; his soul must be denuded of its own sensations and clothed with the base or noble qualities he is called upon to exhibit. I once had an Italian chamber-maid who, returning one evening from seeing me in *Phèdre*, said: 'Oh Madame was so lovely that I didn't recognize Madame.' And no compliment ever went more direct to my heart.

Sarah Bernhardt *The Art of the Theatre* 1925

My eyes are really nothing in particular. . . . God gave me boot buttons, but I invented the dreamy eyelid, and that makes all the difference.

Mrs Patrick Campbell

I belong to the bull moose set. We are people who go to the same vocal teacher in New York. His name is Alfred Dixon and his lessons are remarkable for their simplicity. We just sit and moo. It does wonders for the voice and it's remarkably easy – once you have learned *how* to moo.

Noël Coward

He was the first actor I encountered who prepared to make a laughing entrance by going round doing *ha – ha!* sounds for hours.

George Cukor on **Charles Laughton** quoted in G. Lambert, *On Cukor*

Unless you know your character's mind it's a hollow sound you make.

Judi Dench *Sunday Times* 15 December 1991

I have found that although actors can play any part and shake it off, actresses cannot.

Alan Dent to **Vivien Leigh** 1949 (while Leigh was playing Blanche Dubois); quoted in A. Holden, *Olivier* 1988

With some of us it isn't luck.

Edith Evans to a young actor who wished her luck before a radio play

As a young actress I always had a rule. If I didn't understand anything I always said it as if it were improper.

Edith Evans

Anyone may achieve on some rare occasion an outburst of genuine feeling, a gesture of imperishable beauty, a ringing accent of truth, but your scientific actor knows how he did it. He can repeat it again, and again, and again.

Minnie Maddern Fiske quoted in *Minnie Maddern Fiske*. Her views on Actors, Acting and the Problems of Production, as told to Alexander Woollcott.

Breath, note, tone, word.

Elsie Fogarty fundamental thesis of the founder of the Central School of Speech and Drama, London

The only way to arrive at great excellency in characters is to be very conversant with human nature . . . by this way you will more accurately discover the workings of spirit. . . .

David Garrick

Appear, shine, and, as it were, die.

Jean Genet *Reflections on the Theatre*

You have to spin it all out of yourself, like a spider.

John Gielgud 1961

Generally speaking very good impersonators do *not* make very good actors.

John Gielgud after catching Richard Burton impersonating him; quoted in W. Redfield, *Letters from an Actor* 1971

Theory is the backwash of success.

Cedric Hardwicke

Good actors are good because of the things they can tell us without talking. When they are talking they are the slaves of the dramatist. It is what they can show the audience when they are not talking that reveals the fine actor.

Cedric Hardwicke *Theatre Arts* 1958

The important thing in acting is to be able to laugh and cry. If I have to cry, I think of my sex life. If I have to laugh, I think of my sex life.

Glenda Jackson attrib.

As for me, I find that I act best when my heart is warm and my head is cool.

Joseph Jefferson quoted in Sarah Bernhardt, *The Art of Theatre*

When in doubt, shout – that's the motto.

S. Major Jones, stage manager; quoted in C. Hardwicke, *A Victorian in Orbit* 1961

Whatever might extend my experience of the various aspects of human nature I regarded as needful and imperative study. Under this persuasion I braced my nerves to go through the lunatic asylum. . . . I took from thence lessons, painful ones, that in after years added to the truth of my representations.

William Charles Macready *Reminiscences and Diaries* 1875

Childhood can be a great help to an actor. Your emotions are never so wonderfully clear as then.

Alec McCowen *Sunday Times* 19 January 1992

Any acting that affects and moves an audience is good acting and anything that doesn't, whatever its imposing content or technical dexterity, isn't.

George Jean Nathan
Encyclopaedia of the Theatre 1940

Few people, including actors, know much about the matter and even what the few know is open to question.

Ibid.

Acting is just a bag of tricks.

Laurence Olivier

Sometimes the gods inspire a performance, and then the actor can do no wrong, but the actor must also prepare a performance for the night the gods do not attend.

Laurence Olivier to **Charlton Heston** 1960 quoted in A. Holden, *Olivier* 1988

You American actors are all like football players. You wait until you have the truth in your arms before you start running with the ball. We English start running when the curtain goes up and hope the truth will catch up with us.

Laurence Olivier to **Anthony Quinn** 1960; quoted in A. Holden, *Olivier* 1988

It is next to impossible to produce the effect of great suffering without the actor enduring some degree of it.

Laurence Olivier quoted in J. Mortimer, *In Character* 1983

Acting is like masturbation, one either does it or one doesn't, but one doesn't talk about it.

Eric Portman when asked by a young actor about his technique, 1965; recalled by **Noel Davis**

The most precious thing in acting is the pauses.

Ralph Richardson to a British National Youth Theatre Group, 1961; recalled by **Alan Allkins**

When a part is first put before me for studying, I look it over in a general way to see if it is in Nature, and if it is I am sure it can be played.

Sarah Siddons

Technique alone cannot create an image that you can believe in . . . creativeness is not a technical trick.

Constantin Stanislavski *An Actor Prepares* 1926

An actor should be observant not only on the stage, but also in real life. He should concentrate with all his being on whatever attracts his attention.

Ibid.

To act you must make the thing written your own. You must steal the words, steal the thought, and *convey* the stolen treasure to others with great art.

Ellen Terry quote found in the fly-leaf of her copy of *Romeo and Juliet* used for the Lyceum production with Irving, 1882

Later along in years I heard Ellen Terry sum up in a sentence this everlasting distinction between the actor's art and the playwright's. 'My boy', she said to me, 'act in your pauses. At those moments you are a creator, not a servant of playwrights.'

Ellen Terry quoted by Cedric Hardwicke in *A Victorian in Orbit* 1961

Could you oblige us with a little more light? I think you may not have realized that my comedic effects in this play are almost wholly grimacial.

Maud Beerbohm Tree to the director of *The Mask of Virtue*, who favoured a gloomy lighting effect

Normally an actor has two tracks running – the character you are playing, and a tiny track recording what you are doing and telling you what comes next. When a great actor is *very* good, the role is taking over. He is allowing something to happen through him. . . .

Dorothy Tutin quoted in A. Holden, *Olivier* 1988

TELEGRAMS

HAMLET? OR PERHAPS YOU ONLY
SAW THEM IN JULIET AND ROMEO.

James Agate to the *Radio Times*;
quoted in A. McGill and K.
Thomson, *Live Wires* 1982

DOCTOR WILL CUT OFF MY LEG
NEXT MONDAY. AM VERY HAPPY.
KISSES ALL MY HEART.

Sarah Bernhardt to Mrs Patrick
Campbell, 1916

PERMISSION TO EXHIBIT LEG? FEE
$100,000.

**Manager of the Pan American
Exposition** to Sarah Bernhardt
after hearing her leg had been
amputated

WHICH LEG?

Sarah Bernhardt

TWO TICKETS RESERVED FOR YOU,
FIRST NIGHT PYGMALION. BRING A
FRIEND. IF YOU HAVE ONE.

George Bernard Shaw to
Winston Churchill

CANNOT MAKE FIRST NIGHT. WILL
COME TO SECOND. IF YOU HAVE
ONE.

Winston Churchill to George
Bernard Shaw

ALL MY PLAYS EXCEPTING
CAVALCADE HAVE BEEN VULGARISED,
DISTORTED AND RUINED BY MOVIE
MINDS. AM NOW MIDDLE-AGED AND
PRESTIGE AND QUALITY OF MY
WORK ARE MY ONLY ASSETS FOR
THE FUTURE THEREFORE HAVE
DECIDED HENCEFORWARD NEVER TO
SELL FILM RIGHTS UNLESS I HAVE
ABSOLUTE CONTROL OF SCRIPT,
DIALOGUE, CAST, TREATMENT,
DIRECTOR, CAMERAMAN, CUTTER
AND PUBLICITY. CONVINCED
PRESENT LOSS IS FUTURE GAIN.

Noël Coward to his American
manager Jack Wilson, on
Hollywood bids for rights to *Blithe
Spirit*

AM BACK FROM ISTANBUL WHERE I
WAS KNOWN AS ENGLISH DELIGHT.

Noël Coward to his private
secretary Cole Lesley

LAST SUPPER AND ORIGINAL CAST
COULDN'T DRAW IN THIS HOUSE.

George S. Kaufman (who was working for a stock company in Troy, NY) to his father

AM WATCHING YOUR PERFORMANCE FROM THE REAR OF THE HOUSE. WISH YOU WERE HERE.

George S. Kaufman to actor William Gaxton *during* a performace of Kaufman's *Of Thee I Sing* 1933

YOU MAY AS WELL START BEING A STAR IN WILMINGTON AS ANYWHERE. SO BE GOOD TONIGHT.

Burgess Meredith to Lauren Bacall; quoted in A. McGill and K. Thomson, *Live Wires* 1982

AM CRAZY TO PLAY ST. JOAN.

Anonymous actress to George Bernard Shaw

I QUITE AGREE.

George Bernard Shaw

EXCELLENT! GREATEST!

George Bernard Shaw to Cornelia Otis Skinner, who played in *Candida* on Broadway, 1935

A MILLION THANKS BUT UNDESERVING SUCH PRAISE.

Cornelia Otis Skinner to George Bernard Shaw

I MEANT THE PLAY.

George Bernard Shaw to Cornelia Otis Skinner

SO DID I!

Cornelia Otis Skinner to George Bernard Shaw

NO GIRLS. NO LEGS. NO JOKES. NO CHANCE.

Telegram sent to **Walter Winchell** after the out of town première of *Oklahoma*, in Newhaven, 1943

THANK YOU INDEED FOR YOUR MAGNIFICENT AND GENEROUS REVIEW OF MY WORK. MAY I CONTINUE TO DESERVE IT OF YOU AND THE PUBLIC. GARRICK IS MY YARDSTICK, HE HAD VERSATILITY AND A ROUND FACE TOO. WARMEST REGARDS.

Donald Wolfit to James Agate

HAVE BEEN LOOKING ROUND FOR AN APPROPRIATE WOODEN GIFT AND AM PLEASED HEREBY TO PRESENT YOU WITH ELSIE FERGUSON'S PERFORMANCE IN HER NEW PLAY.

Alexander Woollcott to George S. Kaufman, on his fifth wedding anniversary

ELLEN TERRY

(BY OTHERS)
She has a voice of plum coloured velvet.

James Agate *Ego 1* 1935

(ON HERSELF)
I am not a great actress, I am not indeed. I am only a very useful one to Henry (Irving).

To critic Clement Scott, after his enthusiastic review of *Faust*, 1885

I can pass swiftly from one effect to another, but I cannot fix one, and dwell on it, with that superb concentration which seems to me the special attribute of the tragic actress.

Memoirs 1908

Though I may *seem* like myself to others, I never *feel* like myself when I am acting, but some one else, so nice, and so young and so happy, and always-in-the-air, light and bodyless.

Quoted in *Ellen Terry and Bernard Shaw. A Correspondence* (ed. Christopher St. John) 1933

You can get on without beauty, but it is impossible for an actress to achieve any distinction without Imagination, Individuality and Industry.

Quoted in R. Findlater, *The Player Queens* 1976

E.T. was persuadable – especially on Mondays – less so on Tuesdays. On Wednesdays people around her found it difficult to make her understand what it was they were trying to say – but by the time Thursday arrived she could be counted on to do the very thing they didn't expect. Friday she devoted to telling them that it didn't hurt, and that they must be brave and not cry – Saturday was always a half-holiday, spent in promising her advisers she would be good next week – and on Sunday she generally drove away to Hampton Court, waving her lily white hand.

Edward Gordon Craig (son)
Ellen Terry and Her Secret Self 1931

Even with her head in a bag she would have captured the house.

Ibid.

Ellen Terry played but one part – herself, and when not herself she couldn't play it.

Ibid.

She was large and lovely and gracious and opulent and untidy with everything falling out of her voluminous handbag.

Gwen Ffrangcon-Davies *The Times* 26 January 1991

Her voice has a sort of monotonous, husky thickness which is extremely touching, though it gravely interferes with the modulation of many of her speeches.

Henry James *The Nation* 12 June 1879

She was an extremely beautiful girl and as innocent as a rose. When Watts kissed her, she took for granted she was going to have a baby.

George Bernard Shaw quoted in S. Winston, *Days with Bernard Shaw*

A heartless waste of an exquisite talent. What a theatre for a woman of genius to be attached to.

George Bernard Shaw on Ellen Terry's partnership with Irving at the Lyceum

The perfect symbol in her work of what the true theatre is – an instrument which transformed body, voice, clothes, words, all materials, into spirit – spiritual essence.

Sybil Thorndike quoted in R. Findlater, *The Player Queens* 1976

Our Lady of the Lyceum.

Oscar Wilde

THE THEATRE

The theatre is not a night-school. Its drama illumines philosophy, sociology, politics and the rest by reflection, in that it lights up the philosopher, the sociologist and the politician.

James Agate

The theatre is in reality the Genesis of creation. It will be done.

Antonin Artaud letter 1948

You're not considered seriously in this country [UK] until you've been on the stage and done all that crap.

Dirk Bogarde *By Myself*, Channel 4 TV January 1992

The theatre must be treated with respect. It is a house of strange enchantment, a temple of dreams.

Noël Coward

To save the Theatre, the Theatre must be destroyed, the actors and actresses all die of the plague . . . they make art impossible.

Eleonora Duse quoted in A. Symons, *Studies in Seven Arts*

It is still only in the theatre that for better or worse, glory or disaster, an actor or actress can make direct contact with an audience, a connection without which they are incomplete as artists. It is in the theatre, above all, that the audience may share the rare magnificence of great acting, an experience of instant excellence, truth and joy to which there can be no parallel in the cinema or in the television rooms.

Richard Findlater *The Player Queens* 1976

The theatre is the aspirin of the middle classes.

Wolcott Gibbs *More in Sorrow* 1958

Of all the arts that mankind has invented to clothe its concept of reality and to ornament its leisure moments, none is more suited to the genius of the female of the species than that of the theatre.

Rosamond Gilder *Enter the Actress* 1931

The theatre is ruthless. An actor walks on the stage and within 30 seconds you know whether you want to watch him or not.

Peter Hall *Diaries* 12 June 1974

The theatre is the best way of showing the gap between what is said and what is seen to be done and that is why, ragged and gap-toothed as it is, it has still a far healthier potential than some poorer, abandoned arts.

David Hare quoted in the *Penguin Dictionary of Modern Quotations* 1980

For me, the theatre is the projection on a stage of the interior world.

Eugene Ionesco

Come leave the loathed stage,
And the more loathsome age;
Where pride and impudence (in faction
      knit)
Usurpe the chair of wit!

Ben Jonson *Ode (to himself)* 1631; written after his plays had been poorly received

To my mind there is no sadder spectacle of artistic debauchery than a London theatre; the overfed inhabitants of the villa in the stalls hoping for gross excitement to assist them through their hesitating digestions; an ignorant mob in the pit and gallery forgetting the miseries of life in imbecile stories reeking of the sentimentality of the backstairs.

George Moore *Confessions of a Young Man* 1888

The stage can be defined as a place where Shakespeare murdered Hamlet and a great many Hamlets have since murdered Shakespeare.

Robert Morse 1965

The gathering together for a special occasion is at the very heart of what theatre is.

Adrian Noble *The Times* 7 October 1991

The Theatre, for all its noise and glitter, is a tiny world. Most of the people who work in it do not realise how small it is because they never take the risk of stepping outside it.

J.B. Priestley 1951

The stage is actors' country. You have to get your passport stamped every so often or they take away your citizenship.

Vanessa Redgrave *Newsweek* 10 February 1975

I think the theatre is a wonderful holiday.

Tony Richardson 1966

A change, slight but unmistakable has taken place; the English theatre has been dragged, as Adlai Stevenson once said of the Republican party, kicking and screaming into the twentieth century.

Kenneth Tynan *Curtains* 1961

Whoever condemns the theatre is an enemy to his country.

Voltaire letter to the Paris police commissioner, 20 June 1788

Theatre is a group activity in public. It is one of the few public arenas we have left. It is bold and courageous, like medieval jousting. A muscular place where you get good jokes.

Timberlake Wertenbaker *The Guardian* 4 September 1991

Those Enchanted Aisles.

Alexander Woollcott (book title)

TOURING

Oh, Lilian, I hear you are a perfect *tour de force* playing me! And here I am forced to tour.

Mrs Patrick Campbell to **Lilian Braithwaite** who was playing a character based on 'Mrs Pat' in Ivor Novello's *Party*; quoted in R. May, *The Wit of the Theatre* 1969

God was very good to me. He never let me go on tour.

Edith Evans

Fifteen shillings a week could get you bed and breakfast in a place like Glasgow, but you might find yourself enacting the old gag of leaning against the wall in your overcoat to feel the warmth from the fire in the house next door.

John Osborne *A Better Class of Person* 1981

I remember a landlady who used to split her dining room into two halves: straight actors on the left, variety turns on the right.

Ernie Wise quoted in *Apt and Amusing Quotations* (ed. G.F. Lamb) 1986

Mrs Roosevelt runs the best theatrical boarding house in Washington.

Alexander Woollcott who stayed at the White House while playing in *The Man Who Came to Dinner*

TRAGEDY

Tragedy is an imitation of an action that is serious, complete, and of a certain magnitude, effecting through pity and fear the proper catharsis, or purgation, of emotions.

Aristotle *Poetics* I *c.* 322 BC

Tragedy represents the life of princes; comedy serves to depict the actions of the people.

François D'Aubignac *La Pratique de Théâtre c.* 1660

Sex, flesh, and physicality are the root of tragedy.

Dario Fo *The Independent* 1 April 1992

HERBERT BEERBOHM TREE

(ON HIMSELF)
Oh my God! Remember you're in Egypt. The *skay* is only seen in Kensington.

To an over-refined actor, attrib.

I can stand any amount of flattery so long as it's fulsome enough.

Quoted in M. Beerbohm *From a Brother's Standpoint*

Ladies – just a little more virginity if you don't mind.

While directing a production of Shakespeare's *Henry VIII*; quoted in A. Woollcott, *Shouts and Murmurs*

(BY OTHERS)
Do you know how they are going to decide the Shakespeare–Bacon dispute? They are going to dig up Shakespeare and dig up Bacon; they are going to set their coffins side by side, and they are going to get Tree to recite *Hamlet* to them, and the one who turns in his coffin will be the author of the play.

W.S. Gilbert letter, quoted in H. Pearson, *Lives of the Wits* 1962

His performance as a whole often fell short of high excellence, yet these same impersonations were lit by insight and masterly strokes of interpretation which made the spectator feel that he was watching the performance of the most imaginative of living actors.

Desmond MacCarthy *From the Stalls c.* 1920

With the amount of personal

attention, Mr Tree, which you give to all your presentations, and the care you bestow on every detail, I really don't think you need an actual producer. Nor with the constant supervision you so thoroughly exercise, have you any use for a stage manager. What you really require are a couple of *tame, trained echoes*!

Hugh Moss, after an engagement with Tree; quoted in J. Graham, *An Old Stock Actor's Memories*. (Tree was an old-style actor-manager who produced, acted and directed.)

Even when he was hopelessly miscast Tree's acting was so clever, so inventive, so varied and interesting, that for unalloyed entertainment one wanted rather to see him in a bad play than anyone else in a good one.

Hesketh Pearson *The Last Actor Managers* 1950

A charming fellow, so clever: he models himself on me.

Oscar Wilde quoted in H. Pearson, *Beerbohm Tree* 1956

OSCAR WILDE

(ON HIMSELF)
Who am I to tamper with a masterpiece?

(When asked to make changes to one of his plays)

I have nothing to declare but my genius.

(To customs on his arrival in New York, 1882)

(BY OTHERS)
The solution that he, deliberately or accidentally found, was to subordinate every other dramatic element to dialogue for its own sake and create a verbal universe in which the characters are determined by the kinds of things they say, and the plot is nothing but a succession of opportunities to say them.

W.H. Auden *Forewords and Afterwords* quoted in F.S. Pepper *Dictionary of Biographical Quotations* 1985

From the beginning Wilde performed his life and continued to do so even after fame had taken the plot out of his hands.

Ibid.

That sovereign of insufferables, Oscar Wilde, has ensued with his opulence of twaddle and his penury of sense. . . . With a knowledge that would equip an idiot to dispute with a cast-iron dog, an eloquence to qualify him for the duties of the caller of a hog-ranch, and an imagination adequate to the conception of a tomcat, when fired by contemplation of a fiddle-string, this consummate and star-like youth, missing everywhere his heaven-appointed functions and offices, wanders about, posing as a statue of himself, and like the sun-smitten image of Memnon, emitting meaningless murmurs in the blaze of women's eyes.

Ambrose Bierce 'Greetings to an Aesthetic Visitor', *Wasp* 31 March 1882

Like a many-coloured humming top he was at once a bewilderment and a balance.

G.K. Chesterton *Daily News* 19 October 1910

Paradox with him was only truth standing on its head to attract attention.

Richard Le Gallienne

Oscar Wilde's talent seems to me essentially rootless, something

growing in a glass in a little water.

George Moore

Oscar and George Bernard
Cannot be reconciled.
When I'm Wilde about Shaw
I'm not Shaw about Wilde.

Freddie Oliver

If with the literate I am
Impelled to try an epigram
I never seek to take the credit
We all assume that Oscar said it.

Dorothy Parker

He had the property of making his critics dull. They laugh angrily at his epigrams, like a child who is coaxed into being amused in the very act of setting up a yell of rage and agony. They protest that the trick is obvious, and that such epigrams can be turned out by the score by anyone lightminded enough to condescend to such frivolity. As far as I can ascertain, I am the only person in London who cannot sit down and write an Oscar Wilde play at will. The fact that his plays, though apparently lucrative, remain unique under these circumstances, says much for the self-denial of our scribes.

George Bernard Shaw review 1895, *Dramatic Opinions and Essays* Vol. I 1909

It was rather amusing as it was a complete mass of epigrams, with occasional whiffs of grotesque melodrama and drivelling sentiment.

Lytton Strachey on *A Woman of No Importance;* letter to Duncan Grant, 2 June 1907

When Oscar came to join his God,
Not earth to earth but sod to sod.
It was for sinners such as this
Hell was created bottomless.

Algernon Swinburne

He was over-dressed, pompous, snobbish, sentimental and vain. But he had an undeniable *flair* for the possibilities of the commercial theatre. He got himself into

trouble, poor old thing, by an infringement of a very silly law, which was just as culpable, and just as boring, as an infringement of traffic or licensing regulations.

Evelyn Waugh *Harper's Bazaar* November 1930

What has Oscar in common with Art? Except that he dines at our tables and picks from our platters the plums from the puddings he peddles in the provinces.

J.M. Whistler letter to *The World* 17 November 1886. (Wilde and Whistler were engaged in a long-running feud. In his reply Wilde wrote 'With our James vulgarity begins at home and should be allowed to stay there.')

They sent Oscar Wilde, that poor man, to Reading Jail for doing what all other actors today get knighted for.

Wilfrid Hyde White quoted in D. McClelland, *Star Speak* 1987

Oscar was not a man of bad character; you could trust him with a woman anywhere.

William Wilde (brother) 1895; quoted in H. Pearson, *The Marrying Americans* 1961

TENNESSEE WILLIAMS

(ON HIMSELF)

I changed my name to Tennessee Williams, the justification being mainly that the Williamses had fought the Indians for Tennessee and I had already discovered that the life of a young writer was going to be something similar to the defence of a stockade against a band of savages.

What writers influenced me as a young man? Chekhov! As a dramatist? Chekhov! D.H. Lawrence, too, for his understanding of sexuality, of life in general.

A morbid shyness once prevented me from having much direct communication with people, and possibly that is why I began to write to them plays and stories. But even now, when that first tongue-locking, face-flushing, silent and crouching timidity has worn off with the passage of the troublesome youth that it sprang from, I still find it somehow easier to 'level with' crowds of strangers in the hushed twilight of orchestra and balcony sections of the theatres than with individuals across a table from me. . . .

Introduction to *Cat on a Hot Tin Roof*

I have made a covenant with myself to continue to write, since I have no choice, it is so deeply rooted as a way of existence and a form of flight. . . .

Memoirs

My tragedies are funnier than my comedies. Some of these characters have to laugh. They've got to. Or they'll die.

(BY OTHERS)

Mr Williams's problem is not lack of talent. It is, perhaps, an ambiguity of aim; he seems to want to kick the world in the pants and yet be the world's sweetheart, to combine the glories of martyrdom with the comforts of success.

Eric Bentley *New Republic*

Tennessee Williams has a strong streak of poetry, but I think he has run into the ground rather – what with all those neurotic mothers, castrations and things.

Noël Coward quoted in D. Richards, *The Wit of Noël Coward*

He sometimes ran a purple ribbon through his typewriter and gushed where he should have damned.

T.E. Kalem *Time* 1983; quoted in C. Jarman, *The Guinness Dictionary of Poisonous Quotes* 1991

If a swamp alligator could talk, it would sound like Tennessee Williams.

Rex Reed 1972

Playwright Tennessee Williams often writes like an arrested adolescent who disarmingly imagines that he will attain stature if (as short boys are advised in Dixie) he loads enough manure in his shoes.

Time Magazine

BIOGRAPHICAL INDEX

OF

INDIVIDUALS QUOTED

OR

REFERRED TO IN QUOTATION

ABBOTT George b. 1887
American playwright, actor and producer

Plays

ADAMS Franklin Prince 1881–1960
American writer

Critical Abuse – actors

ADLER (Levitsky) Sara 1858–1953
Russian-born American/Yiddish actress

Greek drama; Method acting (Lee Strasberg)

AGATE James 1877–1947
English dramatic critic and diarist

Actors: Katharine Hepburn; Amateurs; J.M. Barrie; Mrs Patrick Campbell; Critical Abuse – actors; Critical Abuse – plays; Criticism to Critics; Directors; Eleonora Duse; Music hall Vaudeville; Olivier; Plays; Quick Thinking; Ralph Richardson; Shakespeare's Plays – Hamlet *(Gielgud, Olivier); George Bernard Shaw; Telegrams; Ellen Terry; Theatre.*

AINLEY Henry 1879–1945
English actor

Advice

ALBEE Edward b. 1928
American dramatist (*A Delicate Balance*)

Critics; Prejudice

ALLEN Fred 1894–1956
American comedian

Tallulah Bankhead; Star Quality

ALLEN Woody b. 1935
American actor/writer/film director

Show Business

ALLEYN Edward 1566–1626
Elizabethan actor; founder of Dulwich College

Actors – Alleyn

ALLKINS Alan b. 1940
Founder member of the British National Youth Theatre

Technique

ANDERSEN Hans Christian 1805–75
Danish writer and story-teller

Ibsen

ANDERSON Robert b. 1917
American playwright; Playwights

Dressing Room Talk; Playwrights

ANDREWS Julie b. 1935
British actress/singer

Actors – Julie Andrews

ANOUILH Jean 1910–87
French dramatist best known for interpretations of classical Greek drama (*Antigone*)

Playwrights – Anouilh

ARCHER William 1856–1924
British dramatic critic and playwright

Critics

ARISTOPHANES *c.* **448–380** BC
Greek dramatist (*The Frogs*)

Greek Drama; Playwrights – Euripides

ARISTOTLE *c.* **384–322** BC
Greek philosopher

Comedy; Tragedy

ARNAUD Yvonne 1892–1958
French actress

Insults

ARNOLD Matthew 1822–88
English poet and literary critic

Actors – Rachel; Shakespeare

ARTAUD Antonin 1896–1948
French actor/director/playwright

Purpose; Theatre

ASHCROFT Dame Peggy 1907–91
British actress

Peggy Ashcroft; Shakespeare's Plays – As You Like It, Romeo and Juliet

ATKINS Robert 1886–1972
British actor/director

Quick Thinking

ATKINS Eileen b. 1934
British actress

Audience Asides; Shakespeare's Plays – As
You Like It

ATKINSON Brooks 1894–1984
American drama critic (*New York Times*
1926–60)

*Acting; Barrymores (John, Lionel); Critical
Abuse – plays; Dedication; Star Quality*

D'AUBIGNAC Francois *fl.* **1660s**
French writer

Tragedy

AUBREY John 1626–97
English antiquary and biographer (*Brief
Lives*)

*Beaumont and Fletcher; Ben Jonson;
Shakespeare*

AUDEN W(ystan) H(ugh) 1907–73
English poet

Shakespeare; Wilde

AUGUSTINE OF HIPPO St. AD **354–
430**
Christian priest and philosopher

Opprobrium

AYCKBOURN Alan b. 1939
British playwright

Actors – Donald Wolfit

AYE John *fl.* **1920s and 30s**
English writer

Critics; Life

BACALL Lauren b. 1924
American actress

Telegrams

BACON James *fl.* **1960s**
Contemporary American journalist

Shakespeare's Plays – Hamlet *(Richard
Burton)*

BACON Sir Francis 1561–1626
English statesman and philosopher

Life; H.B. Tree

BADEL Alan 1923–82
English actor

Film and Television

BALDWIN Stanley 1867–1947
British Prime Minister 1923–24, 1924–29,
1935–37

George Bernard Shaw

BALZAC Honoré de 1799–1850
French novelist (*Eugéne Grandet*)

Talent

BANCROFT Sir Squire 1841–1926
English actor-manager

Finance

BANKHEAD Tallulah 1903–68
American actress famous for outrageous
behaviour

*Bad Habits; Tallulah Bankhead; Critical
Abuse – plays; Critics – Alexander Woollcott;
Fans; Finance; First Nights; Insults;
Playwrights – Lillian Hellman; Shakespeare's
Plays –* Antony and Cleopatra

BANNISTER John (Jock) 1760–1836
English comic actor

Comedy

BARKER Felix
Contemporary British drama critic

Shakespeare's Plays – Cymbeline

BARKER Harley Granville 1877–1946
English writer/actor/director

Resting

BARKER Howard b. 1946
British playwright

Censorship

BARKLEY Alben W. 1877–1956
United States Senator

Audiences

BARNES Clive b. 1927
British-born American drama critic; most influential in 1970s on the *New York Post*

Critical Abuse – plays; Critics – Clive Barnes; Plays

BARNUM Phineas T. 1810–91
American showman and theatrical producer

Finance

BARRAULT Jean Louis b. 1910
French actor/director

Purpose

BARRIE Sir James 1860–1937
Scottish novelist and dramatist (*Peter Pan*)

J.M. Barrie; Critical Abuse – plays; Method Acting

BARRYMORE Ethel 1879–1959
American actress; sister of John and Lionel

Barrymores; Success

BARRYMORE John 1882–1942
American actor; brother of Ethel and Lionel; famous for his Hamlet

Artistic Integrity; Audiences; Barrymores; Dressing Room Talk; Fame; Shakespeare's Plays – Hamlet; Technique

BARRYMORE Lionel 1878–1954
American actor and musician; brother of Ethel and John

Barrymores; Epitaphs

BARRYMORE Maurice (Herbert Blythe) 1847–1905
English actor who took the name Barrymore from a playbill and emigrated to the United States; he and Georgina Drew (1856–93) were parents of Ethel, John and Lionel

Actors – Maurice Barrymore; Epitaphs

BART Lionel b. 1930
British composer/lyricist/playwright (*Oliver!, Blitz*)

Critical Abuse – plays; Criticism

BAXTER Beverley 1891–1964
English theatre critic

Critics – Kenneth Tynan; Gielgud

BAYLIS Lilian 1874–1937
Founder of the Old Vic and Sadler's Wells theatres

Fame; Finance; Life; Quick Thinking; Technique

BEATON Sir Cecil 1904–80
English photographer and stage designer

Actors – Katharine Hepburn; Playwrights – Somerset Maugham

BEAUMONT Sir Francis 1584–1616
English dramatist; collaborator with Fletcher (*The Maid's Tragedy*)

Beaumont and Fletcher

BEAUMARCHAIS Pierre Augustin Caron de 1732–99
French dramatist (*The Barber of Seville*)

Audiences

BECKETT Samuel 1906–89
Innovative Irish-born playwright (*Waiting for Godot*)

Playwrights – Beckett

BEERBOHM Sir (Henry) Max(imilian) 1872–1956
English writer/caricaturist/theatre critic; succeeded G.B. Shaw on *The Saturday Review*

Comedy; Critical Abuse – actors (Duse); Critics – Max Beerbohm; Criticism; Epitaphs –

*Dan Leno; Failure; Playwrights – Pinero;
Shakespeare; Shakespeare's Plays – Hamlet,
Macbeth; H.B. Tree*

BEHAN Brendan 1923–64
Irish playwright

Purpose

BEHN Mrs Aphra 1640–89
First English woman to work as a
professional writer and dramatist (*The
Rover*)

Playwrights – Aphra Behn

BELLOC (Joseph) Hilaire 1870–1953
Anglo-French writer

G.B. Shaw

**BENCHLEY Nathaniel Goddard
1915–81**
American writer

Method Acting

BENCHLEY Robert 1889–1945
American actor/drama critic (*Life, New
Yorker*); member with Alexander Woollcott
and Dorothy Parker of the Algonquin
Round Table

*Critical Abuse – plays; Critics; Critics – R.
Benchley*

BENÉT William Rose 1886–1950
American writer

Playwrights – Pirandello

BENNETT Alan b. 1934
English playwright/actor

Critics

BENNETT (Enoch) Arnold 1867–1931
British writer (*The Old Wives' Tale*)

Actors; G.B. Shaw

**BENSON Lady Constance (Constance
Featherstonhaugh/Samuel) 1860–1946**
Member of Sir Frank Benson's Shakespeare
company. Married FB in 1888

Advice; Bad Habits

BENSON Sir Frank 1858–1939
English actor, founder of the Shakespeare
Festival, Stratford-upon-Avon

Actors – Frank Benson; Technique

BENTLEY E(ric) C. b. 1916
English-born American theatre critic

Critics; Purpose; G.B. Shaw

BERGMAN Ingrid 1915–82
Swedish actress

Ambition; Star Quality

BERKOFF Steven b. 1937
British actor/playwright (*Kvetch*)

Purpose

BERLIN Irving b. 1888
American composer of popular songs (*God
Bless America*) and musicals (*Annie Get Your
Gun*)

Musicals; Show Business; Success

BERNARD Tristan 1866–1947
French playwright

Audiences

**BERNHARDT Sarah (Henriette
Bernard) 1844–1923**
French actress, 'The Divine Sarah',
regarded as the greatest tragedienne of her
day

*Actors – Duse; Audiences; Costume and
Make-up; Finance; Insults; Life; Quick
Thinking; Shakespeare's Plays – Hamlet; Star
Quality; Telegrams*

BETTERTON Mary c. 1637–1712
English actress, the first to be buried in
Westminster Abbey; married to Thomas
Betterton

Actors – Mary Betterton

BETTERTON Thomas 1635–1710
English actor/dramatist; married to Mary
Betterton

Shakespeare's Plays – Hamlet

BETTY William Henry West (Master Betty) 1791–1874
English child star, 'The Young Roscius', played Romeo, Hamlet and Richard III aged only 12

Actors – Master Betty

BIBESCO Elizabeth *fl.* **1940s/50s**
American writer (*Haven*)

Life

BIERCE Ambrose 1842–1914?
American journalist

Playwrights

BIGGE Sir Arthur 1849–1931
Groom in Waiting to Queen Victoria

Censorship

BILLINGTON Michael b. 1939
English critic and writer

Peggy Ashcroft; Critical Abuse – actors (Peter O'Toole); Olivier

BIRD Robert Montgomery 1806–54
American playwright/novelist

Success

BLAKELOCK Denys 1901–70
English actor

Playwrights; Resting

BLOOM Claire b. 1931
English actress

Shakespeare's Plays – Twelfth Night

BOGARDE Sir Dirk (Derek Van Den Bogaerde) b. 1921
British actor/writer

Fans; Stage Fright; Theatre

BOGART Humphrey 1899–1957
American actor and film star

Method Acting

BOORSTIN Daniel J. b. 1914
American writer

Fame

BOOTH Edwin 1833–93
American actor famous for his Hamlet and Othello

Actors; Actors – Edwin Booth

BOOTH Junius Brutus Sen. 1796–1852
American actor; father of Junius Brutus jun., Edwin and John Wilkes (who assassinated President Lincoln)

Bad Habits

BOOTHROYD Basil 1910–88
British writer and broadcaster

Critics

BOSWELL James 1740–95
Scottish biographer of Dr Samuel Johnson

Actors; Garrick; Shakespeare; Sarah Siddons

BOUCICAULT Dion 1822–90
Irish born dramatist/actor

Epitaphs; Finance; Plays

BOWDLER Thomas 1754–1825
English reformer who, with his sister **Harriet**, published an expurgated version of Shakespeare's works (*Family Shakespeare*) in 1818, giving rise to the expression 'to bowdlerize'

Censorship; Shakespeare

BRACEGIRDLE Anne *c.* **1663–1748**
English actress, brought up by Thomas and Mary Betterton

Actors – Anne Bracegirdle; Reputation

BRADY William A. 1863–1950
American theatrical producer

Finance

BRAGG Melvyn b. 1939
British writer

Failure

BRAHMS Caryl 1901–82
English writer

Beaumont and Fletcher

BRAITHWAITE Dame Lilian 1865–1940
English actress

Insults; Quick Thinking; Touring

BRANAGH Kenneth b. 1961
British actor/director/producer

Success

BRANDO Marlon b. 1924
American actor and filmstar

Acting; Actors; Fame

BRECHT Bertolt 1898–1956
German dramatist/poet with strong
Marxist principles

Playwrights – Anouilh; Purpose

**BRÉMONT Comtesse de fl. late 19th
century**
American? journalist

Insults

BRENNAN Robert E. fl. 1930s/40s
American writer

Critics – Dorothy Parker

BRENTON Howard b. 1942
British playwright

Avant-garde; Comedy; Plays; Purpose

BRIDGES-ADAMS William 1889–1965
English theatre director

Scenery and Lighting

BRIEN Alan b. 1925
English journalist and critic

Shakespeare's Plays – Macbeth *(Simone
Signoret)*

BRIERS Richard b. 1932
English actor

Acting

BRINDLEY Madge fl. 1920s/30s
American actress

Critical Abuse – actors

BROOK Peter b. 1925
British theatre director/producer

*Avant-garde; Directors – Peter Brook; Gielgud;
Purpose; Technique*

BROUGHTON John, 1st Baron 1786–1869
English politician and writer

Kean

BROUN Heywood C. 1888–1939
American columnist and critic

Tallulah Bankhead; Critical Abuse – plays

MASON BROWN John 1900–69
American journalist; theatre critic of *The
Saturday Review of Literature*

*Adaptations; Critics – A. Woollcott; Olivier;
Playwrights – O'Neill; Shakespeare's Plays –
Antony and Cleopatra (Tallulah Bankhead)*

BROWN Pamela 1917–75
English actress

Advice

BROWN Thomas 1663–1704
English satirist

Prejudice

BROWNE Coral 1913–91
Australian actress

Costume; Quick Thinking

BRUCE Lenny 1923–66
American comedian

Motivation

BRYDEN Ronald b. 1927
English critic

Olivier

BUCHANEN McKean *fl.* **mid-19th century**
American actor

Insults

BUCHANEN Robert 1841–1901
British playwright

Actors

BUCKINGHAM George Villiers, 2nd Duke of 1627–87
English courtier and playwright

Critics; Playwrights; Playwrights – Buckingham

BUNNER Henry C. 1855–96
American writer

Shakespeare

BURBAGE Richard *c.* **1567–1619**
English actor; first to play many of the great Shakespearean roles including Hamlet, Lear and Othello

Actors – Burbage; Epitaphs; Shakespeare's Plays – Othello

BURGE Stuart b. 1918
British actor/director

Quick Thinking

BURNEY Charlotte *fl.* **late 18th century**
Sister of Fanny Burney

Fans

BURNEY Fanny (Madame D'Arblay) 1752–1840
English novelist and diarist

Garrick; Shakespeare's Plays – The Tempest; Sarah Siddons

BURNS George b. 1896
American comedian

Actors – Carol Channing; Music Hall

BURTON Richard (Richard Jenkins) 1925–84
Welsh actor and film star. Married to Elizabeth Taylor

Advice; Actors – Richard Burton, Elizabeth Taylor; Bad Habits; Critical Abuse – actors; Insults; Motivation; Shakespeare's Plays – Hamlet, The Tempest

BYRON George Gordon, 6th Baron 1788–1824
English poet

Acting; Sheridan; Sarah Siddons

BYRON H(enry) J(ames) 1834–84
English actor/dramtist specializing in pantomime

Plays

CADELL Selina b. 1953
English actress

Dressing Room Talk

CAMPBELL Ken b. 1941
British actor/writer

Shakespeare's Plays – Hamlet

CAMPBELL Mrs Patrick (née Beatrice Stella Tanner) 1865–1940
English actress renowned for her ready wit; close friend of George Bernard Shaw

Actors – Basil Rathbone; Audiences; Tallulah Bankhead; J.M. Barrie; Costume and Make-up; Insults; Noël Coward; Technique; Telegrams; Touring

CAMPBELL Thomas 1774–1844
English writer; biographer of Sarah Siddons

Actors – Master Betty

CANTOR Eddie 1892–1964
American comedian

Producers – Ziegfeld

CAPOTE Truman b. 1924
American writer

Actors

CARROLL Diahann b. 1935
American actress/singer

Dressing Room Talk

CARSON Jack 1910–63
American actor

Fans

CERVANTES Miguel de Cervantes Saavedra 1547–1616
Spanish writer (*Don Quixote*)

Comedy

CHAMFORT Nicolas 1741–94
French writer who 'lived by his wit'

Comedy

CHANNING Carol b. 1921
American actress

Actors – Carol Channing

CAREW Richard 1555–1620
English (Cornish) poet and antiquary

Prompts

CHAPMAN John 1900–72
American theatre critic of the *Daily News*

Critical Abuse – plays

CHEKHOV Anton 1860–1904
Russian dramatist (*The Cherry Orchard, Uncle Vanya*)

Finance; Life; Plays; Tennessee Williams

CHESTERTON G(ilbert) K(eith) 1874–1936
English novelist and critic

Amateurs; Broadway; Oscar Wilde

CHETWOOD William Rufus d. 1766
English bookseller and dramatist

Reputation – Mrs Woffington

CHRISTIANSEN Marie *fl.* 1930s/40s
American actress

Slips of the Tongue

CHURCHILL Sir Winston 1874–1965
British statesman and Prime Minister 1940–45, 1951–55

Vivien Leigh; G.B. Shaw; Telegrams

CHRYSOSTOM St. John *c.* 347–407
Priest and writer

Opprobrium

CIBBER Colley 1671–1757
English actor/dramatist and Poet Laureate

Actors – Colley Cibber; Finance; Reputation – Anne Bracegirdle

CLARKE Creston 1865–1910
American actor

Critical Abuse – actors

CLIVE Kitty 1711–85
English actress who worked with Colley Cibber and Garrick

Critical Abuse – actors; Garrick

COCHRAN Sir Charles Blake 1872–1951
English impresario

Critical Abuse – actors

COHAN George M. 1878–1942
American theatrical producer/playwright/songwriter

Tallulah Bankhead; The Press; Producers – George Cohan

COLE John 1792–1848
British antiquary and book-seller

Shakespeare's Plays – Hamlet (Kean)

COLEMAN George 1762–1836
English dramatist

Actors – Colley Cibber, John Kemble

COLERIDGE Samuel Taylor 1772–1834
English poet

Beaumont and Fletcher; Kean; Playwrights – Congreve

COLLIER Jeremy 1650–1726
English churchman and moral crusader

Opprobrium; Purpose

COMSTOCK Anthony 1844–1915
English writer

George Bernard Shaw

CONGREVE William 1670–1729
English playwright (*The Way of the World*)

Critics; Playwrights – Congreve

CONNOLLY Cyril 1903–74
British journalist and critic

Noël Coward

COOK, William d. 1824
Irish dramatist

Dedication

COOKE Edmund Vance b. 1866–?
American poet and author

Actors – Edwin Booth

COOPER Lady Diana 1892–1986
Society beauty and occasional actress

Quick Thinking

COOPER Dame Gladys 1888–1971
English actress

Star Quality

CORNEILLE Pierre 1606–84
French tragic dramatist (*Le Cid*)

Audiences; Playwrights – Corneille

CORNELL Katharine 1893–1974
American actress

Actors – Katharine Cornell; Star Quality

COTTRELL Cherry b. 1909
English actress

Shakespeare's Plays – Hamlet

COWARD Sir Noël 1899–1973
English actor/playwright/lyricist/composer; best known for his brittle, witty comedies (*Private Lives, Blithe Spirit*)

Acting; Actors – Gertrude Lawrence; Advice; Ambition; Auditions; Avant-garde; Beaumont and Fletcher; Beginnings; Charity Galas; Chekhov; Child Actors; Noël Coward; Critical Abuse – actors; Critical Abuse – plays; Criticism; Critics – Alexander Woollcott; Dedication; Kitchen Sink Drama; Method Acting; The Lunts; Plays; Playwrights – Somerset Maugham, John Osborne; Quick Thinking; Recognition; Shakespeare's Plays – Richard III (Olivier); Technique; Telegrams; Theatre

CRAIG Edward Gordon 1872–1966
English actor/stage designer/writer; son of Ellen Terry

Irving; Ellen Terry

CRICHTON Kyle 1896–1960
American theatre critic

Critical Abuse – plays

CROSSE Henry fl. 17th century

Audiences

CUKOR George 1899–1983
Hollywood film director

Vivien Leigh; Technique (Charles Laughton)

CUMBERLAND Richard 1732–1811
English dramatist

Garrick

CUSACK Sinead b. 1948
Irish actress

Acting

CUSHMAN Charlotte 1816–76
American actress, famous for playing men's
roles and in the role of Meg Merrilees

Acting; Dedication

CUSHMAN Robert b. 1943
British theatre critic for the *Observer*

Critical Abuse – actors (Elizabeth Taylor)

DALY (John) Augustin 1838–99
American dramatist

Irving

FO Dario b. 1926
Italian playwright/actor

Playwrights; Tragedy

DARLINGTON W.A. 1890–1979
English theatre critic for the *Daily Telegraph*

*Actors – Edith Evans; Beginnings – Olivier;
Critical Abuse – plays*

DAVIES Marion 1900–61
American actress; long time companion of
newspaper magnate William Randolph
Hearst

Critical Abuse – actors

DAVIES Robertson b. 1913
Canadian novelist/actor/playwright

Critics

DAVIES Russell
Contemporary British journalist

Olivier

DAVIES Thomas 1712–85
English actor/bookseller

Playwrights – Congreve

DAVIS Bette 1908–89
American actress and film star

Purpose

DAVIS Noel b. 1929
British actor/casting director

*Audience Asides; Costume and make-up;
Greek Drama; Technique*

DELDERFIELD R.F. 1912–72
English novelist

Actors

DE MILLE Agnes b. 1908
American choreographer/writer

Fame

DENCH Dame Judi b. 1934
British actress

Actors; Peggy Ashcroft; Success; Technique

DENNIS Sandy 1937–92
American actress

Insults

DENT Alan 1905–78
English theatre critic

Technique

DEPARDIEU Gérard b. 1948
French actor

Actors – Gérard Depardieu

DEVINE George 1910–65
English actor/director; co-founder of the
English Stage Company

Directors – George Devine

DICKENS Charles 1812–70
English writer (*David Copperfield, Bleak
House*)

Actors – Charles Dickens; Advice

DIETZ Howard 1898–1983
American lyricist and librettist

Tallulah Bankhead; Failure

DILLER Phyllis b. 1917
American comedienne

Actors – Phyllis Diller

DODD Ken(neth Arthur) b. 1931
British comedian

Comedy; Life

DORAN Dr. John 1807–78
English social historian

Playwrights – Aphra Behn

DOVER Kenneth James b. 1920
English scholar; professor of Greek

Greek Drama

DREW John 1853–1927
American actor, uncle of Ethel, John and
Lionel Barrymore

Actors – John Drew

DRUMMOND William 1585–1649
Scottish poet

Playwrights – Ben Jonson

DRYDEN John 1631–1700
English poet

*Actors – Nell Gwynne; Beaumont and
Fletcher; Life; Playwrights – Buckingham;
Shakespeare; Shakespeare's Plays –* The
Tempest

DUDLEY William b. 1947
English theatre designer

Critics – Kenneth Tynan

DUMAS Alexandre 1824–95
French novelist/playwright

Sarah Bernhardt; Prejudice

DU MAURIER Sir Gerald 1873–1934
English actor-manager

Actors – Gerald Du Maurier

DUNCAN Ronald b. 1914
British playwright

Playwrights

D'URFEY Thomas 1653–1723
British dramatist and song-writer

Opprobrium

**DURANTE Jimmy (James Francis)
1893–1980**
American actor/comedian, known as
'Schnozzle'

Shakespeare's Plays – Hamlet

DUSE Eleonora 1859–1924
Italian actress

*Actors – Eleonora Duse; Critical Abuse –
actors; Theatre*

ELDON John, 1st Earl of 1751–1838
English lawyer and politician

Sheridan

ELLIOTT Denholm 1922–92
English actor

Costume and Make-up

ELIOT T(homas) S(tearns) 1883–1965
American-born poet/critic/dramatist
(*Murder in the Cathedral*)

*Beaumont and Fletcher; Critical Abuse – plays;
Critics – Hazlitt; Musicals; Plays; Purpose*

ELLISTON Robert W. 1774–1831
English actor

*Actors – Robert Elliston; Critical Abuse –
actors*

ERVINE St. John 1883–1971
English playwright and theatre critic

Audiences

ESSLIN Martin b. 1918
Hungarian born critic and writer

Avant-garde; Directors

EURIPIDES 480–406 BC
Greek tragedian

Playwrights – Euripides

EVANS Dame Edith 1888–1976
English actress remembered for her
definitive portrayal of Lady Bracknell in
Wilde's *The Importance of Being Earnest*

Actors – Edith Evans; Shakespeare's Plays –
Macbeth; *Technique; Touring*

EVANS Gareth Lloyd
Contemporary British theatre critic

Playwrights – Harold Pinter

EVELYN John 1620–1706
English diarist

Shakespeare's Plays – Hamlet

FADIMAN Clifton b. 1904
American writer

Playwrights – Clare Boothe Luce

FALLON Gabriel b. 1923
Irish writer

Mrs Patrick Campbell

FELDMAN Marty 1933–83
British actor and comedy writer

Comedy

FERBER Edna 1887–1968
American writer; member of the
Algonquin Round Table

Critics – A. Woollcott; Producers – Jed Harris

FERGUSON Elsie 1885–1961
American actress

Telegrams

FERNALD John b. 1905
American-born theatre director

Audience Asides

FEYDEAU George 1862–1921
French dramatist, author of more than 60
farces

Playwrights – Feydeau

**FFRANGCON-DAVIES Dame Gwen
1891–1991**
British actress, famous for her Juliet, with
John Gielgud, in 1924; played her last
television part aged 100

Advice; Auditions; Ellen Terry

FIELD Eugene 1850–95
Theatre critic of the *Denver Tribune* in the
1880s

Critical Abuse – actors

FIELDING Henry 1707–54
English novelist (*Tom Jones*)

*Actors; Critical Abuse – plays; Shakespeare's
Plays – Hamlet*

**FIELDS W(illiam) C(laude)
Dukinfield 1880–1946**
American vaudeville comedian and film
star

Actors; Actors – Mae West; Advice

FINDLATER Richard b. 1921
British theatre critic

Peggy Ashcroft; Critical Abuse – plays; Theatre

FINNEY Albert b. 1936
British actor

Finance; Shakespeare's Plays – Hamlet

FISHER Eddie b. 1928
American singer

Insults

**FISKE Minnie Maddern (Marie
Augusta Davey) 1865–1932**
American actress

Actors – Minnie Maddern Fiske; Technique

FITZGERALD Barry 1888–1961
Irish actor

Actors – Barry Fitzgerald

FLECKNOE Richard d. 1678
Jesuit priest and playwright

Epitaphs

FLETCHER John 1579–1625
English dramatist, collaborator with
Beaumont

Beaumont and Fletcher

FOGARTY Elsie 1866–1945
Founder of the Central School of Speech
Training and Dramatic Art, London

Technique

FONTAINE Joan b. 1917
American actress

Vivien Leigh

FONTANNE Lynn 1887–1983
American actress, wife of Alfred Lunt

Insults; The Lunts

FOOTE Samuel 1720–77
English actor/dramatist

Critical Abuse – actors; Epitaphs

**FORBES-ROBERTSON Sir
Johnstone 1853–1937**
English actor-manager

Dedication

**FORD John (Sean O'Feeney) 1895–
1973**
American film director

Acting; Actors – Barry Fitzgerald

FOWLER Gene 1890–1960
American writer

Barrymores (John)

**FRÉDÉRICK (Antoine-Louis-Prosper
Lemaître) 1800–76**
French actor of Romantic drama

Actors – Frédérick

GABRIEL Gilbert W. 1890–1952
American theatre critic of *The World*,
1930s

Critical Abuse – plays

GAINSBOROUGH Thomas 1727–88
English landscape and portrait painter

Sarah Siddons

**GARLAND Judy (Frances Gumm)
1922–69**
American actress/singer/dancer

Insults; Stage Fright

GARLAND Robert 1895–1955
American theatre critic

Chekhov; Critical Abuse – plays

GARRICK David 1717–79
English actor-manager; renowned for his
versatility and the naturalism of his acting

*Comedy; Epitaphs; Fame; Fans; Garrick;
Prologues; Scenery and Lighting; Sheridan;
Technique; Telegrams*

GAXTON William 1893–1963
American actor

Telegrams

GENET Jean 1909–86
French playwright/novelist/poet; credited
with creating the 'Theatre of Cruelty'

Technique

GEORGE II 1683–1760
King of Great Britain and Ireland 1727–60

Shakespeare

GEORGE III 1738–1820
King of Great Britain and Ireland 1760–
1820

Shakespeare

GEORGE VI 1895–1952
King of Great Britain and Northern Ireland
1936–52

Ralph Richardson

GERHARDIE William 1895–1977
English writer

Playwrights – Somerset Maugham

GIBBS (Oliver) Wolcott 1902–58
American theatre critic for the *New Yorker*

Critical Abuse – plays; The Theatre

GIELGUD Sir John b. 1904
British actor/director

Actors – Vanessa Redgrave; Film and Television; John Gielgud; Shakespeare's Plays – Hamlet; Technique

GILBERT Sir William Schwenck 1836–1911
English poet/dramatist; librettist of the Gilbert and Sullivan comic operas (*The Mikado, The Pirates of Penzance*); built and owned the Garrick Theatre

Dressing Room Talk; Epitaphs; Insults; Irving; Shakespeare's Plays – Hamlet; Success; H.B. Tree

GILDER Rosamund 1896–1986
American writer and dramatic critic

Theatre

GILDON Charles 1665–1724
English critic and playwright

Actors – Mary Betterton

GILL Brendan b. 1914
American writer

Tallulah Bankhead

GILLIATT Penelope b. 1933
English writer; theatre critic of the *Observer* 1964–68

Peggy Ashcroft; Playwrights – Beckett

GINGOLD Hermione 1897–1987
English comedy actress

Actors – Donald Wolfit; Beginnings; Billing

GIRAUDOUX Jean 1882–1944
French playwright

Plays

GISH, Lillian b. 1893
American actress

Insults

GLENVILLE Peter b. 1913
English director

Film and Television

GOGARTY Oliver St. John 1878–1957
Irish poet and memoir writer

Playwrights – Lady Gregory

GOLDSMITH Oliver 1728–74
Irish playwright (*She Stoops to Conquer*), and novelist

Garrick; Epitaphs

GOODWIN Nat(haniel) Carl 1857–1919
American comedian

Broadway

GONCOURT Edmond de 1822–96
French novelist; founder of the Académie Goncourt

Sarah Bernhardt

GORDON Ruth 1896–1985
American actress; married to writer Garson Kanin

Acting; Critical Abuse – actors

GRAVES Robert 1895–1985
English poet and novelist

Shakespeare

GREENE Sir Graham 1904–91
British novelist

Success

GREENE Robert 1558–91
English dramatist

Shakespeare

GREGORY Lady 1852–1932
Irish playwright associated with the Abbey
Theatre

Playwrights – Lady Gregory

GREVILLE Samuel *fl.* **1767**
First recorded American professional actor

Beginnings

GRIFFITH Hubert 1896–1953
British drama critic and dramatist

Critical Abuse – actors; Olivier

GUEDALLA Philip 1889–1944
English historian and biographer

J.M. Barrie

GUINNESS Mrs *fl.* **1890s**
Member of Frank Benson's Shakespeare
Company

Quick Thinking

GUINNESS Sir Alec b. 1914
English actor

Critics – Kenneth Tynan; John Gielgud

**GUTHRIE Sir (William) Tyrone
1900–71**
English actor and director

*Advice; Directors; Film and Television; Olivier;
Talent*

GWYNNE Nell (Eleanor) *c.* **1650–87**
English actress, mistress of Charles II

Actors – Nell Gwynne

HAGGARD Stephen 1911–43
English actor, co-author with Athene
Seyler of *The Art of Comedy*

Comedy

HALE Lionel 1909–76
British journalist and playwright

Critical Abuse – plays

HALL George b. 1925
Former Director of the Acting Course at
the Central School of Speech and Drama
in London

Dressing Room Talk

HALL Sir Peter b. 1930
British director/producer. Created the
Royal Shakespeare Company 1960;
succeeded Olivier as Director of the
National Theatre

*Peggy Ashcroft; Audiences; Costume and
Make-up; Critics; Directors; Directors – Peter
Hall; Finance; First Nights; Life; Plays;
Playwrights – Brecht; The Press; Rehearsals;
Restoration Theatre; Shakespeare;
Shakespeare's Plays – Hamlet; Success;
Theatre*

HAMMOND Percy 1873–1936
American theatre critic for the *New York
Herald Tribune*

Critical Abuse – plays; Criticism

HAMPTON Christopher b. 1946
British playwright *(Les Liaisons Dangereuses)*

Critics

HANDS Terry b. 1941
British theatre director. Associated most
closely with the Royal Shakespeare
Company

Motivation

HAPGOOD Norman 1868–1937
American theatre critic

Shakespeare's Plays – Hamlet

HARDWICKE Sir Cedric 1893–1964
British actor

*Actors; Actors – Cedric Hardwicke; Critical
Abuse – actors; Film and Television;
Technique*

HARE Augustus 1792–1834
English clergyman and writer; brother of
Julius Hare

Life

HARE David b. 1947
British playwright (*Plenty, Pravda*)

Purpose

HARE Julius 1795–1855
English clergyman and essayist; brother of
Augustus Hare

Life

**HARRIMAN Margaret Case *c.* 1904–
1966**
American journalist whose father (Frank
Case) had run the Algonquin Hotel during
the heyday of the Algonquin Round Table

Tallulah Bankhead

HARRIS Frank 1856–1931
British writer and journalist

Shakespeare; G.B. Shaw

HARRIS Jed 1900–79
American theatrical producer

Critics; Epitaphs; Producers – Jed Harris

HARRIS Richard b. 1932
Irish actor

*Actors – Richard Harris; Shakespeare's Plays –
Cymbeline*

HARRISON Sir Rex 1908–90
British actor and film star

Beginnings

HART Moss 1904–61
American playwright and director

Plays

HAUSER Frank b. 1922
British theatre director

Motivation

HAYES Helen (Brown) b. 1900
American actress, the 'First Lady' of
American theatre

*Actors – Helen Hayes; Critical Abuse – actors;
Fame; Purpose; Theatre*

HAZLITT William 1778–1830
English essayist and theatre critic for *The
Examiner* and *The Morning Chronicle*

*Critics – Hazlitt; Finance; Kean; Shakespeare;
Sheridan; Sarah Siddons*

HECHT Ben 1894–1964
American journalist

Sarah Bernhardt

HEINE Heinrich 1797–1856
German poet and essayist

Playwrights – Schiller

HELLMAN Lillian 1905–84
American playwright (*The Little Foxes*)

*Tallulah Bankhead; Playwrights – Lillian
Hellman*

HELPMANN Robert 1909–86
Australian-born actor/dancer/
choreographer

Musicals

HEMINGWAY Ernest 1899–1961
American war correspondent and novelist
(*For Whom the Bell Tolls*)

Failure; Insults

HEPBURN Katharine b. 1907
American actress and film star

Acting; Critical Abuse – actors

HERFORD Oliver 1863–1935
American writer

Actors

HEROLD Don 1889–1966
American journalist

Noël Coward

HESTON Charlton b. 1922
American actor and film star

Actors – Richard Harris

HICKS Sir (Edward) Seymour 1871–1948
English actor-manager

Amateurs

HILL Benny 1925–92
British comedian

Show Business

HILLER Dame Wendy b. 1912
British actress

Method Acting

HILLGATE Jason
Contemporary British journalist

Shakespeare's Plays – Hamlet

HOBSON Sir Harold 1904–92
English theatre critic for the *Sunday Times* for over 40 years

Shakespeare's Plays – Hamlet, Othello

HOFFMAN Dustin b. 1937
American actor and film star

Advice

HOFFMAN Irving *fl.* 1930s/40s
New York correspondent for the *Hollywood Reporter*

Critical Abuse – plays

HOPE Anthony (Sir Anthony Hope Hawkins) 1863–1933
English novelist (*The Prisoner of Zenda*)

J.M. Barrie; Epitaphs – W.S. Gilbert

HOPE Bob b. 1903
American comedian and actor

Audiences

HOPPER Hedda 1890–1966
American actress turned gossip columnist

Actors – Hedda Hopper

HORDERN Sir Michael b. 1911
British actor

Critical Abuse – actors

HOUDAR DE LA MOTTE Antoine 1672–1731
French poet/playwright

Censorship

HOUSSAYE Arsène *fl.* 1899
Director of the Comédie Française

Playwrights

HOWARD Leslie 1893–1943
English actor and film star

Shakespeare's Plays – Hamlet

HUNT Hugh b. 1911
English writer

Insults

HUGO Victor 1802–85
French poet/novelist (*Les Misérables*), and playwright (*Ruy Blas*)

Playwrights – Victor Hugo

HUNEKER James 1860–1921
American theatre critic for *The Sun* and *The New York Times*

Ibsen

HUNT (James Henry) Leigh 1784–1859
English poet and essayist

Actors – Robert Elliston, J.P. Kemble; Critics

HURREN Kenneth
Contemporary British theatre critic

Critical Abuse – actors

HUXLEY Aldous 1894–1963
British novelist (*Brave New World*)

Greek Drama

HYDE WHITE Wilfrid 1903–90
British actor

Beginnings; Critical Abuse – actors; Directors; Oscar Wilde

IBSEN Henrik 1828–1906
Norwegian poet and dramatist (*A Doll's House, Ghosts*)

Mrs Patrick Campbell; Critical Abuse – plays; Ibsen

IONESCO Eugene b. 1912
Romanian-born French playwright

Playwrights – Ionesco; Theatre

INVERCLYDE Lady June *fl.* 1940s/50s
English actress

Insults

IRVING Sir Henry 1838–1905
English actor-manager. First actor to be knighted for services to the theatre. Enjoyed a phenomenal success with *The Bells*. Ran the Lyceum Theatre with Ellen Terry as his leading lady

Advice; Fame; Scenery and Lighting; Shakespeare's Plays – Richard III; Ellen Terry

JACKSON Glenda b. 1936
British actress and politician

Beginnings; Directors – Peter Hall; Technique

JACOBI Derek b. 1938
British actor

Acting; Advice; Stage Fright

JAMES Clive b. 1939
Australian-born writer and critic

Olivier

JAMES Henry 1843–1916
Anglophile American novelist

Acting; Irving; Ellen Terry

JARVIS Martin b. 1941
British actor

Film and Television

JEANS Ronald 1887–??
English actor

Actors; First Nights

JEFFERSON Joseph 1829–1905
American actor/comedian

Technique

JENNINGS H.J. *fl. c.* 1910
English journalist

Critical Abuse – plays

JEROME Jerome K(lapka) 1859–1927
English playwright and writer (*Three Men in a Boat*)

Beginnings; Critical Abuse – plays; Finance

JESSEL George 1898–1981
American actor/producer

Quick Thinking

JOHNSON Celia 1908–82
British actress best remembered for her role in the film *Brief Encounter*

Actors – Celia Johnson

JOHNSON Richard b. 1927
British actor and film star

Film and Television

JOHNSON Dr. Samuel 1709–84
English lexicographer/critic

Actors; Actors – Thomas Sheridan; Criticism; Epitaphs – Goldsmith, Garrick; Playwrights – Corneille; Prologues; Shakespeare; Sarah Siddons

JONES Henry Arthur 1851–1929
Prolific and successful English playwright (*The Silver King*)

Insults; Playwrights – Henry Jones; G.B. Shaw

JONSON Ben 1572–1637
English poet and dramatist (*Volpone*); contemporary of Shakespeare who appeared in his play *Every Man in His Humour*

Actors – Alleyn, Burbage; Beaumont and Fletcher; Epitaphs; Shakespeare; Theatre

JOUVET Louis 1887–1951
French director/actor

Avant-garde

JOYCE James 1882–1941
Irish writer (*Ulysses*)

G.B. Shaw

KAEL Pauline b. 1919
American film and theatre critic

Insults

KALEM T.E.
American journalist

Tennessee Williams

KAUFMAN George S. 1889–1961
American playwright (*The Man Who Came to Dinner*) and wit

Critical Abuse – actors; Critical Abuse – plays; Epitaphs; Producers – Jed Harris; Telegrams

KAUFMAN Wolfe *fl.* **1940s/50s**
American journalist

Vivien Leigh

KEAN Edmund 1789–1833
The most famous English actor of his day. Renowned for playing the major Shakespearean roles at Drury Lane.

Comedy; Kean; Shakespeare's Plays – Hamlet, Romeo and Juliet

KEATING Fred 1897–1961
American actor

Tallulah Bankhead

KEMBLE Charles 1775–1854
English actor specializing in romantic parts such as Romeo; brother of John Kemble and Sarah Siddons, father of Fanny Kemble

Slips of the Tongue

KEMBLE Fanny (Francis) 1809–93
English actress and writer, niece of Sarah Siddons

Kean

KEMBLE John Philip 1757–1823
English tragedian; brother of Sarah Siddons

Actors – J.P. Kemble; Kean

KENDAL Dame Margaret (Madge) 1845–1939
English actress

Sarah Bernhardt; Child Actors; Quick Thinking

KENNEDY Joseph P. 1888–1969
American self-made multi-millionaire and sometime Ambassador to the United Kingdom

Actors

KERR Deborah b. 1921
British actress best remembered for her role in the film *The King and I*

Actors – Deborah Kerr

KERR Jean b. 1923
American playwright, wife of Walter Kerr

Actors; Adaptations; Audiences; Comedy

KERR Walter F. b. 1913
American journalist and critic; husband of Jean Kerr

Actors – Elizabeth Taylor; Critical Abuse – plays; Critics; Producers – David Merrick

KITCHIN Laurence b. 1913
English writer

Actors

KLEIN John David
Contemporary American theatre critic

Critical Abuse – plays

KNOWLES Sheridan 1784–1862
Irish dramatist

Sarah Siddons

KRETZMER Herbert b. 1925
British journalist and theatre critic

Critical Abuse – plays

KRONENBURGER Louis 1904–80
American theatre critic

Critical Abuse – plays (Mae West)

LACTANTIUS Lucius Caelius *fl.* **4th century AD**
Christian theologian

Comedy

LAMB Charles 1775–1834
English essayist; author, with his sister Mary, of *Tales of Shakespeare*

Finance; Shakespeare's Plays – Hamlet

LANDOR Walter Savage 1775–1864
English poet

Shakespeare

LANGFORD Bonnie b. 1964
English singer/dancer/actress; fomer child star

Child Actors; Critical Abuse – plays

LANGNER Lawrence 1890–1962
American co-founder of the Theater Guild

Dedication

LANGTRY Lillie (Emilie) 1853–1929
Jersey-born society beauty, mistress of the Prince of Wales (Edward VII). Known as The Jersey Lily. Later achieved fame as an actress

Actors – Lillie Langtry; Slips of the Tongue

LAUGHTON Charles 1899–1962
English-born American actor

Critical Abuse – actors; Film and Televison; Method Acting; Shakespeare's Plays – Henry V; *Technique*

LAWFORD Peter 1923–84
British actor, married to President Kennedy's sister

Actors

LAWRENCE D(avid) H(erbert) 1885–1930
English poet and novelist (*Sons and Lovers, Lady Chatterley's Lover*)

Critical Abuse – plays (G.B. Shaw); Shakespeare; Tennessee Williams

LAWRENCE Gertrude 1898–1952
British actress/singer. Close associate of Noël Coward

Actors – Gertrude Lawrence; Critical Abuse – actors

LEAN David 1908–91
British film director (*Lawrence of Arabia*)

Advice

LE GALLIENNE Richard 1866–1947
British novelist

Oscar Wilde

LEIGH Vivien (Vivian Mary Hartley) 1913–67
British actress renowned for her beauty. Star of the film *Gone With the Wind*. Wife of Laurence Olivier with whom she frequently worked

Costume and Make-up (Olivier); Vivien Leigh; Shakespeare's Plays – Macbeth

LENIN (formerly Ulyanov) Vladimir Ilyich 1870–1924
Russian statesman and revolutionary

G.B. Shaw

LENO Dan (George Galvin) 1860–1904
Phenomenally popular English music hall star

Epitaphs

LESLEY Cole (Leonard Cole) 1911–80
Noël Coward's private secretary and biographer

Telegrams

LEVANT Oscar 1906–72
American actor/composer

Actors – Phyllis Diller; Musicals

LEVIN Bernard b. 1928
British writer and critic

Critical Abuse – actors; Critical Abuse – plays; Musicals

LEVINSON L.L. 1905–74
American journalist

Musicals; Producers

LEWES George Henry 1817–78
English writer. Editor and critic of *The Leader*

Actors – Frédérick, Rachel

LEWIS Percy Wyndham 1884–1957
Artist and novelist; born in Maine, USA of English parents

G.B. Shaw

LICHTENBERG Georg Christoph 1742–99
German physicist and satirist

Shakespeare

LILLIE Bea(trice) (Lady Peel) 1898–1989
Canadian born comedienne

Actors – Bea Lillie; Insults (Tallulah Bankhead)

LINCOLN Abraham 1809–65
16th President of the United States. Assassinated during a visit to the theatre

Comedy; Shakespeare

LIPMAN Maureen b. 1946
British actress/writer

Shakespeare; Quick Thinking

LISTER Moira b. 1923
English actress

Critical Abuse – actors

LITTLEWOOD (Maudie) Joan b. 1914
English director, founder of Theatre Workshop

Actors; Producers

LIVINGS Henry b. 1929
English actor

Costume and Make-up

LLOYD Marie (Matilda Alice Victoria Wood) 1870–1922
British music hall star, famous for her risqué songs

Epitaphs; Music hall/Vaudeville

LOGAN Joshua b. 1908
American playwright/producer

Chekhov

LONGFORD Lady (Christine Patti Trew) d. 1980
Irish playwright

Critical Abuse – plays

LOVE Montague 1897–1943
English actor

Critical Abuse – actors

LUCE Clare Boothe 1903–87
American playwright

Playwrights – Luce

LUNT Alfred 1893–1977
Highly successful American actor/producer/director. Married to Lynne Fontanne

The Lunts

McCAMBRIDGE Mercedes b. 1918
American actress

Critics – A. Woollcott

McCAREY Leo *fl.* 1950s
American journalist

Star Quality

MacCARTHY Sir Desmond 1877–1952
English critic

H.B. Tree

MACAULAY Thomas Babington, 1st Baron 1800–59
English historian and essayist

Actors – Anne Bracegirdle; Playwrights – Wycherley

McEWAN Geraldine b. 1932
English actress

Critical Abuse – actors

MACLIAMMOIR Micheàl (Alfred Willmore) 1899–1978
Irish actor. Co-founder of the Gate Theatre in Dublin

Acting; Star Quality

McCOWEN Alec b. 1925
British actor

Beginnings; Vivien Leigh; Technique

McKELLEN Sir Ian b. 1939
British actor

Shakespeare's Plays – Hamlet

MACREADY William Charles 1793–1873
English actor, rival of Kean

Actors – Master Betty; Irving; Technique

McSHANE Ian b. 1942
British actor

Film and Television

MAETERLINCK Count Maurice 1862–1949
Nobel Prize winning Belgian playwright. Renowned for his erudition and involvement in the symbolist movement

Mrs Patrick Campbell; Critical Abuse – plays; Playwrights – Maeterlinck

MAMET David b. 1947
American playwright (*Glengarry Glen Ross*)

Playwrights – Mamet

MANEY Richard 1891–1968
American theatre publicist

Dressing Room Talk

MANKIEWICZ Herman J. 1897–1953
American playwright; co-wrote *Citizen Kane* with Orson Welles

Playwrights – Orson Welles

MARCH Frederic 1897–1975
American actor

Critical Abuse – actors

MARLOWE Christopher 1564–93
English dramatist (*Tamburlaine the Great, The Tragical History of Dr. Faustus*)

Beaumont and Fletcher; Playwrights – Marlowe

MARTIN Mary 1913–90
American actress best known for her role in the musical *South Pacific*

Broadway; Recognition; Talent

MARX Harpo (Arthur) 1893–1964
American actor/comedian; one of the Marx Brothers

Critical Abuse – plays; Oscar Levant

MARX Groucho (Julius) 1890–1977
American actor/comedian; one of the Marx Brothers

Critical Abuse – plays

MARX Karl 1818–63
German founder of international communism

Shakespeare's Plays – The Merry Wives of Windsor

MASSEY Daniel b. 1933
British actor; son of Raymond Massey and godson of Noël Coward

Actors – Gertrude Lawrence; Noël Coward; Star Quality

MASSEY Raymond 1896–1984
Canadian-born actor/director

Critical Abuse – actors

MASSON Tom 1866–1934
American actor/critic

Shakespeare's Plays – Hamlet

MATTHAU Walter b. 1920
American actor

Acting; Film and Television; Vivien Leigh

**MATTHEWS A(lfred) E(dward)
1869–1960**
English actor

Critical Abuse – actors

MATURA Mustapha b. 1939
West Indian-born playwright

Playwrights – Mustapha Matura

**MAUGHAM (William) Somerset
1874–1965**
British novelist and playwright (*The Circle*)

Plays; Playwrights – Somerset Maugham

**MENCKEN H(enry) L(ouis) 1880–
1956**
American writer and critic

Comedy; Finance; Shakespeare

MEREDITH Burgess b. 1908
American actor/director/producer

Telegrams

MEREDITH George 1828–1909
English novelist (*Diana of the Crossways*)

Comedy

MERMAN Ethel 1904–84
American actress/singer

Talent (Mary Martin)

MERRICK David b. 1911
American producer/actor

Critics; Producers – David Merrick

MILES Sir Bernard 1907–91
English actor/manager; founder of the
Mermaid Theatre

Purpose

MILLER Arthur b. 1915
American playwright (*The Crucible*)

Playwrights – Arthur Miller

MILLS Sir John b. 1908
English actor

Audience Asides; Costume and Make-up

MILNE A(lan) A(lexander) 1882–1956
English novelist/playwright (*Mr Pym Passes
By*) and children's writer (*Winnie the Pooh*)

*Actors – Du Maurier; Audiences; Plays;
Playwrights*

MILTON Ernest 1890–1974
British actor

Advice

MILTON John 1608–74
English poet (*Paradise Lost*)

Shakespeare

MITFORD Mary Russell 1787–1855
English novelist and dramatist

Kean

MIZNER Addison 1872–1933
American architect

Actors

MIZNER Walter 1876–1933
American actor/playwright/entrepreneur
and Broadway character

Actors; Finance

**MOLIÈRE (Jean Baptiste Poquelin)
1622–73**
French playwright (*Le Misanthrope, Le
Malade Imaginaire*)

Playwrights – Molière

MOLNÁR Ferenc (Neumann) 1878–1952
Hungarian novelist and playwright (*The Good Fairy*)

Success

MOORE George 1852–1933
Irish novelist (*Esther Waters*); helped found the Abbey Theatre in Dublin

Acting; Motivation; Theatre; Oscar Wilde

MORAND Paul 1889–1975
French diplomat and writer

Broadway

MORE Hannah 1745–1833
English writer

Shakespeare's Plays – Hamlet

MOREHOUSE Ward 1899–1966
American writer

Ziegfeld

MORLEY Robert 1908–92
English actor

Actors; Advice; Playwrights

MORLEY Sheridan b. 1941
English writer and critic, son of Robert Morley

Critical Abuse – plays; Playwrights – Beckett

MORSE Robert b. 1931
American actor

Theatre

MORTIMER John b. 1923
British lawyer/novelist/playwright (*A Voyage Round My Father*)

Plays

MOSS Hugh fl. 1910
English actor

H.B. Tree

MUNI Paul (Muni Weisenfreund) 1895–1967
American-Yiddish actor

Advice

MURPHY Tom b. 1935
Irish playwright

Playwrights – Tom Murphy

NADZO Guido fl. 1930s
American actor

Critical Abuse – actors

NASH (Frederic) Ogden 1902–71
American poet who wrote light/comic verse

Noël Coward

NATHAN George Jean 1882–1958
American writer and theatre critic for *Vanity Fair* and *Newsweek*

Actors; Actors – Eleonora Duse; Tallulah Bankhead; J.M. Barrie; Noël Coward; Critical Abuse – plays; Critics – G.J. Nathan; First Nights; Musicals; Music hall; Plays; Playwrights – Sartre; Shakespeare's Plays – Hamlet

NIETZSCHE Friedrich 1844–1900
German philosopher and critic

Playwrights – Hugo

NIGHTINGALE Benedict b. 1939
British theatre critic

Directors – Peter Brook; Playwrights – Mustapha Matura

NIVEN David (James Nevins) 1910–83
English actor and film star

Acting; Barrymores (John)

NOBLE Adrian b. 1950
British theatre director; Artistic Director of the Royal Shakespeare Company

Theatre

NORTHBROOKE John *fl.* **1570**
English preacher and moralist

Opprobrium

NOVELLO Ivor (David Ivor Davies)
Welsh actor/playwright and composer
(*Keep the Home Fires Burning*)

Actors – Novello; Critical Abuse – plays;
Recognition

NUGENT Frank 1908–65
American critic

Critical Abuse – actors

ODETS Clifford 1906–63
American left-wing playwright

Critical Abuse – plays

OLIVER Freddie b. 1962
British writer

Oscar Wilde

**OLIVIER Sir Laurence Kerr (Baron
Olivier) 1907–89**
English actor/director/producer renowned
for the physical energy of his acting.
Widely regarded as the foremost English
speaking actor of the 20th century. Played
all the great Shakespearean roles, most
notably Richard III, Hamlet, Othello and
Henry V. Married to Vivien Leigh 1940–
61. Director of the National Theatre
1962–73

*Acting; Actors – Deborah Kerr, Anthony
Quayle, Donald Wolfit; Advice; Audience
Asides; Beginnings; Costume and Make-up;
Fame; Life; Motivation; The Press; Purpose;
Shakespeare's Plays – Hamlet, Henry V,
Merchant of Venice, Othello, Romeo and
Juliet; Star Quality; Success; Talent;
Technique*

O'NEILL Eugene 1888–1953
American playwright (*The Iceman Cometh*)

Playwrights – O'Neill

ORIGEN AD **185–254**
Early Christian church father and school
master

Censorship

OSBORNE John b. 1929
English playwright (*Look Back in Anger*).
Pioneer of realism in post-war theatre

*Noël Coward; Criticism; Critics; Directors –
George Devine; Musicals; Music hall; Plays;
Playwrights; Playwrights – J. Osborne;
Rehearsals; Shakespeare's Plays – Hamlet;
G.B. Shaw; Stage Management; Touring*

O'TOOLE Fintan
Contemporary Irish critic and writer

Playwrights – Tom Murphy

O'TOOLE Peter b. 1932
Irish actor and film star (*Lawrence of Arabia*)

*Bad Habits; Actors – O'Toole; Critical Abuse
– actors*

OVID (Publius Ovidius Naso) 43 BC–
AD **17**
Latin poet

Audiences

PAAR Jack *fl.* **1940s/50s**
American actor

Oscar Levant

PACK Major Richardson 1682–1728
English soldier and writer

Playwrights – Wycherley

PAGNOL Marcel 1895–1974
French playwright

Broadway

PALMER Lilli (Peiser) 1914–86
German-born actress working in UK and
America

G.B. Shaw

PARKER Dorothy 1893–1967
American writer/humorist/critic; member of the influential Algonquin Round Table group of critics

Actors – Edith Evans; Critical Abuse – actors (Marion Davies); Critical Abuse – plays; Critics – Dorothy Parker; Epitaphs; First Nights; Oscar Wilde

PATRICK David *fl.* **1903**
English writer and editor (*Chambers Encyclopaedia of English Literature*)

Actors – Colley Cibber

PEARSON Hesketh 1887–1964
British actor and biographer

H.B. Tree

PEMBERTON Brock 1886–1950
American writer

Critics – A. Woollcott

PEPYS Samuel 1633–1703
English diarist

Actors – Nell Gwynne; Shakespeare's plays – Macbeth, Midsummer Night's Dream, Romeo and Juliet

PETAN Zarco
Contemporary theatre director

Directors

PINERO Sir Arthur Wing 1855–1934
English playwright (*The Gay Lord Quex*)

Kean; Playwrights – Pinero

PINTER Harold (Harold Da Pinta) b. 1930
British playwright (*The Birthday Party, No Man's Land*)

Critical Abuse – plays; Playwrights – Pinter

PIRANDELLO Luigi 1867–1936
Italian dramatist (*Six Characters In Search Of An Author*)

Playwrights – Pirandello

PLATO *c.* **427–** *c.* **347** BC
Athenian philosopher, disciple of Socrates

Playwrights – Aristophanes

PLOWRIGHT Joan b. 1929
English actress. Third wife of Laurence Olivier

Olivier

PLUMMER Christopher b. 1929
Canadian actor based in Hollywood

Actors – Julie Andrews

POLLOCK Channing 1880–1946
American playwright and critic

Critics

POPE Alexander 1688–1744
English poet and satirist

Audiences; Garrick; Shakespeare

PORTER Cole 1891–1964
American composer and lyricist

Motivation; Shakespeare

PORTMAN Eric 1903–69
British actor

Star Quality; Technique

POTTER John S. 1806–69
American actor-manager

Finance

PRIESTLEY J(ohn) B(oynton) 1894–1984
English novelist and playwright (*Dangerous Corner, When We Are Married*)

Actors

PRITCHARD Hannah 1711–68
English actress

Dedication

PRYNNE William 1600–69
English Puritan pamphleteer

Opprobrium

QUAYLE Sir (John) Anthony 1913–89
British actor/director/manager; director
of the theatre at Stratford-upon-Avon
1948–56

Actors – Anthony Quayle

QUAYLE Douglas 1904–57
British actor

Advice; Epitaphs

QUAYLE John b. 1936
British actor

Advice

QUILLEY Denis b. 1927
British actor

Critical Abuse – actors

QUIN James 1693–1766
English tragedian of the declamatory
school of acting

Auditions

QUINN Anthony b. 1915
American actor

Technique

RACHEL (Elisa Felix) 1821–58
French tragedienne, famous for her
interpretation of Racine's Phèdre

Actors; – Rachel; Insults

RATHBONE Basil 1892–1967
South African-born actor, famous in the
role of Sherlock Holmes

Actors – Basil Rathbone

RATTIGAN Sir Terence 1911–79
English playwright (*French Without Tears,
The Winslow Boy*)

Audiences

REDGRAVE Sir Michael 1908–85
English actor

Olivier

REDGRAVE Vanessa b. 1937
British actress, daughter of Michael
Redgrave and Rachel Kempson. Holds
radical political views

Actors – Vanessa Redgrave; Advice; Theatre

REED Rex b. 1938
American theatre critic

Tennessee Williams

REYNOLDS Sir Joshua 1723–92
English portrait painter

Garrick

RICH Frank b. 1949
American theatre critic sometimes known
as the Butcher of Broadway

Musicals; Producers – David Merrick

RICHARDS Dick *fl*. 1950s/60s
English show business journalist and
theatre critic

Noël Coward; Kean

RICHARDSON Sir Ralph 1902–83
English actor

*Acting; Actors – Sybil Thorndike; Advice;
Audiences; Criticism; Film and Television;
Ralph Richardson; Shakespeare's plays –
Hamlet, Othello; Technique*

RICHARDSON Tony 1928–92
English theatre and film director (*Tom
Jones*)

Theatre

RIGG Diana b. 1938
British actress

Insults

ROBINSON David
Contemporary British journalist

Actors – Gérard Depardieu

ROBINSON Edward G. (Emanuel Goldenberg) 1893–1973
American actor and film star

Barrymores (Ethel)

ROBINSON Henry Crabb 1775–1867
English diarist

Critical Abuse – actors; Sarah Siddons

ROBINSON Jay b. 1930
American actor/producer

Critical Abuse – actors

ROGERS Ginger (Virginia) b. 1911
American actress/film star/dancer, famous for her screen partnership with Fred Astaire

Advice

ROGERS Samuel 1763–1855
English poet and essayist

Garrick; Scenery and Lighting

ROSE Billy 1899–1966
American impresario and circus proprietor known as The Midget Maestro of Broadway

Tallulah Bankhead; Critical Abuse – plays; Finance; Oscar Levant; Producers – Billy Rose

RUGGLES Eleanor b. 1916
American biographer

Dedication

RUNYON (Alfred) Damon 1884–1946
American journalist and short story writer. The musical *Guys and Dolls* was based on one of his stories

Broadway

RUSSELL Bertrand, 3rd Earl 1872–1970
English philosopher/mathematician/pacifist

G.B. Shaw

RUTHERFORD Dame Margaret 1892–1972
British actress

Actors – Margaret Rutherford

RYMER Thomas 1641–1731
English critic

Shakespeare's plays – Othello

SAINTSBURY George 1845–1933
English writer and scholar

Playwrights – Molière

SAKI Pen-name of H(ector) H(ugh) Munro 1870–1916
British novelist and short story writer

G.B. Shaw

SALINGER J(erome) D(avid) b. 1919
American novelist (*Catcher in the Rye*)

Opprobrium

SANDERS George 1906–72
British actor and film star

Acting; Actors

SARTRE Jean Paul 1905–80
French existentialist philosopher/political activist/literary critic novelist and playwright (*Huis Clos, Kean*)

Actors; Motivation

SCHILDKRAUT Joseph 1895–1964
Austrian-Yiddish actor working in the USA

Insults

SCHILLER (Johann) Friedrich 1759–1805
German dramatist and poet

Playwrights – Schiller

SCOFIELD Paul b. 1922
British actor

Critical Abuse – actors

SCOTT Clement *fl.* **1891**
English theatre critic for the *Daily Telegraph, Sporting and Dramatic News*

Actors; Ibsen

SCOTT Sir Walter 1771–1832
Scottish novelist (*Ivanhoe*) and poet

Audiences

SEVERO Richard b. 1932
American writer

Actors – Monty Woolley

SEYLER Athene 1889–1990
British actress; author, with Stephen Haggard, of *The Craft of Comedy*

Actors – Athene Seyler; Comedy; Costume and Make-up

SHAKESPEARE William 1564–1616
English dramatist and poet, born in Stratford-upon-Avon. Generally accepted as the world's greatest playwright. The most performed dramatist in the world, his 37 plays include *Midsummer Night's Dream, Romeo and Juliet, Twelfth Night, Hamlet, Othello* and *King Lear.*

Actors – Colley Cibber; Advice; Critical Abuse – plays; Epilogues; Epitaphs; Life; Plays; Playwrights – Corneille; Shakespeare; Shakespeare's Plays; G.B. Shaw; Star Quality

SHARIF Omar b. 1932
Egyptian-born actor and film star

Actors – Peter O'Toole

SHAW George Bernard 1856–1950
Irish critic/playwright (*St. Joan, Pygmalion*) with radical beliefs about everything from vegetarianism to capitalism

Acting; Actors; Actors – Eleonora Duse, Cedric Hardwicke; Ambition; Audiences; J.M. Barrie; Beaumont and Fletcher; Mrs Patrick Campbell; Censorship; Costume and Make-up; Critical Abuse – plays; Criticism; Critics; Directors; Epitaphs; Finance; Insults; Irving; Vivien Leigh; Plays; Playwrights; Playwrights – Maeterlinck, Marlowe; Shakespeare; G.B.

Shaw; R.B. Sheridan; Telegrams; Ellen Terry; Oscar Wilde

SHERIDAN Richard Brinsley 1751–1816
Irish politician and playwright (*The School for Scandal, The Rivals*)

Critics; Plays; Purpose; R.B. Sheridan

SHERIDAN Thomas 1719–88
Irish actor; father of R.B. Sheridan

Actors – Thomas Sheridan

SHERWOOD Robert 1896–1955
American playwright (*Abe Lincoln in Illinois, Tovarich*)

The Lunts

SHOALES Ian b. 1949
American critic

Musicals

SHULMAN Milton b. 1913
Canadian-born British theatre critic for the *Evening Standard*

Critical Abuse – actors

SIDDONS Mrs (née Sarah Kemble) 1755–1831
English actress. The foremost tragedienne of her generation

Sarah Siddons; Technique

SIDDONS William 1744–1818
English actor, husband of Sarah Siddons

Sarah Siddons

SIGNORET Simone 1921–85
French actress

Actors – Hedda Hopper; Shakespeare's plays – Macbeth

SIMON John b. 1925
American theatre critic

Critical Abuse – actors; Insults

SINDEN Donald b. 1923
English actor

Advice

SKINNER Otis 1858–1942
American actor

Barrymores (Maurice)

SKINNER Cornelia Otis 1902–79
American actress and diseuse

Telegrams

SMITH Dame Maggie (Natalie) b. 1934
British actress

Beginnings

SOTHERN Edward Askew (Douglas Stewart) 1826–81
English actor who worked successfully for long periods in the United States

Quick Thinking

SPATE Roger
Contemporary British journalist

Critical Abuse – actors

STANISLAVSKI Constantin (Sergeivitch Alexeyev) 1865–1938
Russian actor/producer/teacher; developed a scheme for teaching acting technique based on the psychology of the characters portrayed and the actor's innate capacity for self-expression. This was later developed by Lee Strasberg as 'Method' acting

Advice; Insults; Method Acting; Technique.

STEPHENS Yorke 1862–1937
English actor

Critical Abuse – actors

STERN G.B. 1890–1973
American journalist

The Lunts

STEVENS Ashton 1872–1951
American writer

Actors – Bea Lillie

STEYN Mark
Contemporary British journalist

Musicals

STEYNE Geoffrey fl. 1917
American actor

Critical Abuse – actors

STIRLING Fanny 1813–95
English actress famous for her comedy roles

Actors

STOPPARD Tom b. 1937
Czechoslovakian-born British playwright (*Rosencrantz and Guildenstern are Dead, Jumpers*)

Critical Abuse – plays; Plays; Playwrights – Tom Stoppard

STOREY David b. 1933
English playwright (*Home, The Changing Room*)

Critical Abuse – plays

STRACHEY (Giles) Lytton 1880–1932
English biographer

Oscar Wilde

STRASBERG Lee 1901–82
American director/producer/teacher; found r of the Actors' Studio in New York where he worked with actors using the methods developed by Stanislavski

Method Acting

STRINDBERG (Johan) August 1849–1912
Swedish playwright (*Miss Julie, The Dance of Death*)

Playwrights – Strindberg

STUBBES Philip d. 1593
English Puritan pamphleteer

Opprobrium

SWAFFER Hannan 1879–1962
American critic

Critical Abuse – plays

SWINBURNE Algernon C. 1837–1909
English poet and critic

Playwrights – Marlowe; Oscar Wilde

SYDNEY Sir Philip 1554–86
English poet

Scenery and Lighting

TASHMAN Lilyan 1900–34
American actress

Ambition

TALMADGE Norma 1897–1957
American actress

Fans

TAYLOR Elizabeth b. 1932
British-born American actress and film star
(*National Velvet, Cat on a Hot Tin Roof*)

Actors – Richard Burton, Elizabeth Taylor

TEMPEST Dame Marie (Mary Susan Etherington) 1864–1942
English actress

Actors – Marie Tempest

TENNYSON Alfred, Lord 1809–1902
English poet

Playwrights – Ben Jonson

TERRY Dame Ellen 1847–1928
English actress; her partnership with Henry
Irving at the Lyceum dominated London
theatre in the late 19th century

*Advice; Beginnings (Olivier); Irving;
Shakespeare's Plays – Macbeth; G.B. Shaw;
Star Quality; Technique*

THOMAS Dylan 1914–53
Welsh poet (*Under Milk Wood*)

G.B. Shaw

THORNDIKE Dame Sybil 1882–1976
British actress who played the title role in
the first production of Shaw's *St. Joan*

Actors; Actors – Sybil Thorndike; Ellen Terry

**TOLSTOY Count Leo Nikolayevich
1828–1910**
Russian novelist (*War and Peace*) and
philosopher

*Censorship; Chekhov; Critical Abuse – plays;
Shakespeare*

**TREE Sir Herbert Beerbohm 1853–
1917**
English actor-manager, half brother of Max
Beerbohm; Tree was a flamboyant
character actor and keen rival of Henry
Irving

*Advice; Bad Habits; Clubs; Directors; Fame;
Playwrights; Shakespeare's Plays – Hamlet;
H.B. Tree*

TREE Lady Helen (Maud) 1863–1937
English actress most successful in comic
roles. Married to Herbert Beerbohm Tree

Technique

TREWIN J(ohn) C(ourtenay) 1908–90
British theatre critic for the *Observer*

Failure; Vivien Leigh

TRINDER Tommy 1909–89
British comedian

Pantomime

TROLLOPE Frances 1780–1863
English novelist/travel writer; mother of
Anthony Trollope

Shakespeare

TROUGHTON Patrick 1920–87
British actor

Acting

TURNER Michael R.
British writer

Method Acting

TUTIN Dorothy b. 1930
English actress

Technique

TWAIN Mark (Samuel Langhorne Clemens) 1835–1910
American writer (*Huckleberry Finn*) and wit

Comedy

TWIGGY (Lesley Hornby) b. 1949
British actress and model

The Press

TYNAN Kenneth Peacock 1927–80
Inovative British theatre critic who worked closely with Olivier at the National Theatre

Actors; Actors – Katherine Cornell, Orson Welles; Noël Coward; Critics; Critics – Tynan; Gielgud; Insults; Vivien Leigh; Olivier; Playwrights; Playwrights – Congreve; Shakespeare's Plays – Macbeth; *Theatre*

USTINOV Sir Peter b. 1921
British actor/writer of Russian descent

Comedy; Critics; First Nights; Playwrights – Brecht; Shakespeare

URE Mary 1933–75
British actress

Actors

VAN ANDA Carl 1864–1945
American journalist. Editor of the *New York Times*

Critics – A. Woollcott

VANBRUGH Sir John 1664–1726
English architect and playwright (*The Relapse, The Provok'd Wife*)

Playwrights – Vanbrugh

VAUGHAN William 1577–1641
English poet and colonial pioneer

Playwrights – Marlowe

QUEEN VICTORIA 1819–1901
Queen of Great Britain and Ireland 1837–1901

Censorship; Irving; Shakespeare's Plays – King Lear

VOLTAIRE François Marie Arouet de 1694–1778
French writer and philosopher

Censorship; Playwrights – Congreve, Vanbrugh; Shakespeare; Shakespeare's Plays – Hamlet; *Theatre*

WALDORF Willela *fl.* **1940s**
American theatre critic for the *New York Post*

Insults

WALLER Edmund 1606–87
English poet

Audiences

WALPOLE Horace 1717–97
English novelist (*Castle of Otranto*) and letter writer

Opprobrium

WARDLE Irving b. 1929
British theatre critic for *The Times*

Critical Abuse – plays

WARNER Jack 1892–1978
Hollywood producer, founder of Warner Brothers

Barrymores (John)

WARRISS Ben b. 1909–93
British comedian, one half of the partnership Jewell and Warriss

Comedy

WAUGH Evelyn 1903–66
English novelist (*Brideshead Revisited, Scoop*)

Oscar Wilde

WEIR George *fl.* **1920s**
English actor

Bad Habits

WELLES (George) Orson 1915–85
American actor/writer/director. Best
known for his films *Citizen Kane* and *The
Third Man*

*Actors; Failure; Playwrights – Orson Welles;
The Press; Shakespeare*

WELLS H(erbert) G(eorge) 1866–1946
English novelist and sociologist (*War of the
Worlds*)

Shakespeare; G.B. Shaw

WERTENBAKER Timberlake b. 1929
American-born playwright

Theatre

WESKER Arnold b. 1932
British playwright (*Chips With Everything*)

Kitchen Sink

WEST Mae 1892–1980
American actress/producer/writer
(*Diamond Lil, She Done Him Wrong,
Catherine Was Great*); famous for one liners
redolent with sexual innuendo

*Actors – Mae West; Audiences; Critical Abuse
– plays; Epilogues*

**WHISTLER James Abbot McNeill
1834–1903**
American painter who worked mainly in
England

Oscar Wilde

WHITE E.B. 1899–1985
American writer

Critics

WHITE Thomas 1550–1624
English Puritan writer

Opprobrium

WHITELAW Billie b. 1932
British actress who worked closely with
Samuel Beckett

Dedication

WHITING John 1917–63
British playwright (*Marching Song, The
Devils*)

Actors

**WILDE Oscar Fingal O'Flahertie
Wills 1854–1900**
Irish playwright (*Lady Windermere's Fan,
The Importance of Being Earnest*) and wit; his
aphorisms are frequently quoted

*Acting; Actors; Advice; Audiences; Critical
Abuse – plays; Criticism; Critics – M.
Beerbohm; Epitaphs; Irving; Plays;
Playwrights; The Press; Shakespeare's Plays –
Hamlet, Macbeth; G.B. Shaw; Success;
Ellen Terry; H.B. Tree*

WILDE Robert *fl.* **1610**
English writer

Ben Jonson

WILDE William 1852–98
Brother of Oscar Wilde

Oscar Wilde

WILDER Billy b. 1906
American film director

Actors – Walter Matthau

WILDER Thornton 1899–1975
American playwright (*Our Town, The Skin
of Our Teeth*)

Playwrights; Playwrights – Wilder

WILDING Michael 1912–79
British actor, one of Elizabeth Taylor's
husbands

Actors

WILKINSON Tate 1739–1803
English actor and mimic

Sarah Siddons

WILLIAMS Robin b. 1952
American actor and film star

Bad Habits

WILLIAMS Tennessee (Thomas Lanier) 1914–83
American playwright (*A Streetcar Named Desire, The Night of the Iguana*). His outspoken plays were usually set in the southern United States

Tallulah Bankhead; Critical Abuse – actors; Insults; Vivien Leigh; Playwrights – O'Neill; Purpose; Tennessee Williams

WILLIAMSON Nicol b. 1938
English actor

Actors

WILLIS Ted (Baron Willis) 1918–92
British playwright

Shakespeare

WILSON Earl b. 1907
American actor

Tallulah Bankhead

WILSON Jack (John) 1899–1961
Friend and American business manager of Noël Coward

Telegrams

WINCHELL Walter 1879–1972
American journalist and gossip columnist

Broadway; Critics; Critics – A. Woollcott; Finance; First Nights; Insults; Oscar Levant

WINN Godfrey 1908–71
English journalist

Playwrights – Somerset Maugham

WINTER William 1836–1917
American theatre critic

Ibsen

WINTERS Shelley b. 1922
American actress

Acting; Opprobrium

WISE Ernie (Wiseman) b. 1925
British comedian, one half of the Morecambe and Wise partnership

Touring

WODEHOUSE P(elham) G(renville) 1881–1975
British novelist, creator of Bertie Wooster and his butler Jeeves

Critics

WOFFINGTON Peg *c.* 1714–60
Irish actress

Reputation

WOLFIT Sir Donald (Woolfitt) 1902–68
English actor-manager with a flamboyant acting style who toured widely in Shakespeare and the classics

Quick Thinking; Shakespeare's Plays – Twelfth Night; Touring

WOOD Peggy 1892–1978
American actress

Insults

WOOLF Virginia 1882–1941
English novelist (*To the Lighthouse, Orlando*)

Playwrights – Aphra Behn

WOOLLCOTT Alexander 1887–1943
American actor/playwright/theatre critic for the *New York Times*, member of the Algonquin Round Table

Audiences; Sarah Bernhardt; Mrs Patrick Campbell; Critical Abuse – plays; Insults; Playwrights – Feydeau, Wilder; Telegrams; Touring

WOOLLEY Monty 1888–1963
English actor

Actors – Monty Woolley

WYCHERLEY William 1640–1716
English Restoration playwright (*The
Country Wife*)

Playwrights – Wycherley

WYNDHAM Horace 1873–1970
English writer

Melodrama

YATES Mary Ann 1728–87
English actress

Critical Abuse – actors

YEATS W(illiam) B(utler) 1865–1939
Irish poet and playwright

Mrs Patrick Campbell

ZANGWILL Israel 1864–1926
English-born Jewish writer

G.B. Shaw

ZEFFIRELLI Franco b. 1923
Italian theatre and film director

Olivier

ZIEGFELD Florenz 1869–1932
American producer and Broadway
impresario

Producers – Ziegfeld

ZOLOTOW Maurice b. 1913
American writer

First Nights; Oscar Levant

INDEX

OF

PLAY TITLES

ABE LINCOLN IN ILLINOIS
Critical Abuse – actors

ABIE'S IRISH ROSE
Critical Abuse – plays

AFTER THE FALL
Playwrights – Arthur Miller

THE AMOROUS PRAWN
Critical Abuse – plays

ANNIE
Musicals

ANNIE GET YOUR GUN
Show Business

ANTONY AND CLEOPATRA
Audience Asides; Tallulah Bankhead;
Vivien Leigh; Shakespeare's Plays

ANYTHING BUT THE TRUTH
Critical Abuse – plays

THE APPLE CART
Artistic Integrity

ARMS AND THE MAN
Advice; George Bernard Shaw

AS YOU LIKE IT
Epilogues; Life; Shakespeare's Plays

THE BARRETTS OF WIMPOLE
STREET
Critical Abuse – plays

BETRAYAL
Critical Abuse – plays

BIARRITZ
Critical Abuse – plays

BITTER OLEANDER
Critical Abuse – plays

BITTER SWEET
Audiences

BLITHE SPIRIT
Critical Abuse – actors

BLITZ
Critical Abuse – plays

THE BLUEBIRD
Beginnings

BOEING BOEING
Critical Abuse – plays

THE BOYS IN THE BAND
Audience Asides

THE BUCCANEER
Critical Abuse – actors

THE BURGOMASTER OF
STILEMONDE
Critical Abuse – plays

BUY ME BLUE RIBBONS
Critical Abuse – actors

LA CAGE AUX FOLLES
Musicals

CAESAR AND CLEOPATRA
Critical Abuse – actors

CAMELOT
Critical Abuse – plays

IL CAMPIELLO
Critical Abuse – plays

CANDIDA
Telegrams

CANDLELIGHT
Insults

THE CAT SCREAMS
Critical Abuse – plays

CATHERINE WAS GREAT
Critical Abuse – plays; Epilogues

CAVALCADE
Telegrams

THE CHERRY ORCHARD
Audience Asides; Chekhov

CLASH BY NIGHT
Critical Abuse – plays

THE COCKTAIL PARTY
Critical Abuse – plays

THE CRITIC
Critics; Plays; Purpose

CYRANO DE BERGERAC
Critical Abuse – actors

DAZZLING PROSPECT
Critical Abuse – plays

A DEAD SECRET
Critical Abuse – actors

THE DOLL'S HOUSE
Ibsen

DON QUIXOTE
Opprobrium

DOUGLAS
Shakespeare

DR FAUSTUS
Critical Abuse – actors

THE DUCHESS OF MALFI
Peggy Ashcroft

THE DUENNA
Sheridan

EASY VIRTUE
Noël Coward

EDWARD II
Critical Abuse – actors

THE EXCITERS
Tallulah Bankhead

FALSE GODS
Costume and Make-up

FAUST
Ellen Terry

FEDORA
Mrs Patrick Campbell

FIFTH COLUMN
Failure

FLOWER DRUM SONG
Musicals

FOLLOW THE GIRLS
Critical Abuse – plays

THE FOX
Insults

FRESH FIELDS
Critical Abuse – plays

THE GAZEBO
Critical Abuse – actors

GHOSTS
Mrs Patrick Campbell; Ibsen

GONE WITH THE WIND
Critical Abuse – plays

GYPSY
Child Actors

HAIR
Critical Abuse – plays; Musicals

HALFWAY TO HELL
Critical Abuse – plays

HAMLET
Advice; The Barrymores; Beerbohm Tree;
Beginnings; Dressing Room Talk;
Epitaphs; Gielgud; Irving; Plays; Ralph
Richardson; Shakespeare's Plays; Theatre

HEARTBREAK HOUSE
Critical Abuse – plays

HEDDA GABLER
Critical Abuse – actors

HENRY IV
Bad Habits